DEAD IS FOREVER

A NOVEL OF CRIME

ALSO BY DAVID CRAY

Bad Lawyer

Little Girl Blue

What You Wish For

Partners

DEAD IS

A NOVEL OF CRIME

FOREVER

DAVID CRAY

CARROLL & GRAF PUBLISHERS

NEW YORK

DEAD IS FOREVER

Carroll & Graf Publishers
An Imprint of Avalon Publishing Group Inc.
245 West 17th Street
11th Floor
New York, NY 1001

AVALON
publishing group incorporated

First Carroll & Graf edition 2005

Library of Congress Cataloging-in-Publication Data is available.

ISBN: 0-7867-1440-9

Printed in the United States of America
Interior design by Maria E. Torres
Distributed by Publishers Group West

10 9 8 7 6 5 4 3 2 1

ONE

ALLOW ME, IF YOU WILL, a mercifully brief introduction. My name is Philip Corvascio Beckett. In appearance, I am nondescript: average height and weight; neither handsome nor homely; neither fat nor thin. My eyes—blue, or green, or hazel, depending on the light—are neither widely spaced nor closely set; my nose, mouth and chin are well formed, a tribute, Father would insist, to my breeding. They are, nevertheless, entirely inconspicuous.

I could go on to describe my teeth, hands and feet, but I'm sure you get the point. If I attract attention at all, it's only because I dress rather well by New York standards. I avoid T-shirts, athletic shoes, and all garments bearing conspicuous logos. As a matter of pride, I will not be a walking billboard, a patsy for the marketing departments of corporations interested solely in the remaining balance on my credit card, pitiful though it may be.

Benny Abraham, my best friend, has another explanation for my aversion to the dress-of-choice for third-millennium Americans. I will state it for the record, but it should be understood that Benny denies the principle of principle. Guilt and fear, he insists, account for all inhibitions, while conscience is a device invented by human beings to shield themselves from the necessity to act.

"You were born a snob, you were raised a snob, and you're still a snob," Benny explained. "It's simple."

But I'm not. I can't afford to be. The vast majority of my respectably middle-class income is derived from a trust fund left to me by my mother, Luna Corvascio Beckett, who died twenty years ago when I was thirteen. The fund provides me with a quarterly check, but its multi-million-dollar principal is unavailable until the death of my father. At which time, presuming I live that long, I will inherit so many millions it will no longer matter.

I could always work, I suppose, but not only do I despise routine, I have a positive talent for leisure. I can spend hours over breakfast at Sharpers' outdoor café, on the corner of Hudson and Perry Streets. Or over carefully spaced cocktails at the bar inside. Or engaged in the most trivial conversation with friends or lovers. Or on a bench in Central Park, or the Battery, or Washington Square, or . . .

A deep breath is in order. A sigh, really, in contemplation of a single character flaw that drives me to occasional work, and to which I will return later in this introduction. What takes precedence here is my closely held belief that I put in my time, dutifully overachieving for the better part of fourteen years, and have no further obligations to anyone but myself.

First came Choate, prep school to the moneyed class, where in addition to maintaining honor-roll status throughout, I captained the chess and judo teams. Harvard University followed, then Wharton, as I navigated the trail blazed by three prior generations of Becketts. It all was very expected, and I'd had enough, by the time I received my M.B.A. from Wharton, to know that I would never take that final step into the promised land. Though I had climbed the mountain and could see Zion spread before me, I would never assume my place at the helm of Beckett Industries.

A gap followed. Between striving and indolence. I'd been filling my days with productive tasks for so long that cold-turkey withdrawal (as Benny would put it) was not a realistic possibility. Instead I withdrew gradually, earning, over the course of two years' employment by Fisher Security, a license issued by the New York Police Department to conduct private investigations. I resigned my position with Fisher Security on the day my boss, Silena Fisher, put the license in my hand.

"I invested a lot of time and money in you," Silena argued. "You're in my debt."

"You know, Silena," I cheerfully explained, "that's exactly what Father said."

Father, if I may understate the facts by a considerable degree, was very unhappy when I told him that I would never occupy the office he'd set aside for me on the day I entered Harvard. I was the son, and the firstborn, and now he would have to settle for my sister, Regina, who was not only talented, but had a true vocation. Ten years later, she sits to the right of the regent, and looks forward to the passing of the crown. It will be a long wait; Father is in excellent health and has been working so hard and for so long that he has no other life. Regina will be covered by Father's shadow, as Father was covered by Grandfather's shadow, until she is well into middle age.

My father's unhappiness gave me no joy. As far as I can tell, I harbored no secret wish to see him suffer. I know that I endured weeks of discussion, patiently explaining that I lacked obsession, and thus would make a poor captain of industry. "I'm not driven," I insisted. "And I like people too much. I couldn't possibly make the hard decisions."

Motivated by the pressing demands of his financial empire, Father eventually dismissed me with a final gift, a two-bedroom condominium in an utterly nondescript apartment house on East Twenty-seventh Street. Perhaps it was an attempt at irony. Certainly I was being told what I was worth. But in truth it suited me perfectly, and that second tiny bedroom soon became the focus of the single flaw that stands between a modest workload and pure indolence.

There are four objects displayed in this bedroom cum gallery. The largest is eleven inches high, the smallest, a mere three and a half. All were carved from blocks of jade, three in the late nineteenth century and one (oddly, the least expensive) in the eighteenth. I could describe these objects in great detail and with great satisfaction, but I promised to keep this introduction brief. Thus, suffice it to say that while my trust fund pays for life's necessities, it does not support a continuing, self-indulgent passion for Chinese antiques.

So, from time to time, and only at the behest of friends or when a case truly interests me, I work. I have no office and I carry no business cards. I do not *market* my talents. Nevertheless, rarely does a week pass without a call to the phone service I employ to separate my professional and personal lives. My chums of long ago, my schoolmates, have gone on to better things. Many of them work for large corporations or law firms. Others have entered the family business. Either way, from time to time, one or another finds himself or herself in need of my very discreet and rather expensive services.

At the time this story begins, I'd become enamored of a pale yellow vase carved in the shape of a dragon-fish leaping from a turbulent sea. Not only was the vase exquisite, my other pieces were in varying shades of green and I'd long wanted to add pink, white and yellow jade to my collection. Unfortunately, the vase would be auctioned in a mere two weeks and I was several thousand dollars short of a serious bid.

The vase was superbly carved and had that translucent quality that distinguishes jade from all other stone. The best jade does not so much reflect light as broadcast it, as if the source of the light were within the object. My vase positively glowed in the private viewing I'd arranged through a friend at Sotheby's and I'd been lusting after it ever since. I couldn't lose it to mere indolence, to sloth, to sheer inertia; I had to get off my gainfully unemployed duff and go to work.

To that end, on a Wednesday morning in early spring, I made a long series of unproductive phone calls. The first three went to individuals whose business I'd recently turned down. They were unanimously sorry, but they'd gone elsewhere. The next ten or twelve went to law offices I'd serviced in the past. Unanimously, they were pleased to hear from me, but though each promised to keep me in mind, their present needs were being adequately handled by the firms they ordinarily employed. They would call, of course, if . . .

When I restored the telephone's receiver to its cradle for the last time, I'd made three expensive lunch dates but was no nearer my goal. Still, the effort had induced a keen appetite and I left my apartment for Sharpers, convinced that I was through for the afternoon. It was a beautiful spring day, cool in the shade and warm in a mid-April sun that rose high enough to bathe the outdoor café in near-miraculous light. Seated at a table to the right of the door, Sharpers' owner, Benny Abraham, looked positively angelic. His bald pate, as he leaned over his newspaper, had the incandescence of a halo.

Before I could take my seat, Luisa Czernowitz appeared bearing a pot of Earl Grey tea, a cup, and a saucer. A sculptor perpetually in search of a gallery, Luisa had been waiting tables at Sharpers for several years and we'd long ago become friends. We had dinner occasionally, and took in the occasional movie, but neither expected our relationship to advance.

"We're just not compatible," she'd earnestly explained many months before. "I'm in search of a soul mate, while you're a philanderer to your bones."

I might have protested my innocence. In truth, I'd never cheated in the course of an affair. The only charge that could honestly be laid at my door is that my affairs tended toward brevity. But Luisa has a very wide mouth that opens into a very wide smile, a purely delighted (and delightful) smile, which I knew I'd sorely hate to lose. She favored me with that smile as I slid into a molded plastic chair across from Benny.

"It's a perfect day to do nothing," she said. "You must be in seventh heaven." Her light brown hair, backlit by the sun, seemed on fire.

"You're right about the day," I sighed, "but wrong about the state of my euphoria. I'm looking for work."

"In that case, let me get you a drink."

"A well-cooked western omelet with a side of bacon will do nicely." I poured the tea. "It's not like I actually *found* work."

Dropping his newspaper, Benny straightened in his chair. No more than five-six, he had the sort of torso generally associated with Russian weight lifters, and I suspect that in times past he was quite the formidable fellow. But now, as he neared his sixtieth birthday, he'd grown soft around the jowls and waist, while his bandy legs seemed too frail to carry his bulk.

Benny Abraham was still a bookmaker at the time this story begins. He'd been plying his trade for the better part of four decades. Earlier in his career (a career that had seen him imprisoned twice), he'd dealt with a clientele that needed occasional coercion. A formidable appearance, he'd told me, was a definite asset that tended to *prevent* violence.

When I met Benny, I was twenty-three, while he was a couple of years short of fifty. He'd taken me under his wing, teaching me lessons about the street that I would have been a long time learning on my own. I'd repaid the kindness by introducing him to friends and acquaintances, mostly school chums, who not only liked to gamble, but who could afford to lose. Gone were the fifty-dollar bettors who had to be chased down at their jobs, replaced by gentlemen wearing hundred-dollar ties who honored their gambling debts as a matter of honor.

"Your sister was here," Benny announced as he lit a narrow Dominican cigar. "She went to your apartment."

"Regina?"

"That's what she said."

"It couldn't be."

"Kid, she arrived in a chauffeur-driven Rolls."

I sipped at my tea and pondered. Regina and I were not close. For one thing, she thought me a fool to voluntarily surrender what she'd obsessively coveted. (Always self-centered, Regina had difficulty with any point of view not her own.) Beyond this, or so I believed, she harbored a grievance so irrational that it could not be acknowledged. All through college and grad school, whenever I was home for a visit, Regina inevitably found an opportune moment to vent her frustration at life's manifest injustice. My inheritance of the object of all her desires, the family mantle, was simply a matter of genitalia. Her grades were as good as mine, her achievements every bit as grand, yet her fate was to sit on the boards of various charities, to produce an heir for a husband who had no more claim to his position than I, and to be certain that each piece of crystal or cutlery laid out for dinner parties sparkled or gleamed.

Though her ambitions had been realized, Regina was not transformed by my abdication. Instead, she continued to embrace her victimization, and to resent my having presented her with Father's patrimony as if it were a gift to give. It's the only reasonable explanation I can devise for the slights she handed out like Christmas candy whenever our paths crossed at one or another of Father's residences. Regina had never been to my apartment, nor had she invited me to her Park Avenue digs. When she wished me summoned to the odd wedding, funeral, or dinner party, she handed the job to her personal secretary, Marge Hansen, who knew me well enough to call Sharpers before trying my apartment.

So, what did she want with me? It had to be important, of course, and it had to be very, very private. These are two angles I'd exploited many times in the past. As a general rule, the more important and the more private, the more clients are willing to pay to resolve the former while maintaining the latter. Not Regina, though. Regina would expect me to donate my services. Family being family.

I closed my eyes and summoned the image of a wonderfully carved dragon-fish leaping from a sea of yellow waves. I opened my eyes to find Regina marching toward me from the corner of Hudson and Perry streets.

Regina was wearing a beige suit with a long jacket over a pale yellow blouse. The narrow lapels of the jacket were piped with muted gold velvet, while the gold in her ears, across her throat, and over her left breast, exactly matched the sheen of her blond hair.

"I've been looking for you," she announced. "We need to speak." Her cold blue eyes moved to Benny Abraham, their intent unmistakable. Regina required privacy.

Benny's face lit up as he slowly raised his head, then a hand. His small dark eyes positively glittered. "I'm Benny Abraham," he announced. "We got a lotta friends in common."

Regina ignored his hand for as long as possible, then offered her fingertips for a very brief squeeze. "Regina Beckett."

Benny nodded and said, "Well, you kids probably want a little privacy" before returning to the *Daily News*. It was his table and he wasn't going anywhere.

"I'd be grateful if you'd take a ride with me," Regina said without so much a glance in my or Benny's direction.

"Certainly," I replied. "It would be an honor."

TWO

I ROSE, THEN PRECEDED REGINA to the car and opened the door. She preceded me into the back, then slid across the seat, her eyes facing front. The partition, I noted, had been raised. The information she was about to impart was too sensitive for the ears of a servant.

The Rolls pulled into the flow of traffic, instantly drawing the curious glances of drivers and passengers in surrounding vehicles. Though I felt on display, Regina seemed oblivious.

"This is very difficult for me," she declared. "Very, very difficult."

In profile, Regina was quite attractive. Her skin was flawless, the tilt of her nose and chin somehow diffident. Unless you looked directly into her eyes, she might have been Grace Kelly at her most innocent. "Regina," I encouraged, "whatever the apparent differences in our lives and values, you and I are family. You can tell me anything."

She nodded thoughtfully. "This concerns our cousin, Audrey."

"The Countess?"

Audrey Beckett, daughter and only child of Alfred Beckett, Father's older brother, was ten years my elder and the acknowledged Beckett ugly duckling. At age twenty-four, overweight and homely enough to be conspicuous at family gatherings, she'd met and been courted by the very handsome Count Sergio D'Alesse, formerly of Turin. Almost before the family could react, the impeccably old-world D'Alesse had charmed the socially inept Audrey Beckett all the way to the altar. His charm, however, had not transformed her into a swan. Instead, upon realizing that D'Alesse, utterly without resources of his own, expected to maintain a lifestyle in keeping with his noble lineage, she'd first become sullen, then increasingly isolated as the years passed and she failed to produce an heir.

"Countess? I presume that's a joke."

"On whom?"

Her lips curled into a mischievous smile and I remembered an ambition-free time when she'd been my playful little sister. "On the Beckett family name, of course."

"Heaven forfend."

Regina blew a little cough into her hand. "Spring allergies," she explained as she straightened her skirt. "I should be indoors."

I was tempted to declare that the Rolls was an eyeblink away from hermetically sealed, but checked myself. Allergies weren't the point, anyway. No, the point was that her decision to seek me out was causing her some discomfort and it was my fault.

"We could go to my apartment?" I suggested. When Regina responded with a shudder, I followed with, "What would you like to do?"

She turned, her mouth tight as her eyes swept my body, from my cordovan loafers to my English tweed jacket to the cut and style of my hair. I think she was disappointed to find me reasonably presentable. "D'Alesse is in debt."

"Aren't we all."

"This is a gambling debt."

"How much?"

"Forty thousand dollars."

"Can I assume that he and Audrey don't have the money to cover the debt?"

"If they did, I would never have heard of it."

"And her family is unwilling to help?"

"It's not the first time, Philip. Nor the second or the third or the fourth."

I straightened my legs and folded my arms across my chest. Regina, whether she knew it or not, was making it much easier for me. "Tell me who came to whom?" I asked.

"Pardon?"

"Call it curiosity. Did Audrey approach Uncle Alfred? Or did D'Alesse have the courage to make the pitch himself?"

"This is serious, Philip. Sergio has been threatened."

"Threats? Does that mean the count went into the hole with a bookie?"

Regina drew up her shoulders. "I don't know the sordid details. And I wish you'd stop using phrases like 'went into the hole.' It makes you appear common."

I looked out the window and into the eyes of a turbaned cab driver. He grinned, nodded, then accelerated away. Perhaps he thought I was Brad Pitt. "Why don't you just give D'Alesse the forty thousand? After all, you spent more than that on your last trip to Paris?"

She didn't answer, because the answer was obvious to both of us. Father had forbidden it. The answer to the next question was obvious as well, but I asked anyway: "If you've decided to abandon D'Alesse to his well-deserved fate, why do you need me?"

"We don't want him attacked, Philip."

"Because you fear for his safety? Or because you prefer that the affair remain private?"

Regina surprised me by smiling. "From D'Alesse's point of view, I can't see that it matters." She rolled the partition down a few inches, then said, "Take me to the office, Thaddeus."

A black gentleman of the old school, Thaddeus had been with Regina for a decade. He nodded, muttered, "Yes, ma'am," as the partition closed.

"I have appointments," Regina explained, "all afternoon."

"Then you'd best get to the point. What exactly do you want me to do?"

She raised a hand, the gesture as vague as her reply. "I'm not the private investigator. I suppose you'll think of something appropriate."

"At the moment, the most appropriate item that comes to mind is my fee."

"Your fee?"

"Persuading a bookmaker to abandon a forty-thousand-dollar debt is an inherently dangerous pursuit. It screams for compensation."

Regina's face lit up. "If I paid you," she asked, "would I be your client?"

It was neatly done. As my client, she would gain a measure of control over any information I turned up. Father would be pleased.

"I want seven thousand to start, Regina." That would be enough to give me an excellent shot at the auction. "And a thousand dollars a day, plus expenses."

Over years of dealing with my former peers, I'd come to accept my station. I was good for a lunch, a slap on the back, even an admiring glance from time to time. But I was no longer of their class, and the gulf between our respective incomes mirrored a psychological gulf that I had no desire to bridge. I was there, after all, for the money, and I suspect that Regina knew it. In any event, she took a checkbook from her purse and began to write.

"It's not," she explained, "as if they don't have resources."

"Audrey and the count?"

"Audrey has a very generous trust fund. But . . ."

"Let me guess. It's mortgaged to the hilt."

"Several years ago, D'Alesse convinced Audrey to arrange a loan using the fund as collateral. The money is gone and nobody knows where. Bad investments, I suppose. Now their quarterly income is dedicated to paying the interest on the loan."

She tore the check free and passed it over. I noted that it was drawn, not from her personal funds, but from the account of Halstead Financial Services, a company with which I was entirely unfamiliar.

I folded the check and slipped it into my pocket. The Rolls was fighting heavy traffic on Eighth Avenue as we neared the Lincoln Tunnel and the Port Authority Bus Terminal at Forty-second Street. As a scratch or a ding or a dent would be unthinkable, Thaddeus was undoubtedly holding his breath. For Regina and myself, on the other hand, the Rolls was so silent we might have been watching a movie through its windows.

"Anything else I should know?"

"You seem dispirited, Philip."

It was my turn to change the subject. "What happens if I fail?"

"We've been paying D'Alesse's bills for a long time. Too long. Besides, Audrey knows we're prepared to protect her."

I finally got the message. "But only if she leaves him. Is that about it?"

"He's a laughingstock, Philip. And so is she." Regina crossed her legs, then rearranged her skirt. Her expression was entirely serene. A family decision had been made and Audrey's feelings were no longer relevant. Perhaps they'd never been. Not being privy to the decision-making process, I couldn't be sure, but I did know Audrey's fate if she accepted the family's offer. With little hope of remarriage and no fortune of her own, she would become, for the most part, a nonentity. The exception would be at family gatherings, where she would be an embarrassment.

"What's Audrey's position in all this?"

"If you're asking me whether she still loves him, I'd have to assume not. D'Alesse is a clown. How does one love a clown?" She opened her bag and dropped the checkbook inside. We were nearing the Beckett Building on Sixth Avenue, and her attention was already drifting. "We've told Audrey that we're willing to pay D'Alesse's gambling debt this one last time if she files for divorce. You might let her know that our decision stands."

Was she referring to herself and Father? Or to herself, Father and Uncle Alfred? Or was her 'we' royal in nature? I didn't know and was afraid to ask.

"I assume the count is eager to cooperate?"

"He's expecting you."

The Rolls pulled to the curb and Thaddeus jumped out to open the door for Regina. I followed her to the sidewalk and for a moment we stood together on the corner. Twenty feet away, flanking the entrance to the headquarters of Beckett Industries, a pair of fountains sprayed jets of sparkling water into the sunlight. I watched a small shimmering rainbow form and dissolve in the drifting mist, then decided to walk the couple of miles to the D'Alesse apartment. Regina, on the other hand, would disappear into the artificial light and filtered air of her office suite on the forty-seventh floor; her Rolls would be waiting at the curb when she decided to call it a day.

"Would you phone me?" Regina asked. "Tonight?"

"Without fail."

She nodded thoughtfully, then, in lieu of a parting embrace, raised her handbag and shook it.

THREE

"PHILIP, YOU LOOK ABSOLUTELY WONDERFUL. How do you do stay so trim?"

The count was a tall, very lean man whose narrow face was bisected by a scimitar of a Roman nose. His mouth was small, his eyes dark and slightly protruding, his firm jaw properly aristocratic. He took my hand between his palms as I entered the two-bedroom apartment that he shared with Audrey on York Avenue, greeting me as if we were old friends who'd been apart too long. I accepted his attention while I searched his eyes for the panic Regina had spoken of, but I found them merely intense. The count was drawing me into his sphere, a trick I'd seen him perform many times in the past.

"Please," he quickly added, "I have expresso brewing, and the most wonderful biscotti. Make yourself comfortable while I do the service."

Though he'd been living in the United Stated for decades, the count's accent was still apparent. I understood it to be well-cultivated, and part of his lovable rogue package, the only sympathetic persona to which he could reasonably aspire. To an extent, I sympathized; we were, after all, in nearly identical positions. The difference was that I kept as far away from the Becketts and their peers as possible. I did not attend their parties, except on family occasions. Nor did I attend galas, or charity balls, or benefit concerts at Lincoln Center. Unlike the count, I knew my place.

I made myself comfortable in a sagging upholstered club chair, then crossed my legs and glanced around. Despite the upscale York Avenue address, the room was simply a cube. The well-worn furniture clustered beneath the window was of department store quality, and the walls, except for ghost-like rectangles over which pictures had once proudly hung, were badly in need of painting. A large mahogany breakfront, the only expensive piece in the room, stood with its display shelves empty. At one time it had housed the pre-Columbian artifacts Audrey had been collecting for decades.

Though I pride myself on a carefully nurtured tolerance, I found myself repulsed. The count had blown it all. The paintings, the sculpture, the pottery, the trust fund. He'd tossed away everything, save the loyalty of his wife, and now even that was in jeopardy. Would he go back to Italy? Or would he work the upscale resorts in search of another meal ticket? Of one thing I was certain: the count was in his early fifties and had never held a job. He wasn't about to carry a lunch pail.

"Ah, Philip, here were are." The count crossed the room bearing a stainless steel tray. In times past, it would have been toted by a servant. "Please, allow me to pour." He set the tray on a glass coffee table, then filled the tiny cups. "And the biscotti, please. I have a friend who brings them from Bay Ridge in Brooklyn."

I dutifully nibbled and sipped before muttering the obligatory compliment. "Excellent, Sergio. Worth the effort."

"*Grazie.*" He beamed at me for a moment, then said, "But you haven't told me how you stay in such condition. Look at me. Three times each week, I go to the gymnasium, and yet my waist becomes larger and my chest smaller." He threw up his hands. "What can I do?"

"Stiff upper lip is the only thing that comes to mind. Audrey's not here, I assume."

"No, unfortunately." His mouth curled into a little circle of disappointment. "We didn't know you were coming."

"Regina didn't speak to you?"

Again, the moue of disappointment. If he'd had his way, we might have exchanged pleasantries for another hour before we got down to business. "Yes, of course we spoke." He took a pack of Gitanes from the coffee table and lit one up. "Your sister, Regina, she is very . . . powerful. As a girl, she was not so intense."

"I wouldn't know about her intensity," I responded rather meanly. "I rarely see her these days."

He was sitting forward on the couch, leaning toward me, his cigarette pinched between his middle and ring fingers. "Ah, but she persuaded you to . . . assist me with my problem."

"Regina's paying me, Sergio." It was as close as I would come to explaining that Regina, and not he, was my client.

"It is business, then." His tone was free of disdain or contempt. "Well, I seem to have gotten myself into some difficulty, Philip. Entirely my own fault, I must admit."

The count told his story very well. And why not? He was an entertainer by nature and by necessity, a charmer who could make the most trivial conversation seem profound. He filled his tale with sweeping gestures. He lied about every peripheral matter. But I was reasonably certain the pertinent facts were accurate. The count was smart enough to know that his very bones depended on it.

The lies concerned his situation prior to meeting Prentice Cook about a year before. According to the count, he and Audrey (whom he described as "an absolute saint, an angel") had been doing well, their lives dominated by social engagements, as were the lives of their peers. It was, in fact, in the course of just such an engagement that their downfall began. He and Audrey were in Turin, following the wedding of the count's nephew to the daughter of a Brazilian industrialist, when they decided to accompany a number of fellow revelers on a trip to Monaco. Among them was an insurance executive with an impressive pedigree named Prentice Cook.

"A fabulous night, Philip. I couldn't lose. The dice were magic in my hands."

Cook had stood next to the count throughout the evening, making heavy bets on the pass line, and they both had gone home big winners. When they'd met the next day at breakfast, the conversation had naturally turned to other gambling adventures. A series of tales (embellished, no doubt) had followed, and for once the count had to play second fiddle. Cook had gambled in every part of the world.

Though he was intimately familiar with the various games offered by the casinos, Cook's specialty was poker. In poker, he explained, you compete against the other players instead of the house. If they play badly and you play well, over the long run you come out a winner. It was that simple.

"Prentice tells me that he travels constantly within the United States on business, that he finds a game no matter where he goes. He tells me that some of these games have been going on for many years because the players are too important to be arrested, even though authorities know of their existence. Of course, I asked him if he had knowledge of a such a game in Manhattan. I was curious, merely, and trying to be polite. The man spoke fluent Italian. He was dressed like a gentleman."

As it happened, Prentice Cook, whose gentlemanly countenance the count never again saw, did know of a game suitable to the count's station. The game took place on the third floor of a town house/art gallery on East Fifty-seventh Street. It began shortly after the gallery closed, then continued through the night.

"Prentice gives me this." The count held up half of a fifty-dollar chip that had been cut in a zig-zag pattern. "With this, he explains, I will be admitted to play either dice or poker. Both are available."

Still motivated by curiosity, the count soon made his way to the town house, where he discovered, to his delight, that Prentice Cook had not exaggerated. The staff bowed and scraped; the other players, men and women, were the right sort; and the atmosphere was suitably illicit. Not only that, he'd won his first hand at poker, then continued to win for the next three months.

The games played at the poker table were five- and seven-card stud. Any player could bet or raise the entire amount in the pot, while the smallest acceptable bet was ten dollars. At the end of the night, the big loser might be out five thousand, the big winner up the same amount.

More often than not, over those early months, the count was the big winner, and by the time his lucky streak came to an abrupt end shortly after the turn of the year, he'd not only accumulated thirty thousand dollars in winnings, he believed himself supremely skilled at the art of poker.

"Then I lose ten thousand dollars in one night. My cards are fantastic, but always someone has better. After that, it's as if my cards are cursed. I can do nothing right. Nothing."

The count fell as swiftly as he'd risen. Within a month, his thirty grand having evaporated, he was digging into his own pocket. Within six weeks, he was offering his marker. The first time, he'd been hesitant. Normally, he covered his losses with a check. But his marker was graciously accepted. After all, gentlemen pay their debts. If they can.

"Now, all is gone and they threaten to break my bones." He waved his arms as if mystified by the turn of events.

The truth was that most of Audrey's money had vanished long before the count began to play poker. The game was simply the last in a long series of blunders that stretched back to the first days of his marriage. Still, there was no reason to puncture the count's balloon. My job was to rescue the man without paying his debt, and to keep the matter private. As yet, I had no idea how (or *if*) I was going to accomplish either.

"Tell me about the poker game, Sergio. Does the house compete against the other players?"

"No, and this is the best. The ante is twenty dollars, which the house keeps. There is no reason for them to be dishonest."

Was he joking? The reason for the house to cheat and the reason they operated the game in the first place were identical: money. "Is there a house dealer?"

"Carlos, a very quiet man. Very steady."

"But he doesn't play."

"No. But with the dice, we compete against the house. As in a casino."

I finished my expresso and laid the cup on the tray. "The chip you showed me. Will it get me into the game?"

His smile was rueful as he passed the chip to me. "Players lose and they stop coming. There is often the need for new players."

"But the people running the game, they never change?"

"Always the same. The continuity, it reassures."

I sat for another few minutes while the count described John Caroll, the man who operated the club, then rose to leave. The count followed me to the door, and again pressed my hand between his palms. "You must not put yourself in danger on my account," he told me. "I need a bit of time, but that's all. My fortunes. . . ." He spread his hands, palms up, as if showing me that he'd concealed nothing. "My fortunes will soon be improved. All Mr. Caroll need do is wait."

"Don't worry, Sergio," I replied in an effort to forestall any further outburst of empty bravado. "I never deliberately put myself in danger. But if I did, it would be entirely for my own sake, not yours."

FOUR

IT WAS JUST AFTER SIX when I got to Sharpers. The west side of Hudson Street was in deep shadow and the afternoon warmth had died off in the face of a rising breeze. The outdoor tables wcrc deserted, the dining room nearly so. The bar, on the other hand, was jammed. It was happy hour. Cocktails were half price, domestic beer was two dollars per bottle, the lighting was reasonably subdued. There was, as they say, nothing not to like.

The patrons were young and single, office workers on their way home after nine or ten hours spent hundreds of feet above the Earth in soft-walled cubicles. As just the thought of it was enough to make me cower, I sympathized with their plight and with their solution. Each weekday, they emerged from their labors slightly bewildered, like workers of old, as I imagined them, emerging at the end of the day from a coal mine. Without doubt, they were equally in need of the release offered by alcohol and conversation.

Pausing to exchange a word or two with casual acquaintances, I made my way to the rear of the building. Sharpers was one of New York's older taverns. The bar, booths, and wainscoting, though scarred, were solid oak; the pine floorboards were twelve inches wide. They gave slightly as I approached Benny Abraham's booth, which was separated from the barroom by a door leading to the kitchen. On the wall opposite, a second door leading to a large storeroom and to the basement further isolated Benny from the general din.

"Hey, Philly, how'd it go with the sister?"

Benny's small face, made even smaller by the girth of his neck and spread of his shoulders, was expressionless, as befitted a man both successful and slow to anger. I saw nothing in his dark eyes, pursed mouth, or stubborn chin to indicate his thoughts or feelings, but I didn't expect to. It was only after knowing Benny for many months that I came to realize that, in general, he meant exactly what he said. Benny wasn't asking about Regina because it was the polite thing to do, though it undoubtedly was. He was asking because he wanted to know.

"The game's afoot, Benny."

Benny's eyes, round as marbles and dark enough to seem all pupil, were overhung by semi-circles of shaggy salt-and-pepper eyebrow. These semi-circles rose a millimeter as he replied, conveying what I understood to be unbridled amusement.

"*Afoot?*" he asked.

"The 'afoot' part's a little weak," I admitted, "but we *are* talking about a game."

"And what game would that happen to be? If you don't mind my askin'."

"Poker."

Now that I had his full attention, I went on to describe (without naming names, of course) the parameters of the case. Benny waited me out, then took the stub of a cigar from an ashtray on the table and jammed it between his teeth without lighting up. "The guy who runs the game," he asked, "would he go by the name John Caroll?"

"That's him."

"Do ya know that his real name is Gaetano Carollo?"

"Now I do."

Benny shook his head, at what I wasn't sure, then abruptly changed direction. "So whatta ya wanna do here?" he asked.

"The first thing I need to know is if the game's honest. The rise and fall of the gentleman in question seems rehearsed. As if Caroll and his people have done it before."

"Find the mark. Clean him out." Benny cupped his mouth, then called out, "*Next.*"

His response cheered me. "So, it's possible? Caroll—or Carollo —might be stupid enough to risk the game itself? Because you know what would happen if the players found out." I paused as Joe Deter, one of the bartenders, entered the storeroom, then disappeared into the basement. "I mean the game must turn a nice profit without cheating."

"Forget about the marks wisin' up. That's not gonna happen."

"Why not?"

"Because you got a bunch of amateurs up against a bunch of professionals. Besides, from what you told me, Caroll's not tryin' to clean out everybody who walks through the door. He's pickin' his spots. That means you got winners every night and winners never suspect they were in a rigged game." Benny glanced away for a moment, then turned back to me. "If the game's crooked, are you gonna bust it?"

"Are you asking if I'm going to inform the other players?"

"Exactly."

"My aim here is to have the count's debt forgiven."

Benny nodded judiciously, but I could almost hear the wheels turning. "Carollo runs a small crew. Five years ago, I woulda said he was connected. But now, with the Gottis out of circulation, there's nothing much to connect to. On the other hand, Caroll would burn you in a heartbeat if you threatened the game. You might wanna keep that in mind."

I looked at my watch. It was past six-thirty and I had an eight o'clock date that I intended to keep. "Unless the game is crooked and I can prove it, none of this matters. I need to know what to look for."

"You say the mark played poker?"

"Exclusively."

"And there was a house dealer who didn't play?"

"That's right."

"Forget the dealer altogether. He could be dealing seconds, bottoms . . . it don't matter because you're not gonna see it happening. Look for the shill, the guy who wins the big pots. If the house don't play, there's gotta be a shill." He pulled the cigar from his mouth and ground the butt into the ashtray. This despite the fact that it wasn't lit. "Now with craps you got a different situation. There's not that many ways to gaff dice and they can all be spotted if you know how to look."

I left Sharpers thirty minutes later, at seven o'clock, much the wiser, and took a cab to my apartment, where I began to dress for my date. Magdalena Santos (Maggie to one and all) was the daughter of a Spanish diplomat and a British novelist. Her first ten years were spent in London, her next fifteen in Paris, where she received a degree in international law, and the last five in New York working for Exxon. Her job, as she'd described it on our first date, was to guide mega-tons of crude oil from beneath the earth or the sea, through the treacherous shoals of regulation, to their final resting place in the upper atmosphere.

Maggie's self-deprecating humor was in direct contrast to her appearance, like a surprise concealed beneath some greater gift. Her large eyes were a dark liquid brown, her flawless complexion that mysterious shade between yellow and brown that so easily becomes sallow. Her mouth was very generous, and the brief good-night kisses we'd shared had left me filled with a speculation that in no way stopped at her lips. Maggie's passion was ballroom dancing; she'd taken me along to the Continental Club on our second date. As we'd circled the dance floor in a slow waltz, my fingers on the unyielding swell of her hip, her breasts lightly brushing my chest, I'd surrendered to the commingled odors of her perfume and her flesh. It was as simple as that, and if I'd had my way. . . .

Well, my *way*, or so I'm fond of explaining to my friends, often at great length, is anticipation. The hours, days or weeks between when we know we will and when we do can be the most exquisite time in an affair. Even the most trivial aspects of life seem erotically charged; the rain is mysterious, the sun glorious, the breeze along the avenues a pure delight. There's a foolishness to it, of course, a foolishness that grows sharper as I grow older, but at that time I was in love and in lust, and I really didn't give a shit.

On the other hand, I was greatly concerned with the simple fact that I was going to have to disappoint her. After dinner, Maggie expected to return to the Continental Club for an evening of Latin dance. She'd promised to teach me to tango, and I'd been secretly practicing all week. Unfortunately, with the count already threatened, his problem couldn't be put off. I would gamble, not dance, the night away, and I needed to arrive early to secure a place at the craps table with a view of the poker game.

I took a pearl-gray blazer from the closet and laid it on the bed. The blazer, which had come from the sales rack at Paul Stuart, was woven of a wool as soft and smooth as velvet. I quickly added a slate-blue cashmere sweater, charcoal trousers, and a pair of highly polished English oxfords. The shoes were more than a decade old, and the supple leather molded to my feet as I laced them up.

Old leather and old money. I wanted John Caroll, when I introduced myself, to absorb both impressions. I wanted him to imagine an inexhaustible bankroll, a bankroll that dwarfed the count's, a *Beckettsian* bankroll. I wanted to tempt him to ignore any suspicions aroused by the connection between the Beckett family and Sergio D'Alesse.

Maggie was waiting when I arrived at Café Argentine a few minutes after eight. Her eyes were soft with what I hoped was anticipation, her smile warm and intimate.

"I'm late," I apologized as I sat alongside her on a red leather banquette. Our lips met just as a waiter arrived to ask if I wanted a cocktail. I ordered a Scotch sour, Black Label, and settled back. Maggie's vodka martini, a lemon twist curled at the bottom, rested on a blue napkin by her right hand.

"I hear you're working."

I'd been introduced to Maggie by Luisa Czernowitz. At the time, they'd been mere acquaintances. Now they were best friends. "The call of the wild antique," I explained. "A summons no man dares ignore."

Maggie nodded. I'd shown her the vase as it appeared in the catalog, and though she made the right noises, I knew she was profoundly unimpressed. Not with the quality of the object, nor with its intrinsic beauty, but with my need of it. That need was something only another collector would appreciate, one of those facts of life (like Regina's disdain) I'd long ago learned to accept.

"When is the auction?"

"Two weeks."

"Do you think you'll snatch it up?" On many levels, Maggie was a study in contrasts. Her features were purely Mediterranean, her accent London-educated, and her idioms, because she'd been so many years away from Britain, very American. I found the mix charming, though I suspected that it masked a complex, somewhat reckless personality.

"I'll be able to make a realistic bid. It's an auction, after all. If somebody else wants it more than I do . . ." I glanced away from her. The walls behind and across from where we sat were decorated with elaborately woven gaucho blankets. At the far end of the room, the horns and skull of a bull (or a cow, or a steer) hung almost protectively above a highly polished leather saddle.

Maggie put a finger under my chin and turned my head until I faced her. "Is something wrong, Philip?"

"I don't want you to think," I said, "that I'm putting a seven-inch vase ahead of you." That was true enough. I didn't want her to think anything of the kind, even if it was true. "It's just that the case . . ." My drink arrived at that moment and I took a healthy sip before I continued. "Let me tell you about the case," I said.

She leaned in my direction, her black hair drifting forward to narrowly frame her face as I outlined the family's position, along with the strategy I hoped to pursue. Only this time, I emphasized the plight of the victim. "They've already bled the man dry," I concluded. "The problem is that they don't know it."

Maggie shook her head vigorously. "His family will come through for him," she declared. "To keep the matter private, if for no other reason."

"You don't know this family." If I was free to elaborate, I would have told her that Regina was capable of any sort of treachery. Father as well. That was a good part of the reason I'd kept my distance for the past ten years. "Look, the point here is that I can't take you dancing."

"And you want to take me gambling instead." She laughed, raising her arms. "Do I need to change?"

She was wearing black slacks and a white silk blouse. The blouse was buttoned to a lace collar that circled her throat, and its full sleeves were trimmed with lace at the cuffs. Beneath the collar, a red velvet ribbon, tied in a simple bow, added a touch of color. It was a perfect outfit for an evening of tangos. It would do for John Caroll as well.

I tried to explain the potential for danger, going so far as to reveal Caroll's birth name: Gaetano Carollo. But Maggie would not be deterred. As I spoke, her eyes grew wider, as did her smile. Would I disappoint her twice? On one level, I think she was offering a dare, but I only knew her well enough to be certain that I wanted her.

"You look perfectly fine," I finally told her. "But if you want to come along, you'll have to pay a price."

"And what would that be?"

"I want to conceal a tiny video camera in your shoulder bag. And I want you to point it exactly where I tell you."

She reached out to squeeze my thigh. "Dominate me, big boy," she whispered. "I love it."

FIVE

THE WINDOWLESS DOOR LEADING TO John Caroll's club was off to the side of the shuttered display windows protecting the treasures within Galerie Française on East Fifty-seventh Street. It opened at a touch and I let Maggie precede me into a narrow hallway leading to a flight of stairs. Against the wall to our left, a whippet-thin, square-jawed little man, wearing a blue uniform a shade lighter than that worn by the city police, sat behind a small desk. Located just above his Big Apple Security badge, a name tag identified him simply as TONY. Tony's job, as the count had described it to me, was to keep the riff-raff away. As we apparently did not fit that category, he merely smiled, gestured to the stairway, and said, "Good luck, folks."

The casino was on the third floor (the first, second, fourth, and fifth floors of the converted town house were occupied by the gallery) and the stairs were narrow and poorly illuminated, with sharp switchbacks between landings. It was all very atmospheric, but in the event of a fire—or trouble of any kind—it would be hell coming down.

By contrast, the casino was very bright. A pair of brass chandeliers over the craps tables, and a third over the poker table, augmented a dozen sconces fixed to the wall at regular intervals. There wasn't a shadow in the place.

I stood in the doorway for a moment and allowed my eyes to adjust to the light while I surveyed the room. The tables, I noted, were first-rate; the felt covering them might have been installed that day. A thick red carpet with a gold border, also in perfect condition, ran from the stairs to a small bar sealing off the end of the room closest to the windows overlooking Fifty-seventh Street. Six leather armchairs, arranged in facing pairs, fronted the bar. The chairs looked comfortable, and would have been appropriate in any of the city's top-drawer private clubs.

When Maggie and I finally stepped into the room, we were immediately approached by our host, John Caroll, who was exactly as the count had described him. Tall and broad, with a leonine head surmounted by a mane of red hair, the man was immaculately groomed. Every hair was in place and the half-moons on his finger-nails had the luster of pearls. His banker-blue, double-breasted suit fit him perfectly, while his gold cuff links and matching tiepin were both expensive and inconspicuous. He'd gone to a lot of trouble, this Gaetano Carollo, to perfect an image that couldn't possibly be natural to him. Without doubt, he would take at least as much trouble to protect it.

"Good evening." Caroll's smile was fixed, his gaze, beneath a prominent brow, curious but unthreatening. "I'm John Caroll."

"Philip Beckett," I replied, offering my hand for a brief squeeze. "And this is Maggie." Though I had the count's chip in my pocket, I didn't offer it.

"Delighted to meet you, Mr. Caroll," Maggie said.

Caroll's smile widened at Maggie's British accent. "John," he said. "Please."

"All right, John," Maggie replied with a wink. "But I want to warn you. I'm feeling very lucky tonight. You may not be so friendly by the time I'm through with you."

John was about to reply when we were interrupted by a voice from the craps table. "Phil? Is that you, old buddy?"

I recognized the man walking toward us, though I hadn't seen him in more than fifteen years. As the only black student in my class at Choate, and a star athlete, Louis Porter had been something of a celebrity. Always affable, he'd never seemed at a loss in any social setting.

"Well," Louis said to John Caroll, "it look like you've finally hit the big time. This is a man whose pockets reach his cuffs." Louis, apparently, was unaware of my fall from grace.

Our host tapped me on the arm and winked. "Take me for my shirt," he said. "I need a new one, anyway." Then he drifted off to greet an entering group of players while I introduced Louis Porter to Maggie. Like Caroll, Porter seemed delighted by Maggie's accent. As I watched his eyes flick over her body, I recalled that John Caroll's gaze hadn't dropped below Maggie's throat. He was too professional for that.

Louis, Maggie and I made small talk for a few moments before exchanging the obligatory promise to "get together soon." Then I offered Maggie my arm and we sauntered off. As intended, I chose a spot at the craps table that offered a clear view of the poker table in the center of the room. It was still quite early and the atmosphere surrounding us was charged with positive energy. After all, there were as yet no losers.

Three people, two men and a woman, were seated at the poker table, but the game hadn't started. The craps game, on the other hand, was in full swing, and Maggie, who understood the game, was eager to go. After I purchased a thousand dollars worth of chips (which, as far as I was concerned, fit the category of billable expense), I let her do all the betting. Not that I expected her skill to matter all that much. No, what I thought, or *hoped*, was that John Caroll would try to set me up the way he'd set up the count.

Maggie and I had discussed our strategy in the cab on the way over. She would begin with fifty-dollar bets, always on the pass line, then raise the bet on my signal. I would throw the dice when they reached me, but would otherwise remain aloof while I studied the poker and dice games.

We held our own for the next hour. The poker game was up and running by this time, and both craps tables were full. When the dice came around to me, I tapped Maggie's foot with my shoe. She turned so that the pinpoint lens of the tiny camera concealed in her shoulder bag focused directly on my hands, then opened the bag's zipper a few inches, and slipped her fingers inside to set the camera going. Finally, her fingers re-emerged, clutching a little packet of tissues.

"Coming out."

The stickman tossed the dice in my direction, and I let them roll to a stop. Each die showed a four on its upper face.

"You feeling lucky?" I asked.

Maggie cocked her head, then raised the bet to a hundred dollars. With a wink, I scooped up the dice with my right hand, then cupped them in both hands for what appeared to be a good shake. In fact, I was pinching the dice against my palms so they wouldn't tumble, while at the same time reversing my hands, so that when I re-opened them, the bottoms of the dice were exposed to the camera. Again, each die showed a four, a fact I'd noted on my previous roll and had now documented.

The dice were what, in a bustout game, are called tops. An ordinary die carries a different number on each face, from one through six. A top carries only three numbers, repeated on opposite sides. The deception rests on the fact that you can only look at three sides of a die at any one time and no adjoining sides of a topped die bear the same numbers. You have to turn the die over to spot the gaff, something I would never have thought to do on my own.

Although tops are available in many different combinations, this particular pair carried only a two, a four, and a six. They could not roll a seven, which gave me a huge edge. If I rolled any number except boxcars on my first toss, I had to win.

Earlier, Benny Abraham had instructed me to watch the stickman. "If the stickman touches the dice with his hands, he's most likely switching in a gaffed pair. Otherwise, he'll move the dice with the stick, which is what he's supposed to do in the first place."

The stickman—whose name was Clyde—though he used the stick to distribute chips, was, indeed, handling the dice. Though I didn't see him make the switch (and I was looking), I was certain the gaffed dice hadn't been introduced by another player because I received a pair of normal dice after making three consecutive passes and quickly sevened out.

* * *

I took a step back, at that point, in order to concentrate, not on the poker game, but on Maggie. She was standing in front of me and slightly to the left so that her right buttock and hip were poised before me in a manner that frankly fired my imagination. So much so, that the first time she leaned over the table to place a bet, I thought the seemingly deliberate thrust of that hip and buttock to be solely imagined. And thus my joy when she turned to face me at one point, standing close enough for our bodies to lightly touch along their full length while she looked up at me with eyes so brazen that I finally realized it was not.

Maggie was having a great time. With the game and with Philip Corvascio Beckett whom she'd apparently decided to bed on that very night. To an extent (though I did bend down at one point to kiss the nape of her neck), I'd resisted. There was a job to be done, after all, a burden to be manfully borne, and I needed to concentrate. But once I'd determined that John Caroll's little club was actually a bustout joint, I had all the leverage I needed, whether or not the poker game was being dealt straight up. If news of those gaffed dice should reach the other players, Caroll would be out of business in a week. Somehow, I didn't think he would risk that for the dubious pleasure of thrashing Count Sergio D'Alesse. Or me, for that matter.

"What do you say to a drink?" I asked Maggie. "And a break."

"Done." She scooped up her chips and led me across the room. Except for a pair of cocktail waitresses and a pair of bartenders, the area near the bar was deserted. The night was still young, and everybody wanted to play.

The bartender who strolled up to us, Shawn according to his name tag, wore a white shirt beneath a kelly-green vest, and a black, clip-on bow tie. "What can I get you folks?" he asked.

John Caroll approached before either of us could reply. "I'd offer to buy your drinks," he said, "but the drinks are free and it would only make me look bad." He flashed a purely professional smile, then added, "How're you folks doin'?"

"We're up a few hundred." As she spoke, Maggie slipped the fingers of her right hand beneath the cuff of my sweater and caressed the inside of my wrist. "And I'd like a glass of red wine."

Caroll turned to the bartender. "The bordeaux, Shawn. The Pichon Lalande." A moment later, Shawn arrived bearing a pair of wineglasses along with a bottle of wine, which he opened with an unnecessary flourish before offering the cork, which I refused. Finally, he filled our glasses halfway, then slipped off to join his buddy at the far end of the bar. As Maggie raised her glass in a silent toast, she leaned forward and up, as I leaned forward and down, my only thoughts of the pressure of her mouth and the texture of her lips.

"Have you spotted the shill?" she whispered into my ear.

As I have difficulty splitting my attention between sex and all other aspects of the known universe, the best response I could manage was an interrogatory grunt.

"You know what I did today, Phil? I mean *all* day."

I leaned against the bar, put the heel of my right foot on the rail. A smile, unbidden though not unwelcomed, pulled at the corners of my mouth as I recovered my equilibrium. "I have no idea."

Her arm slid around my waist, and her hand rose lightly to my chest. "I spent my entire day attempting to have a Liberian tanker bearing a cargo of Exxon crude admitted to the port of Maputo, in Mozambique. According to the harbormaster, the tanker had a leaking oil pump that would have to be repaired before the ship could be allowed to enter Maputo Bay. The parts to complete this repair, unfortunately, were not available. But in a few days, perhaps a week, at a cost of . . ." She flicked her wrist and shook her head. "This is fun," she declared. "Do you do this every day?"

"Not if I can help it." I stroked her shoulder, then kissed her cheek. Maggie had been unhappy at her job for some time, a position with which I was entirely sympathetic. "What's this business about 'spotting the shill'?"

"The fat man with the red face. He's the shill."

I shook my head. "It's too early. Anybody at that table could just be lucky."

"Phil, it's obvious."

"How so?"

"Four out of five times, he drops out on the first bet. But when he does stay in, it's always a big pot and he almost always wins." She tapped me on the chest. "Plus, you can see it on his face. He knows when a good hand is coming. You watch him for an hour, you'll see it."

"Watching a fat, red-faced man play poker for the next hour is not exactly what I had in mind for our immediate future."

This time her lips rose to meet mine. "It's been a perfect night for me," she declared, her tone amused, "and I expect it to end perfectly." Her fingers slid across my mouth, preventing a reply. She was in charge of this scenario, this foreplay, and while I was invited to play my part, I was to play it within the confines of the script.

Fortunately, it was a good script, and now that I understood my part, I was better able to concentrate. Maggie was right about the fat man with the red face. He sat just to the left of the dealer and dropped out of nearly every hand, surrendering his ante in the process. Most of the time, he slumped in his chair, his mouth slightly open, as if the weight of his cheeks and jowls were dragging at his jaw. His mouth tightened, however, and his jaw rose to prominence, on those hands he played. Even before he'd so much as glanced at his hole cards.

The signal was simple enough. On each hand, after the cards were cut, the dealer rapped the table, then declared, "Pot's right," before dealing the first card. On most hands, he rapped with his knuckles or the heel of his closed fist; but when it was the shill's turn to win, he rapped with the tips of his fingers. *Pay attention, schmuck, because here it comes.*

The other players were predictably oblivious. With the shill out of most hands, there were plenty of chips moving around and there were several other winners at the table. Nevertheless, by the end of the night, the shill, though he did not win every contested hand, would be among the winners. I wondered how much he was getting to betray his peers. Benny had told me that the mechanic, the dealer, usually received fifteen percent of the action, but I hadn't asked about the shill.

I touched Maggie's shoulder and said, "How we doin'?" We were standing at the far end of the craps table on the west side of the room and she'd been trying to set up the camera to record the dealer's signal and the fat man's reaction to it.

"I took my best shot," she replied. "If I haven't got it now, I never will." She leaned back against me and smiled. "You ready to call it a night?"

I was ready, or, rather, I would have been if the fat man hadn't chosen that moment to take a break. He gathered his chips, stood up, and walked over to the bar, where my schoolboy chum Louis Porter already stood. A moment later, they were engaged in conversation.

"Phil, do you see what I see?"

"I do."

"You check it out. I'll cash us in."

I walked over to the bar, where I took a place next to Louis and ordered a Perrier.

Louis turned to me with a smile. "How're you doing?"

"I'm up a bit, and I'm taking it with me. How about you?"

He looked across at Maggie as she approached us, then said, his voice respectfully wistful, "If I had her to go home with, I'd cash in, too. You're a lucky man."

"Hello, Louis," Maggie said a moment later. "How're you doing?" She slid her arm beneath my jacket and around my waist, the gesture seeming to me wonderfully casual, yet at the same time entirely calculated. I covered her hand, then began to caress the tips of her fingers. My sense of touch was so acute at that moment, I might have traced the whorls and ridges of her fingerprints.

"Up and down, mostly down," Louis responded with a smile. "By the way, do you know Graham Winokur?"

The fat man interrupted before Louis could introduce us. "We haven't had the pleasure," he said. "I'm Graham Winokur."

"I'm Maggie Santos," Maggie said, "and this is Philip Beckett."

I can't speak for what was going through Winokur's mind, but he responded to Maggie with a nod, then focused his attention on me. "If you're Philip Beckett, Junior, then I know your family."

Actually, I was Philip Beckett III, a designation I despised. "How do you know my family?" I asked.

"I'm handling a piece of one of their IPOs." He struggled to get his hand into the interior pocket of his suit jacket, but the jacket was too tight, and he had to unbutton it before he could remove a small billfold. His shirt was too tight, as well, especially at the collar, which he'd fastened beneath his tie with a collar bar. Perhaps he'd chosen his wardrobe for its slimming effects, but it looked to me as if the pressure of his collar and belt had forced his blood into his extremities. If he took off his shoes and socks, his feet would be as red as his face. "Here, take my card," he insisted. "I mostly do institutional investments, but I have a few private accounts."

As Maggie excused herself to visit the ladies' room, I glanced down at Winokur's business card to find the name of his firm, Winokur, Champion, Berwick, and its address, Twenty Broad Street.

Mother, when she was alive, would have pronounced Mr. Winokur hopelessly bourgeois. In her world, as in the world of my father, the world in which I'd been raised, one simply didn't make one's pitch in a social setting. It was crass, crude, cheap, common; it was purely vulgar. Nevertheless, I was properly grateful (a mark, no doubt, of how far I'd fallen), because Graham Winokur had just set himself up for the sort of deal he could not refuse.

I stared at his card for a moment, then snapped it against my thumbnail. "Actually, I *have* been meaning to make some changes. Do you think you can find some time for me tomorrow? Say, around one?"

SIX

AT THE TOP OF THE stairs, on our way out, Maggie and I exchanged perfectly insincere platitudes with John Caroll. Yes, of course, we would return soon. Yes, we would give him a chance to get even. Ha, ha, ha.

At the bottom of the stairs, Maggie offered a thank you to Tony, who held the door while he recited the official line: "Hope to see you folks real soon."

On the street, we linked arms and strolled toward Lexington Avenue in search of a cab. Above us, small clouds, illuminated by the reflected light of a million streetlamps, showed milky white against a starless black sky. My right arm circled Maggie's shoulders. Her left curled around my waist as we leaned into each other.

It was a perfect Manhattan moment, and erotic as hell. Maggie's free hand rose up to tug at the lapel of my coat and our lips met in a kiss that might have gone on for an hour despite the cold. I felt drawn into Maggie, through her lips and her tongue. Her wind-whipped hair slapped against my face as though searching for purchase. I'd never wanted a woman more.

We stepped away from each other as a cab pulled to the curb, but our eyes remained locked for a moment longer. I knew what Maggie was looking for, because I was searching for the same thing. Everybody wants to be wanted, to be passionately, mindlessly desired. That's what I saw in her dark eyes, and that's what she must have seen in my own, because at the moment there was nothing else to see.

I opened the door to the cab and stepped back to let Maggie enter. As she passed, she caressed the side of my face, her touch somehow firm and erotic at the same time. I followed her into the cab, and closed the door behind me as she ordered the cabbie to drive us to West Seventeenth Street between Seventh and Eighth avenues. The driver grunted assent, his voice barely audible through a scratched and yellowed partition that offered at least the illusion of privacy. I followed Maggie across the seat, my mouth reaching for hers, my fingers already in her hair. Her lips met mine eagerly, hungrily, and I was the first to break away.

"You're a marvel," I told her. "You're utterly unique."

She grasped my hand, pulled it to her lips, and began to nibble at my index finger. "It wasn't me who walked away from one of the largest fortunes in the world," she said. "Speaking of *unique*." She took my finger in her mouth while her hand dropped to my knee and began to move upward.

"Please, Maggie," I protested. "I'm too old to leave my game in the backseat of a car, and you're old enough to regret it if I do."

I might have protested again when she backed off, but the look in her eyes, the flush on her cheeks, the rise and fall of her breasts . . . We were sitting with our backs against the doors of the cab, riding block after block as we made love with our eyes. I'd told Benny that my many brief affairs were part and parcel of my search for the perfect woman. Now I was being put to the test, and I felt certain, as we got out of the cab, that I would never find a better woman than Maggie Santos. If I lost her, I would be convicting myself of the charge Benny Abraham, a faithful husband for thirty years, had leveled.

"What you are," he'd insisted, "is a common pussy hound. The women you screw? You don't even know they exist. All you want is the conquest."

We left a trail of clothing, from the door of Maggie's apartment, to the couch twenty feet away. We were a long time getting there because the removal of any article of clothing required the flesh beneath to be touched, to be kissed, to be savored. If the nap on her carpet had been a bit higher, I don't think we'd have made it at all.

For a long time afterward, we lay on the sofa, head back, eyes closed. Then I finally broke the silence.

"You were right," I told her as I forced my body between hers and the back of the narrow couch.

"About what?"

"About it being a perfect night."

"It is," she agreed as she turned her head to kiss me, "and the best part is that it's not over yet."

After quick trips to the bathroom, we entered her bedroom a few minutes later. Our ostensible purpose was to view the tape Maggie had recorded, since the bedroom was where she kept her television. But as I watched her fit the minitape into an adapter, then slide the adapter into the VCR, I wanted her as much as I'd wanted her before we'd entered the apartment. Most of the women I'd known, especially in the early stages of an affair, covered themselves after making love, if only with a sheet. I can't speak for their motivations, but Maggie seemed completely unaware of her nudity. Or so I thought until she turned down the satin spread, hopped between the covers, and fixed me with a frankly evaluating gaze.

"You know something?" she finally said as I climbed in behind her. "You're better-looking naked than dressed."

Before I could respond (before I could even decide whether or not I'd been flattered), she pressed the TV's remote control, and we were off and running.

The black-and-white picture on Maggie's twelve-inch TV was not only of predictably poor quality, it jiggled relentlessly. Nevertheless, the essentials were all there. The fours on the tops and bottoms of the dice were clearly visible. If anything, Winokur's come-to-attention each time the dealer tapped his fingertips against the edge of the table was more obvious than it had been while the game was in progress.

The television was on a dresser (a nice dresser, by the way; French provincial and of Drexel Heritage quality) near my side of the bed. I was on my side with Maggie lying against my back. She'd thrown her right leg across my own and was rubbing her heel against my knee in a way that seemed to me speculative. Maybe I was getting to know her better, because after a moment, she said, "Tell if I'm wrong. The problem here is how to get this tape to John Caroll without getting killed in the process. That about it?"

"I've a way around that problem." I dropped onto my back and looked up into her eyes. Despite her sweat-matted hair and the line of mascara running from the corner of her left eye, I found her absolutely gorgeous.

"Tell me."

"I'm going to muscle Winokur into doing the job for me." I folded a pillow in half and forced it beneath my head. Now our faces were inches apart. "He's the one who has the most to lose."

"And not Caroll?"

"Caroll's a criminal. If you close him down on Fifty-seventh Street, he'll lick his wounds and open up somewhere else. But Winokur's a stockbroker catering to a small, select clientele. He has nowhere else to go. If word gets out that he's a crook, not only will his clients vanish, he'll be blackballed by every legit brokerage on the Street."

Maggie nodded, then caressed the left side of my face. Again, I pronounced the gesture speculative. "I need to tell you something," she said. "A confession."

"Something I need to know?"

"Before we go any farther."

I took a deep breath, then announced, "All right, I'm ready."

"The fact of the matter," she told me, "is that I drool."

"Drool?"

"While I'm sleeping. I drool on my pillow. Or on anything else too close to my mouth."

"How often?"

"Every night."

"Without fail?"

"Without fail."

"What if I were to sleep with my head at your feet?"

"Then you'll probably wake up with soggy toes."

I wanted to tell her that she was amazing. But I'd already used the word too many times. Instead, I pulled her up until she was sitting across my belly, then took her face between my hands. "Right now," I admitted, "there's only one approach to this drooling problem that really appeals to me."

"And what's that?"

"Let's not go to sleep."

SEVEN

THOUGH WE LASTED INTO THE wee hours, we did eventually fall asleep. I was accustomed to late hours (after all, I had, for the most part, no schedule to keep), but Maggie seemed out of sorts when I opened my eyes to find her wriggling into her skirt. According to the clock on the night table, it was ten minutes after ten, which left me with plenty to time to do what I had to do. Maggie's work ethic, on the other hand, the ethic demanded of all upwardly striving corporate lawyers, required her to arrive at her desk an hour early. Now she would be two hours late.

I sat up in bed, then waited until she turned to me before I said, "Hi."

Her features softened as she looked at me. My heart softened as well. She was wearing a maroon business skirt over a pair of ultra-sheer pantyhose, and a plain black bra. A charcoal blazer and a white blouse hung from hangers on the closet door.

"Keep your eyes in your pants," she said. "Right now, I'm hearing the slosh of crude oil against the hull of a tanker. For me, it's the siren's song."

I couldn't ignore her bitter tone, not when she'd already made her dislike of her job clear, but I didn't want to advise her, either. Like most men (especially men of the very patriarchal class into which I was born), I have a strong tendency to offer advice I can't take. It's pitiful, really.

"Maybe," I offered, "today will be the day when somebody invents the electric fuel cell that renders fossil fuels obsolete."

Maggie slid into her blouse and quickly buttoned it to the top. The blouse was collarless and made of an appropriately opaque fabric. "We'd kill her," she said. "Without doubt."

"Then I guess you're stuck." I got out of bed and struggled into yesterday's underwear, then into my wrinkled trousers. "You mind if I use your phone?"

"Go ahead."

A moment later, I was speaking to Regina, who began her workday no later than seven o'clock. "You promised to call me last night," she instantly accused.

"I was tied up." In fact, in the heat of the moment, I'd forgotten Regina entirely.

"I waited until one."

"I'm sorry."

"Sorry? What you are, Philip, is unreliable. Which is why I opposed using you in the first place. Now, either you work for me or you don't. Which is it?"

"You wanna fire me, Regina, I wouldn't blame you."

"But would you return the money?"

Though I knew, from years of experience, that playing tit-for-tat with my sister was as futile as human experience gets, I sometimes strung her along, strictly for my own amusement. The thought of losing my vase, however, was anything but amusing. "I've already deposited your check," I lied.

Her voice tightened down as she went for the rhetorical kill. "I could always stop it."

I wanted to say, *you do that and I'll come up there and rip out your fucking fingernails.* But not only was I too well-bred for that approach, I knew it wouldn't do me any good. No, there was only one course of action open to me: self-abasement. Regina wasn't going to quit until I took it.

"Regina," I said, "I promise that I'll call you whenever I promise to call you. From this moment forward. Without fail."

In lieu of a victory salute, she sniffed once, then again, then asked, "Have you made any progress?"

"Some." For purely practical reasons, I keep my clients as ill-informed as possible until I produce a tangible result. "And there's more to come if you can find it in your heart to do me a little favor."

"That's why you called me?"

"Regina, please, it's ten o'clock and I have a lot of work to do."

She sniffed again, this time in disdain, but said, "What is it you want?"

"I want to borrow your car and driver for a few hours."

"You want the Rolls?"

"I need to put up a front." My reasons for wanting the Rolls were, in fact, more complex. At some point I was going to have to speak directly to John Caroll and I wanted our surroundings to preclude the possibility of serious bodily harm. To my knowledge, no human being had ever been murdered in the back of a Rolls-Royce. "I could always rent a limo and bill it to you, Regina, but I couldn't guarantee privacy or the discretion of the driver."

When I hung up the receiver a few minutes later, after having secured Regina's cooperation, Maggie was fully dressed and sitting next to me on the edge of the bed. The expression on her face was properly sympathetic. "That didn't sound like much fun," she said.

"I wanted you to know," I explained, "that what I do isn't all thrills and excitement."

"Why?"

"Why?"

"Why do you want me to know about your work?"

Lacking the courage to take the conversation any farther, my response was typically male. I turned and laid my hands on Maggie's shoulders, half-expecting her to pull away. After all, not only was she late for work, she was fully made up, and what I had in mind would require an emergency repair. But she reached for me without hesitation, her eyes closing as her mouth opened. I kissed her lips, her eyes, her ears, until, finally, she sighed and stood.

"I haven't fallen for anybody in a long time," she said as she trotted off to the bathroom. "I forgot how good it feels."

* * *

I found the Rolls, with Thaddeus at the wheel, standing next to the fire hydrant in front of my apartment building when I emerged, briefcase in hand, a little before noon. Freshly showered and dressed, I was wearing my best suit (a charcoal Ungaro I'd purchased last year for the wedding of a second cousin) over a powder-blue shirt and a red tie dotted with gold fleurs-de-lis.

The ride downtown was predictably slow, and I was late for my one-o'clock appointment. Nevertheless, Winokur's secretary, presumably well briefed, didn't seem to mind. All smiles, she rose to open her boss's door, and a moment later I was perched on the unyielding seat of an armchair in front of his desk.

It was quite a desk. Bowl-shaped and cut from a single piece of granite, its blood-red top was highly polished, while its gray sides were as rough and irregular as the slopes of a mountain. The problem was that it was much too big for Graham Winokur's small office. It reeked of the sort of vanity I'd always associated with the profoundly second-rate.

"Coffee, Phil," Winokur asked, "or something stronger?"

"No thanks, Graham. I'm pressed for time."

"Right." Winokur's grin was suffused with equal measures of narcissism and greed. "So, what can I do for you?"

I leaned forward, then, with great deliberation, and tapped the desktop with my fingertips before settling back in the chair.

Winokur blinked once, then twice, as his eyes swept the room. "I'm sorry," he said, still smiling. "I don't see what you're getting at."

Taking my time about it, grinning all the while, I did the whole bit again. Tap, tap, tap. Finally I said, "You should be happy, Graham. When I tap like this, it means I'm gonna deal you a good hand. Which is more than you deserve."

He closed his eyes for a moment, presumably in an effort to form a strategy. Should he continue to deny, maybe force me to produce hard evidence? Or should he play his hole card right away? Finally, he opened his eyes and fixed me with what I assumed to be a baleful stare. "Do you have *any* idea who you're fucking with?"

I have another, darker side, a side I was completely unaware of before going to work for Silena Fisher. Fisher Security did a fair amount of work for bail bondsmen, and from time to time, each of her investigators was assigned to return an accused felon to the jurisdiction of the court. Like any other soldier anticipating combat for the first time, I was afraid that I'd panic, flee, disgrace myself. But I'd felt no fear whatever on the afternoon I cornered Martin Crowell on West Thirty-eighth Street. Not even when he'd promptly knocked me on my narrow ass. I'd grabbed his leg as he tried to flee, then calmly applied a judo technique I'd learned at Choate. The technique didn't work exactly as intended, but it must have annoyed Crowell, because he stopped trying to get away and concentrated, instead, on the more enjoyable task of beating me to death.

Fortunately, the police arrived before Crowell accomplished his purpose, and my injuries were limited to a scalp laceration and a few bruises. But how well I'd fought wasn't the point. The point was that I hadn't been afraid, not even when it became clear that Martin Crowell was too much for me to handle by myself. The point was that I'd fought hard and with a savagery I could not have predicted. The point was that I enjoyed combat and I wasn't about to be intimidated by a card cheat.

"I'm fucking with *you*, Graham." I explained. "But you don't have anything to worry about. I just want you to run a little errand for me."

More than likely, Winokur had been expecting me to make an attempt at blackmail. When I didn't, his mouth opened slightly and his eyes darted from his hands to the desktop.

"I want you to take a ride," I continued. "I've got a videotape that John Caroll needs to see."

"And you want me to show it him?"

"Exactly."

"No fucking way."

"You afraid he's gonna hurt you?"

Winokur laughed. "Hey, if you've got the balls, why don't you show it to him yourself? I'll give you his home address."

"The only thing you need to fear," I said, "is what will happen to your livelihood if your clients discover that you're a thief."

He slapped his palms on the desk, the gesture closer to a tantrum than a threat. "Who are you to call me a thief?"

"I'm the guy who caught you, Graham. And I have the video to prove it."

"Yeah?" He swiveled his chair across the room, then opened a large cabinet to reveal a television with a built-in VCR. "Let's see what you got."

Winokur watched the tape with his back to me. He said nothing, but his shoulders gradually dropped as the tape played out. All along, he'd been imagining himself to have the aplomb of a cat burglar. Now he had to face the facts. He was just another fat guy who couldn't hold his water.

"It wasn't like you think," he said without turning around. "I was deep in the hole."

I listened to the whir of the rewinding tape for a moment, then asked, "Do we have to go through this?"

"Yeah, we do." He turned to face me, his expression very intense. Apparently my charge had struck close to home.

"Why?"

"Because if you were in my position, you would've done the same thing."

I shrugged. "All right, let's get it over with."

"They picked me up one night, Caroll and a pair of goons, and they took me into the basement of this house in Queens. Caroll took out a gun, cocked it, and put it to the back of my head. He told me I had two choices. I could work off the debt or I could leave my face on the floor. Guess which one I picked?"

EIGHT

AN HOUR LATER, I WAS sitting in the back of the Rolls waiting for John Caroll (or for his murderous minions) to emerge from the San Remo, one of New York's landmark apartment buildings. Located on Central Park West, the Art Nouveau San Remo is organized as a co-operative, which means that residents, in lieu of buying or renting their apartments, purchase shares in the co-op, shares that are not freely sold to the first individual to appear with the money. Instead, applicants must prove themselves worthy by securing approval from notoriously finicky boards of directors. Richard Nixon may have been the most prominent applicant ever to be turned down by a co-op board, but he was far from the only applicant.

In the meantime, Gaetano Carollo, aka John Caroll, had made it past the board of the San Remo, in the process securing himself a rather prestigious slice of the American dream. And that meant, to me as I analyzed the situation in the back of the Rolls, that despite Graham Winokur's unpleasant experience (assuming he'd told me the truth), John Caroll was not a street criminal. He did not, for example, come home from the club, exchange his suit for a leather jacket and a ski mask, then go out to hijack trucks. The very cultivated image he projected at the club spilled over into his everyday life. He would listen to reason.

This was important because the message I'd instructed Winokur to convey to John Caroll was unequivocal. This was Caroll's one chance. If we couldn't reach an immediate understanding, the essence of which I would reveal only to him, I would go public with the tape.

Caroll took his time thinking it over, but when he finally emerged forty minutes after Winokur went up to fetch him, he was again immaculately groomed and dressed.

"Nice touch," he said as he slid in beside me. "The Rolls, I mean."

I responded by removing an envelope from the briefcase I carried and tossing it in his lap. "Last night's profit," I explained. "It was good of you to let me win, but the money represents a conflict of interest and I can't accept it."

He looked down at the envelope, then back at me, a smile playing at the corner of his mouth. "You got serious balls, kid, *serious* balls. You know what could happen to you here?"

"I'm a Beckett," I bragged. "My family belongs to the gang that runs the world.

Caroll laughed. "Is that the best you can do?"

"I'm afraid it is."

A momentary silence followed as Caroll inspected the interior of the Rolls. His fingers caressed the leather seat, then the burled walnut partition between ourselves and Thaddeus. Caroll was smiling again. "I got the money to own one of these," he told me. "What I don't have . . ." He shook his head. "Why don't we get down to business?"

"By all means." I folded my hands in my lap. "Sergio D'Alesse . . ."

"That fucking deadbeat?" Caroll's eyebrows rose to his hairline. "You're risking your ass for that deadbeat?"

"What are you telling me, John? That you cheated him fair and square?"

He calmed down immediately. "Something like that," he admitted.

"Well, you're not gonna get paid." I raised my hand to forestall a response. "D'Alesse doesn't have the money and the family's not willing to bail him out. No matter what you do to him."

"He's that much of a bum?"

"He is."

"And what about the tape?"

"Forget D'Alesse and I'll forget the tape."

"See, Phil, that's my problem. I mean, how do I know, say six months from now, you won't show the tape anyway? The players, they're your people. They belong to the gang that runs the world." He tapped his chest, his smile still in place. "Me, I belong to a gang that runs a lousy craps game. In the long run, you got no good reason to protect me."

"Are you telling me you're willing to tear up Sergio's marker?"

Caroll sighed. "It was a bluff, all right. We don't break people's legs. Violence is bad for business." He tapped my knee. "Not that I couldn't make an exception if that tape became public."

I stared at Caroll for a moment. I was strongly tempted to explain that I had no loyalty to my class, but in the end I held back. Not only because I didn't want to appear weak, but also because I felt his threat was pro forma. We'd put our cards on the table and now it was time for me to concentrate my attentions on Maggie Santos, who was to meet me after work at Sharpers, where I'd treat Benny Abraham to a well-deserved dinner.

"Point taken," I finally said, hoping that was what he wanted to hear. "With a little luck, we'll never see each other again." I glanced at my watch. "Well, time to give Sergio the good news."

"You're telling me to get lost?"

"Not in so many words, John."

Caroll smiled. "You got balls, kid, and I like that. You ever decide to change professions, give me a call."

I dismissed Thaddeus after phoning the count to let him know I was on my way over, then quickly left the car. I don't recall subjecting my encounter with John Caroll to even the most cursory analysis. Instead, what preoccupied me as I crossed Central Park West and entered the park, was whether to describe the confrontation over dinner, or save it for pillow talk later. Benny was my best friend, and we were ordinarily quite open with each other, but I wanted to re-create the intimacy of my prior evening with Maggie. As I've already said, I'd had a number of very intense, and very brief, affairs over the years. Each began with a long calculated seduction (though it was not always I who played the part of the seducer), followed by passion, followed by an abject failure to take the next step.

To a certain extent, I understood the process. Shortly after graduating from Wharton, at Father's insistence, I'd undergone counseling. Until then, without ever considering the matter in depth, I'd assumed that my childhood, and Regina's as well, were relatively normal. As young children, we rarely saw Father, who was perpetually occupied by the business of protecting the family's interests. Mother was equally remote, though every evening after finishing our dinners, we were ushered into her sitting room by our respective nannies. Fully made up and dressed for her own dinner—right down to the precious stones at her throat, on her fingers, and in her ears—Luna Corvascio Beckett was an incredibly handsome woman. There was never a time, not even years later, when I wasn't awed in her presence. As a young child, I was afraid even to approach her, and can vividly recall my nanny, a middle-aged Irish woman named Brigid, urging me forward to kiss Mother's proffered cheek.

I don't want to belabor the point, or to claim that my very privileged childhood was somehow a time of deprivation. But what I learned in the course of my therapy was that the highly ritualized art of seduction can be every bit as formal as the children's hour in one of the many homes of Luna Corvascio Beckett. The problems emerge later. After the seduction, after that first series of passionate nights, when the carefully cultivated personas break down, one must learn either to embrace a fully realized human being, or to back away.

Backing away had been my specialty since the night, at age sixteen, when I'd lost my virginity to Elizabeth Turlow in the course of a debutante ball at the Waldorf-Astoria. Consummated in a broom closet, our liaison was over almost before it began.

Central Park is New York City's playground, an ongoing carnival in which I ordinarily take great delight. On that afternoon, however, as I made my way across the park toward York Avenue, I was oblivious to the sunbathers in the Sheep Meadow, or to the hordes of excited children at the zoo on the east side of the park, or even to an impromptu jug band playing for contributions near the East Sixty-fifth Street entrance to the park. The inescapable reality was that I was tremendously drawn to Maggie Santos and didn't want to lose her a week, or a month, or even six months, down the line. My problem was that I had (or *felt* I had) nothing to offer besides story-book romance. I could supply little touches like the pima cotton bath towels I'd laid out when I'd gone home earlier to change, or the royal blue terry cloth robe I'd purchased several days before at Henri Bendel's specifically for Maggie's use, or the candles on the dresser, or the bouquet of crimson tulips on the nightstand. But those were not the stuff on which long-term relationships are built, and I knew it.

I carried my thoughts with me all the way to the count's apart-ment, where I rang the intercom several times but received no answer. I suppose that my suspicions should have been aroused, but I simply assumed that the system was out of order and applied my PI skills to the problem. I stepped back onto the sidewalk and waited for a resident to appear, in this case an elderly woman pushing a red shopping cart. When she inserted her key into the lock, I came up alongside her, smiled and said, "Let me get this for you," as I pushed the door open.

The woman looked me over, then returned my smile. "Thank you," she said as she entered the lobby and I followed her inside.

The count's apartment was on the third floor, two flights up, and I took the stairs instead of waiting for the elevator. When I emerged, the long narrow corridor with its gray walls and gray carpeting was deserted. I walked up to the count's door and rang the bell. No answer. I rang again, producing the same result, then knocked, then finally turned as the elevator opened to reveal my cousin Audrey.

"Philip?" Her eyes widened, and her mouth opened in surprise. The reaction was over almost before it started, but I recall won-dering if she'd become one of those fearful women who take every male below the age of seventy for a mugger.

"Audrey," I said, "It's good to see you again."

"And you," she responded, smiling now as she bussed my cheek. She was wearing a thick woolen coat that emphasized her large hips and larger derriere. Ringlets of her already thinning hair protruded from beneath a shapeless knit cap. She seemed, as always, slightly out of breath, as if perpetually responding to some emergency known only to herself. "Did you ring the bell?"

"No answer."

"Sergio likes to nap in the afternoon," she explained as she unlocked the door and pushed it open. "He's probably asleep."

But Count Sergio D'Alesse of Turin was not peacefully asleep in his bed. He was seated at a Formica-topped breakfast table in the apartment's little dining area, slumped forward, his face lying in the remains of a raspberry tart. His left hand dangled alongside the chair's tubular frame, while his right, extended across the table, clutched a fractured demitasse cup. At the back of his head, a wormlike streak of already-drying blood meandered from a small, blackened hole in his skull, through his neatly clipped hair, and onto the collar of his white-on-white, pinpoint oxford dress shirt.

NINE

"HE'S DEAD?" AUDREY'S TONE WAS inquisitive, as if the matter were under dispute.

"Listen to me." I put my arm around her shoulder and tried to gently guide her back into the hallway. "We've got to get out of here and call the police."

Shaking me off, she stumbled over to her husband. "Poor bastard." She reached down as if to take his hand, then shuddered and half-fell into the chair beside him. "Poor worthless bastard."

My own thoughts were bouncing through my brain like John Caroll's gaffed dice. Except for the need to leave, the only thing I was sure of was that everything was wrong. *Everything.*

"We've got to get out of here," I repeated as my eyes swept the short hallway leading to the bedroom. "Whoever did this might still be in the apartment."

Audrey responded with a snort. "This is my home," she declared with a wave of her free hand. "Be it ever so homely."

I was close enough to smell the alcohol on her breath. Unless I dragged her through the door, Audrey wasn't going anywhere. "You know I loved him," she told me. "You know I did."

"We have to be practical." I gave it one last try. "The door was locked. Your husband's killer could be inside the apartment."

Audrey's grin was cold. "How do I know he's not standing in front of me?" Before I could even guess at a response, she added, "And the door wasn't locked. You could have opened it by twisting the knob."

My thoughts slowed abruptly. I was almost certain I'd heard the snap of the tumbler as it retracted. Was Audrey lying? Was she mistaken? Although she'd been drinking long enough to become, if not belligerent, at least stubborn, she didn't appear to be drunk.

"Are you sure?" I asked. I might have saved my breath. Audrey had already turned back to her husband. The practicalities were left to me.

Despite the business with the lock, I found myself wishing that I was armed as I walked down the hall and pushed the bedroom door open to reveal an empty room. Distinctly relieved, I quickly checked the closets, then the bathroom, then stopped long enough to formulate some sort of strategy. The police had to be called, but what Audrey had said about my possibly having killed her husband was a position those same police might well embrace. I'd spoken to D'Alesse from the Rolls perhaps forty minutes before, then walked across town. In that time, I'd seen nobody I knew, and done nothing to attract attention, and could not, therefore, verify my whereabouts (in which the cops would undoubtedly show great interest) at the time the count was killed.

The phone in the bedroom began to ring before I could decide my next move. I let it go for a bit, hoping Audrey would pick up, but she didn't move a muscle. Finally, I answered.

"Who is this?" As always, Regina's tone was imperious.

"It's Philip," I replied.

"Philip? What are you doing there?"

"I came over to let the count know that he was off the hook for the forty grand. Unfortunately, someone killed him before I could deliver the good news."

"Killed? What are you talking about?"

"Sergio's dead, Regina. Shot in the back of the head."

She took a minute to think it over, then asked, "Have you phoned the police?"

"I was about to do just that when you called."

She sniffed once, as if I'd failed, not for the first time, to perform some elementary task. "Do you want me to send an attorney over?"

"Yeah, for Audrey."

"What about you?"

"I think I'll find my own. See you later." I hung up before she could respond, then called Benny Abraham at Sharpers. I realized that the cops might check the phone logs and draw the wrong conclusion, but it had to be done. Benny listened while I briefly explained the situation, including a request that he send his personal lawyer, Arthur Howell, to the D'Alesse apartment. He agreed without hesitation.

"Is that it?" he finally asked. "Anything else I can do?"

"Yeah, Maggie Santos is supposed to meet me at Sharpers. We were going to treat you to dinner, believe it or not. I want you to tell her that I might not make it."

Benny knew Maggie by sight, but I had yet to introduce them. "Don't worry, kid. I'll see she's taken care of. Meanwhile, keep your mouth shut until Arthur shows up. The cops'll probably slap you around, but, hey, you're the kinda guy I know could take it. See ya."

He hung up, laughing, and I quickly dialed 911 to report the D'Alesse homicide. When the operator asked for my name, I told her that I'd be at the scene when the cops arrived, then went in search of Audrey. I found her in the kitchen. She was pouring coffee beans from a paper sack into one of those brewers that grind the beans automatically. "I'll be having company soon," she explained. "I want to be ready."

As she spoke, her hand began to shake, spilling beans onto the counter and floor. I took the bag from her hand, then led her to a chair in the living room. I would have guided her out of the apartment, but I was sure she wouldn't go.

Once I got Audrey settled, I walked through the apartment, this time with my wits about me. As far as I could tell, nothing was out of place. I checked the door leading into the apartment next, but found no indication of forced entry, not even the sort of minuscule scratches that might be left by a pick. Finally, without disturbing his body, I examined the wound in Sergio's skull.

The count had been shot, dead center, in the back of the head, evidently with a small-caliber weapon because there was no exit wound. I put my finger to the back of my own head and realized that, awkward as it was, D'Alesse could have pulled the trigger himself. This was important, because the gun that killed him (and which I noticed for the first time) was resting on the floor beneath his chair.

Standing beside the count, I was still trying to remember how closely I'd examined his body upon entering the apartment, when the first cops to respond knocked on the door. They were uniformed patrolmen, Coniglio and Acerrez by their name tags, and as mismatched as it's possible for partners to be. Except for a monk's fringe around his ears, the middle-aged Coniglio was completely bald. His rumpled uniform was stained at the collar, and the skin on his face and neck was as ruddy as the walnut grip on his ancient Smith & Wesson revolver.

By contrast, Acerrez, who appeared to be in his early twenties, was all spit and polish. His uniform fit him so perfectly, it might have been sewn by the London tailor who made Father's suits. "Somebody reported a shooting?" he asked.

I stepped back and Acerrez, without saying a word to his partner who remained in the hall, strode past me and up to the body. He put his fingertips to the count's throat, then announced, "He's dead," before turning back to me and asking, "You wanna identify yourself?"

"My name is Philip Beckett."

"And you, ma'am?" he said to Audrey, who was still in the living room.

"Audrey D'Alesse," she replied. "I'm his wife."

"The victim's?"

"Yes, the victim's."

Acerrez nodded, then glanced at his partner and raised his eyebrows. Coniglio bit at his lower lip, then said, "I'm gonna have to ask you step into the hall, Mr. Beckett. We gotta clear the scene."

"Mrs. D'Alesse?" Acerrez approached Audrey and offered his hand. "Please. We need to clear the apartment until the detectives arrive."

Audrey locked her hands beneath her breasts. "This is my home."

"I know that, ma'am, but it's also a crime scene." Clearly uncomfortable, Acerrez shifted his weight from one foot to another. "We want to catch whoever did this," he finally said. "We need . . ."

"How do you know," Audrey declared as her upper lip curled into a little sneer, "that *I* don't know who did this? How do you know I didn't *do* it myself?"

When I felt Coniglio's hand on my shoulder, I flinched, and he quickly pulled it away. "C'mon," he said, "we're gonna take a little walk."

Coniglio was just doing his job. After what Audrey said, he didn't have any choice. We were suspects and had to be separated.

"You don't have any weapons on ya?" Coniglio asked as we walked to the end of the hall furthest from the stairwell. Though his belly strained the buttons of his regulation blouse, he moved with the casual grace of a bear on a log.

"I don't."

"You wanna show me some ID?"

I retrieved my billfold, then passed over my driver's license. I did not offer my PI's license.

"Philip Beckett," Coniglio said. "Whatta you do for a living?"

Despite his expression demonstrating little more than profound indifference, I decided to cut him off. If possible, I wanted to postpone giving a statement until I had a chance to discuss the question of client confidentiality with my lawyer. I knew I couldn't protect John Caroll, whose threats were on the record, but I hoped to keep Regina out of it. The sad part is that I was certain she would assume I hadn't made the attempt in the event that I failed.

"Officer," I declared, "I'm not going to give a statement until the detectives arrive."

"Is that right?" Coniglio's eyes ran up and down my body. "Nice suit," he finally said.

"Thank you."

"Nice tie, nice shirt, nice shoes. I'll bet you got a nice watch, too. And a nice car."

I didn't respond to his taunts. Without doubt, Coniglio was an officer of the old school. If our conversation was taking place thirty blocks uptown, he'd convey his contempt with his fists. As it was, he quickly settled into virtual immobility.

The wait was short, a mere ten minutes before waves of police and city personnel began to arrive. The paramedics and the Crime Scene Unit came first, six men and two women. With Sergio immediately pronounced dead, CSU began to work the scene while the paramedics retreated. An assistant medical examiner and a pair of morgue attendants arrived next. The AME went directly to the body while the attendants slouched in the hallway, chatting among themselves. A patrol sergeant, accompanied by a lieutenant, showed up a few minutes later. The lieutenant, a short blond woman, looked at Sergio for a moment, then shook her head before turning to the elevator as a pair of detectives, both male, both wearing microfiber trench coats, emerged.

No one approached Coniglio or myself, not even after the detectives arrived. There was no rush, of course, because I wasn't going anywhere until they released me. I might have used the time for any number of constructive purposes, but I chose to wallow in self-pity instead. My conversation with John Caroll had left me with a distinct sense of accomplishment. After only a single day, I'd earned enough to contend for my dragon-fish vase, and that freed me to return to what I did best, which was nothing, and to my burgeoning affair with Maggie Santos. Now, like it or not, I was so deeply involved in a homicide investigation that I'd felt it necessary to summon an attorney. Until Arthur Howell arrived, I didn't think it could get any worse.

All along, the cops had been politely confronting residents, then escorting them to their respective apartments. But when the elevator doors opened and Arthur Howell stepped out, the closest officer, a sergeant, squared his shoulders as if preparing for a fight. Perhaps it was because Arthur Howell was a very dark black man, or maybe it was the pearl gray cashmere topcoat and matching homburg, or Howell's imposing height, or maybe the sergeant simply recognized him.

Though not quite a celebrity, Howell was well known in New York legal circles. Impeccably mannered, he was an absolute bulldog in the courtroom, as well as a sharp negotiator who could plea-bargain with the best of them. Cops hated him. Prosecutors feared him. Most defendants couldn't afford him.

I watched Arthur pass his business card to the sergeant, then announce, his deep bass tones easily carrying the length of the corridor, "I represent Philip Beckett. I want to confer with my client."

The sergeant hemmed and hawed for a moment, then, predictably enough, called in the blond lieutenant. She listened to Arthur's request, then fixed me with a hard, speculative look before shrugging her shoulders. A moment later, Arthur and I were huddled together with Coniglio fifteen feet away.

Though not friends, Arthur and I knew each other well enough to exchange greetings before I half-whispered my story into his ear. I left nothing out and he didn't speak until I finished.

"You made no statement to the police?"

"I identified myself, but that's it."

Howell's skull was large and his features, especially his eyes, were generous. Now he fixed me with his warmest smile. "I don't think I've ever had a consultation with an innocent client this early in the game. It's a first for me."

As Howell was undoubtedly charging me by the nanosecond, I let his observation stand and cut to the chase. "I need to know whether I'm legally allowed to protect my client's privacy. It may sound pretentious, but privacy is very important to the Beckett family."

"Philip, please." His smile still in place, he put his hand on my shoulder. "You have every right to refuse to give a statement until you're subpoenaed to appear before a grand jury."

"And that's it? I can walk away?"

"No, Philip, it's not." He gave my shoulder a manly squeeze. "I hate to be the bearer of bad news, but if you decide to exercise your constitutional rights, more than likely you'll be arrested and charged with murder."

TEN

I WAS STILL CONSIDERING ARTHUR'S gloomy hypothetical when the elevator doors opened to release Wendell Turcotte, partner at Turcotte, Pendleton, Brown, the white-glove law firm that had handled the Beckett family's affairs. Turcotte was there, not only to represent Audrey, but to make sure I understood my role in the affair. After speaking briefly to his client, he approached Arthur, shook hands, then told me, "I've assured the detectives in charge that they can expect complete cooperation from the Beckett family," before turning away.

Perhaps a half hour later, after passing a nitrate test performed on my hands by a Crime Scene officer with a severe case of psoriasis, I was sitting in the back of an unmarked Ford Taurus with Arthur alongside. Detective Kirk Mulligan sat in front, the tape I'd made at John Caroll's club on the seat next to him. He listened attentively while I gave a complicated statement. Then he stared at me for a long moment, his sad blue eyes so clear they might have been drops of paint.

"You say that Mr. D'Alesse didn't respond when you buzzed the intercom?" he finally asked.

"That's right."

"Weren't you alarmed?"

"I assumed the intercom wasn't working."

"But," he insisted, "you weren't alarmed."

"I'd spoken to Sergio maybe forty minutes before and he was in good spirits. Remember, as far as I knew, I'd gotten his debt forgiven. If there were other problems in his life, I wasn't aware of them."

"Did you know him well?"

"Aside from exchanging a few words at family gatherings, I didn't know him at all."

Mulligan nodded, as if he'd been expecting this very response. "When you got upstairs, did you try the door?"

"Audrey arrived before I got the chance."

"How did she react when you told her there was no response to your knock?"

"She told me that her husband was probably asleep."

"Didn't that seem strange? I mean, the victim was expecting you."

"I suppose it should have, but I don't recall thinking much of it. Audrey had her keys out and we were inside a minute later."

We went back and forth, examining various aspects of my statement, for more than an hour. During that time, I held back only a single detail. Though I supposed that Mulligan would eventually find out, I did not tell him that Maggie Santos had accompanied me to John Caroll's little casino. Perhaps I was being overly protective (certainly I had no sense that Maggie was unable to care for herself), or perhaps I simply wanted to withhold some little piece of information because I was angry. Not with Detective Mulligan, who remained exquisitely polite throughout, but with my sister and my father.

The way I saw it, as I submitted to Mulligan's patient interrogation, I was purely a dupe. Someone in the family had used me. The alternative—that a heretofore unknown enemy just happened to execute Sergio D'Alesse while he was under threat from John Caroll—strained credulity.

Kirk Mulligan's eyes didn't leave my face as he continued to probe. He was putting everything on the record. Should I become a viable suspect later, there would be no squirming room.

"What made you decide to walk from Caroll's to the D'Alesse apartment?" he asked for the second time. "Why didn't you have the chauffeur drive you?"

"Look outside, detective. It's a beautiful evening and it was a beautiful day." When he appeared unconvinced, I added, "I love to walk, especially in Central Park. Besides, I didn't see any need to hurry. I was delivering good news."

"That's another thing that's bothering me here. You told me you weren't close to the victim. You also told me that the victim didn't hire you. So how come you didn't just give him the good news over the phone and have done with it?"

"Sergio and Audrey are family, detective. I wasn't going to dismiss him with a phone call."

"You felt you had to deliver the news in person, but you weren't in any hurry to get there. That about it?"

"That's about it," I admitted.

He changed directions abruptly, as he'd been doing all along. "Do you have a license to carry a concealed weapon?"

"Yes."

"How many weapons do you own?"

"One, a 9mm Browning. It's on a shelf in my closet."

"And . . ."

My expensive attorney, who'd been silently observing (while no doubt calculating his fee), finally interrupted. "We've been over this before, detective, and it's growing late."

Mulligan frowned. "I'm just trying to get to the bottom of this mess." His sad eyes moved from Arthur's to mine. "You gotta concede, what with you having opportunity, and the means lying on the floor next to the victim, it's a fuckin' mess."

"I passed the nitrate test and I'll pass a lie detector test. I didn't kill Sergio D'Alesse. I had no reason to kill him."

"You've already said that," Mulligan observed.

"That's the problem," Arthur rejoined. "He's already said *everything*. At least twice."

Mulligan sighed. "Just a couple more questions?" His tone was pleading, but I think he was amused.

"Shoot."

He stared at me for a moment, then laughed. "That was a joke," he observed.

"Yes," I agreed, "a joke." I looked out the window, at a short black man, almost a midget, who stood beneath a red awning on the other side of the street. He had a crutch beneath his left arm and a tin cup in his right hand. As pedestrians approached, he shook the cup but was otherwise motionless.

Mulligan cleared his throat—"you told me that John Caroll"—he glanced at his notes—"You said that Caroll threatened to harm you if the tape became public. Did I get that right?"

"You got it right."

"Do you think he meant it?"

"I think he would have gone to great lengths to protect the game." I rolled on before Mulligan could interrupt. "He would even go so far as to forgive D'Alesse's debt. Or to allow me to pressure him. As long as the game wasn't jeopardized, he was willing to compromise."

Mulligan smiled again. This time his smile was positively feral. "That's not where I was going, Phil. That's not the point." He reached down, started the car, then turned back to me. "No, the point I'm making here is that now John Caroll's game *is* threatened. Not only that, you've made him a suspect in a homicide. Whatta you think he's gonna do when he finds out?"

ELEVEN

I STOPPED FEELING SORRY FOR myself the minute I parted company with Arthur Howell and Detective Kirk Mulligan. I wasn't upset by the three-thousand-dollar retainer I paid Arthur (with much more to follow if I was charged), or by Mulligan's insistence that I keep a ten-o'clock appointment at the Manhattan North precinct to give a written statement on the following morning. I wasn't overly concerned with John Caroll, either. After all, there were others who knew he'd threatened the count. I was thinking of Maggie. It was close to eight o'clock by that time and she'd been waiting for me at Sharpers for at least two hours. I didn't think she'd leave, but I did think she might be angry because I hadn't called her directly, and I wasn't sure how well she'd take to Benny Abraham, either.

The cab ride downtown was as slow and miserable as cab rides get in Manhattan. There'd been an accident inside the Queens-Midtown Tunnel, and the East Side was jammed in the Thirty-fourth Street area. To avoid the problem, we, along with hundreds of other seasoned Manhattan drivers, detoured west to Fifth Avenue, where we ran into an emergency Con Edison dig that continued for blocks.

"No matter where you try," Gregori Pandopolis apologized as he pulled to the curb in front of Sharpers some forty minutes after I entered his cab, "is always the same. New York is course of obstacles."

I accepted his apology, tipped him well, then walked into the bar. The happy-hour crowd had already departed and the regulars, far fewer in number, had arrived. I was greeted by several friends as I made my way over to Benny Abraham's enclave, but I put them off with a gesture. Benny, already grinning, was facing me. Alongside him, his nephew Paulie Abraham stared at me through narrowed eyes. Paulie, Benny's heir apparent, handled the bookmaking operation's day-to-day activities. He didn't like Philip Beckett, and never lost an opportunity to make his feelings known.

Maggie was seated across from Benny and Paulie. Her black hair, which was loose and fell to her shoulders, gleamed red and gold in the light of the small neon signs over the bar. She was wearing the same charcoal jacket I'd watched her put on that morning and the sight of it reminded me of the soft shoulders beneath.

"See, Maggie," Benny announced as I approached, "didn't I tell ya he'd make bail?"

With some difficulty, Maggie executed a half-turn on the narrow seat before raising her eyes to meet mine. What I saw in them surprised me. Beyond the obvious worry, I recognized a level of personal caring that I immediately (and quite involuntarily) associated with the word *love*.

I slid in beside Maggie, wanting to take her in my arms and hold her for the next week. All along, I'd been obsessed with my own emotions. *Did* I love her? *Could* I love her? Could I love at *all*? Not once had I considered Maggie's feelings. Worse still, I couldn't recall being concerned with the feelings of any of the women I'd been with, despite my having taken great efforts to please them.

Maggie took my face between her hands and kissed me on the forehead. "Was it bad?" she asked.

I smiled at her. "I'm the lily-white son of one of the richest men in the world, and I had a lawyer. How bad could it have been?"

"Benny told me they might arrest you."

"You had to think so, too," Benny quickly defended himself. "Or else you wouldn't have asked me to send Arthur."

"I still think so." I nodded at Paulie Abraham, who had yet to acknowledge my presence, and he reluctantly nodded back. Paulie had a big problem, which his uncle recognized but could do nothing about. He wanted to be a rough tough gangster when he was a little skinny weasel. If he could have settled into his weaselity, he would have been a lot happier. As it was, he felt the need to play the hard-ass, no matter how inappropriate the occasion.

"You think you'll be arrested?" Maggie bit at her lower lip.

"For all of the above-named reasons, plus the fact that I didn't kill Sergio D'Alesse, I'd have to say it's unlikely. But it's still possible."

"What are you going to do about it?"

The question was so simple, I wondered why I hadn't considered it before. "I don't want to do anything," I said. "I'm already out Arthur's fee. . . ."

"He charged you?" Paulie snarled before turning to his uncle. "What'd I tell ya, Uncle Benny? I told ya that prick would take the kid's money."

Paulie's use of the epithet in front of Maggie was a calculated act of disrespect, but typical Paulie Abraham. He needed to show dom-inance when the sad truth was that I could have squashed him like a bug. After my battering at the hands of Martin Crowell, fugitive felon, I'd thought it prudent to reacquaint myself with the martial arts. My experience with judo at Choate had led me to believe that I could handle myself in any situation. Not so.

I studied at half a dozen schools before settling down at the Sunshine Gym on West Thirty-seventh Street. Located on the second floor of a loft building that housed a gaggle of garment industry merchants, the gym was the home of Doug Rosten's School of Self-Defense. Devoid of mystical pretense, Doug's system reduced the art of street survival to its essentials. Accept pain; give pain.

But, of course, for Benny's sake, I didn't respond to Paulie's taunts. With no children of his own, Benny was not only fond of his nephew, Benny needed him. Paulie ran the business efficiently and was straight with the money.

"Arthur shouldn't have charged you," Benny explained. "He owes me big time. I'll make sure he doesn't cash the check."

I looked at Maggie, and wished myself anywhere else. "I'm going to pay my own tab, Benny," I said without looking at him. "That way my lawyer won't confuse the issues before him." I could almost hear Regina make the identical claim when I'd demanded a fee.

"The kid don't want a favor, Uncle Benny," Paulie said. "You believe this?"

Benny waved him off. "Enough, Paulie. Enough, already."

"Look, guys," I took Maggie's hand and started to rise, "I've had a real long day, and I know you've got business to conduct, so—"

"Before you take off," Benny said, "there's something I gotta tell you."

I sat down, but continued to hold Maggie's hand against my thigh.

"See," Benny continued, "after I spoke to you and Arthur, I started thinkin' that sooner or later, most likely sooner, John Caroll was gonna feel some heat. I also figured that he might not be too happy with this turn of events."

"So you warned him," I said. "And now he owes you a favor."

"There's that," Benny agreed, "which I admit I thought about in advance. But look, Phil, this guy, Gaetano Carollo, also called Johnny the Gent, is not someone you should take lightly." He drummed his fingers on the table, then looked from me to Maggie and back to me again. "After I told him that you were a personal friend of mine, I pointed out he was the one who made the threats, and there was no way he could be kept out of it. Too many people knew."

"Did he buy it?" As I asked the question, I flashed from Graham Winokur's story to John Caroll's polished appearance, then to my initial reaction upon finding Sergio D'Alesse's body. Everything was wrong. *Everything.* The only question was whether I gave a damn.

"I couldn't see into his brain, but I think so. He's gonna close down the club for a couple of months, then open somewhere else. By the way, did you tell Carollo you were going over to see D'Alesse?"

"I think so."

"Well, he said you did, and he also says to remind you that you're his alibi."

It made sense. I'd been sitting in the Rolls when Caroll walked back into the San Remo. If I'd asked Thaddeus to drive me crosstown, I would have been at the D'Alesse apartment ten minutes later.

I again made my farewells, and this time got almost to the front door when Luisa Czernowitz called to me from the bar. "Hey, Phil, somebody phoned for you. Maybe ten minutes ago. They left a phone number."

Though I was pretty sure who that somebody was, I accepted the slip of paper Luisa offered, then was surprised to find Father's number.

"It's from my father," I told Maggie. "A summons, no doubt."

Her eyes grew curious as she watched me punch Father's number into the keypad. I think she was wondering how I'd handle it if my family asked me to choose between them and her.

We weren't long in finding out. Father's ancient butler, Calder Hallmark, answered on the third ring. He put me through, not to Father, but to Regina.

"Where have you been?" she demanded.

"Shouldn't that be, 'How have you been'? In light of what I've *been* through."

"Wendell and Audrey are here, Uncle Alfred and Aunt Charlotte as well. We're all waiting for you."

Wendell, of course, was Wendell Turcotte of Turcotte, Pendleton, Brown.

"How is Audrey doing?" I asked.

A loud sniff. "You'll find out when you get here."

"That'll be tomorrow afternoon, at the earliest."

"Pardon me?"

"Regina, I gotta run. It's been a long day."

"Father wants you here tonight."

The ultimate weapon, but I wasn't biting. "Give Father my apologies."

"The family," she countered, "is in mourning."

There was a touch of desperation in Regina's final argument. Father had commanded her to fetch me and she was going to have to tell him that she'd failed. It was not a position to be relished.

"At ten o'clock tomorrow morning, I've got to give a written statement to the police. I'll be over as soon as they let me go."

"You're impossible."

I hung up, knowing it would make her even madder, but it was the only way to get off the phone. Maggie took my arm, and as I looked into her eyes, I felt the tension melt away. I'd decided, long before, that Father's wealth and its eventual disposition was the only sword hanging over my head. As long as I was willing to forgo that wealth, and I was, the sword would remain in its scabbard. Where it belonged.

We had dinner at a quiet Italian restaurant on Greenwich Avenue after making a quick stop at Maggie's, where she picked up a change of clothes. At the restaurant, we discussed the case over bottles of ice cold Dos Equis beer made even colder by frosted mugs. Maggie listened carefully, then jumped on the two essential facts. First, John Caroll had no obvious reason to murder Sergio D'Alesse. Threaten him? Sure. Slap him around? Okay. But you can't collect a gambling debt from a corpse. Second, the count knew and trusted his killer, as the position of the body, the lack of any evidence of forced entry, and the undisturbed apartment amply demonstrated.

"When you think about it," Maggie said as the waiter set her risotto on the table, "there aren't all that many suspects."

"No, not so many." Just who those suspects might be was not something I wanted to think about. Maggie, on the other hand, was as eager as ever.

"Your family," she declared, "is right in the middle of this."

"That's why I intend to walk away and let the police find Sergio's killer. Personally, I don't want to know."

Maggie put her fork down and regarded me for a moment. "I'm being pretty insensitive here," she finally said. "Even for me."

"Nobody likes to be used," I responded, avoiding her comment in the process, "and that's exactly what . . . what *somebody* did."

"Do you mean your sister?"

"I suspect my sister, and my father, and perhaps Audrey as well."

"Suspect?"

"It's early yet, Maggie. Too early to draw conclusions."

We ate in silence for a moment. Maggie's appetite, I noted, was keen, while my own was much diminished, not only because of the day's events, but because my overcooked gnocchi had the texture of boiled newsprint.

"Phil," Maggie finally said, a quizzical half-smile playing on her lips, "did I understand you right?"

"About what?"

"Did you imply that John Caroll murdered your cousin's husband?"

I slid my plate a few inches toward the center of the table, hoping the pastries would be fresh. "Yes, I did."

"But how? You left him on Central Park West."

"He didn't pull the trigger. He sent someone else to do it. An employee, maybe, or someone hired for the occasion."

Maggie fixed me with a speculative stare. "Haven't we already established that Caroll didn't have a motive?"

"We've only established that D'Alesse's gambling debt wasn't the motive. Perhaps Johnny the Gent had another motive to kill D'Alesse."

"Which would be?"

"Because someone in my family paid him to."

"Why?"

"Why is the mystery part, the part I don't know."

After a moment, Maggie returned to her meal. She ate quickly, the movements of her fork sharp, and I suspected that she was angry. I was wrong. After finishing, she laid her fork on her plate, then said, "This must be very hard for you."

I shrugged before replying. "I'm not close to my family," I told her. "And now you know why."

"Ah." She swept her hair away from her face, then sipped at the beer in her mug. "Then you don't mind talking about it."

We were sitting across from each other at a small table. If we'd been close enough, I might have kissed her. As it was, I smiled and took her hand. "I don't mind," I said, "as long as I don't have to become involved."

The waiter took that moment to deliver the dessert menu, and Maggie gave herself time to think by carefully perusing it. Finally satisfied, she asked me if I wanted to share an order of pumpkin fritters in a sauce of wet walnuts. I quickly agreed, though I couldn't recall ever coming across a wet walnut. After assuring us that we'd made a wise decision, the waiter, a typically youthful twenty-something, spun on his heel and marched off.

Maggie watched him walk away, then turned to me and said, "There's something cold inside you, and I think you're afraid of it."

It was the sort of moment that I'd come to dread, and I was very sorry to see it emerge so early in the game. Yes, there was (and is) something cold inside me, something I've always taken great pains to hide.

Maggie opened her bag and removed a cell phone. A moment later, she was speaking to a subordinate named Brill. It was nearly ten o'clock.

"How're those citations coming along?" she asked.

I couldn't hear Brill's end of the conversation, but Maggie's went something like this. "Uh-uh, Brill, I want it on my desk when I arrive tomorrow morning. . . . I don't care, Brill. Just fix the damn computer. . . . Brill, am I not making myself clear? On my desk. Tomorrow morning."

She hung up and stared at me for a moment, then said, her wistful tone utterly opposed to the terse commands of a moment before, "When I was a student, in Paris, we were all radicals. My girlfriends and myself. We were radical feminists and we thought that we'd change the world simply by putting our feminine genes behind an upper-management desk. Not so, Phil. The business of business is profit. If you don't produce it, you won't be long for the corporate world. Or for the investment world, or the political world. 'Fire in the belly and steel in the heart.' That's the way my first manager put it, and that's the way I've lived it. In the eyes of my peers, I'm a success."

Though I was mesmerized by Maggie's revelation (and understood that it was offered in an attempt to make me feel more comfortable), I had no ready response. Fortunately, our waiter offered me a respite by appearing at our table bearing a plate of pumpkin fritters. By themselves, the fritters would have been okay, but they were smothered in a very sweet syrup, and the wet walnuts turned out to be merely limp.

"So," I finally said, "all successful executives are either bastards or bitches. Is that what you're saying?"

"Hearts of steel," she replied. "No beating hearts allowed."

"I'm not sure I see where you're going with this."

She replied without hesitation. "What I'm saying is that we should find the individual or individuals who murdered your cousin-in-law and ram it up his, hers, or their asses. And we should do it with malice aforethought."

TWELVE

A FEW MINUTES LATER WE were out the door and strolling toward my apartment, two miles away. The long walk, as erotically charged as our cab ride on the previous evening, became an end in itself. The night was cool enough to draw us close, but not so cold that we felt a need to hurry. On nearly every block, Callery pear trees threw up sprays of small white flowers turned pale yellow by the light of the streetlamps. We stopped often, to kiss, to look into each other's eyes. It's a wonder we weren't mugged.

As I opened the door and held it for Maggie to enter, I realized that we'd barely spoken since leaving the restaurant. It occurred to me that neither of us was the sort of person who needed to fill every silence with the spoken word. It was a comforting thought to a man who looks forward to spending an afternoon on a bench in Central Park.

I followed Maggie inside, locked the door behind us, then turned to find Maggie holding a small, foil-wrapped box. She opened the box, laid the cover aside, then flipped through several sheets of tissue paper before extracting a bar of soap molded in the shape of a leaping yellow fish.

"If you get the vase, it's a victory prize," she said. "If you lose, it's a consolation prize."

She went on to explain that the soap, made at her request by a friend, had two virtues, the lesser of which was that it gave off the bracing odor of sandalwood. The greater, which Maggie did not so much describe as demonstrate a few minutes later as we stood beneath a pulsating showerhead, was that it was saturated with some essential oil that made human skin so slippery that nothing could be held, while everything could be touched. At one point, I felt that Maggie's hands were inside my body.

We were a long time getting into the bedroom, long enough to make me forget about the unlit candles on the dresser, or Maggie's blue robe which was hanging on a hook on the bathroom door, or the very concept of pillow talk. I slid under the covers, drew her into me, then (oaf that I was and am) fell asleep.

I woke up a bit after three o'clock, chasing the tail end of a dream that slid from my consciousness as if it'd been greased with Maggie's fish-soap. Afterward I lay semiawake as the dream was gradually replaced by a memory that came to me in a series of nearly static scenes.

One night, many years before, Regina and I were ushered into Mother's presence. After receiving her customary buss, Mother issued her customary directive: "Why don't you children play?"

Though our lives were devoted to the same end, our civilizing, Regina and I were rarely in each other's company except during the children's hour in the evening. That was why, at Mother's command, we ordinarily retired to some individual pursuit, a puzzle or a book, where we passed the hour in near silence. Not this time.

"Let's," Regina said, "play St. George and the Dragon."

Perhaps, as the elder, it would be been more natural to reject the suggestion out of hand. Instead (for reasons long ago lost to me), I went along. That first time, we had to imagine the dragon I destroyed to save Regina, the fair maiden. But as the weeks passed, whether I was Sir Francis Drake rescuing the brave Regina from a pirate's den, or Robin Hood freeing Maid Marian from the clutches of the sheriff of Nottingham, our role-playing became more and more elaborate. We carried props into the room, wore costumes, created elaborate dialogue that we recited with great passion.

The game brought Regina and I closer for a time, though we never achieved our unstated goal. We desired our mother's approval, desired it with the unalloyed simplicity of children; the roles we played were the roles we believed would please her. It was that simple, and that pathetic.

These memories flashed through my mind, like a series of photographic slides, one rapidly succeeding another, until I found myself clinging to a final image as I became fully awake. I saw Mother again seated on her Victorian armchair. The chair was upholstered in blue velvet, and Mother sat erect, as if there were no give in the cushioned seat beneath her. Her arms were folded in her lap, her neck long and noticeably straight. A tiny smile dominated her lips, as though frozen in place by the subdued pink lipstick she wore. The smile was both enigmatic and utterly serene. It could not be read because it never left her mouth. We had nothing with which to compare it.

Maggie stirred alongside me, then rolled onto her back. Within seconds, a thin line of saliva trailed from the corner of her mouth to the pillow. I snatched a tissue from a box on the nightstand, then carefully wiped her lips. A waste of time.

I flipped the tissue in the general direction of the wastebasket and let my head drop to the pillow. Maggie's body smelled of sandalwood and salt. I wanted to touch her, to claim her, but I knew she would have to be up in a few hours if she was not to be late for work a second day in a row. In the highly charged atmosphere she'd described, two consecutive days of tardiness would start tongues wagging. Those tongues would say that perhaps Maggie Santos isn't star material after all. Perhaps we've made a mistake. Perhaps it would be better for all concerned if she remained at the same desk for . . . say the next thirty years.

Eventually I dropped into a very deep sleep from which I was only gradually aroused by the bright trill of the telephone. I sat up, wiped my eyes, and glanced at the clock. It was five minutes after five o'clock.

"Phil?" The voice on the other end of the line, though I couldn't place it, was familiar.

"Who is this?"

"It's Detective Mulligan."

Knowing the games had begun, I deliberately used Mulligan's first name. "I'm an early riser, Kirk. Always have been. Say, you haven't been up all night, have you?" Somehow, I refrained from adding, *You low-life piece of shit.*

"Goes with the territory, but I'm home now and I'm gonna try to catch a nap. That's why I'm calling. See, I've made arrangements to get statements from your sister and your cousin later this morning. We're gonna do it at your father's place on Park Avenue around eleven. I was hopin' you'd come by at the same time, lemme kill three birds with one stone. I'm gonna be really jammed in the afternoon."

"Fine. This morning at eleven, see you then."

"Between eleven and noon. I'll get there as soon as I can."

I laid the receiver in its cradle, then rolled back and let my head drop to the pillow. Maggie was sitting up in bed, her expression serious.

"That was Detective Kirk Mulligan. I'm to appear at my father's apartment at eleven to give a formal statement."

Maggie slid down next to me. "Last night, after you fell asleep, I couldn't stop thinking about you being a suspect. I'd tell myself, *No, this can't be right; it's too crazy.* But the sad truth is that you could easily be arrested."

"I don't think so, Maggie. I really don't."

"Listen to me, Phil. I'm a lawyer." Her tone was sharp enough to preclude an immediate response, and she quickly continued. "They're going to find your fingerprints in the apartment."

"That's because I was there on the prior day."

"You were exiting the scene when Audrey arrived."

"I wasn't even *entering* the scene. I was knocking on the door."

"You left John Caroll, then took a cab to the D'Alesse apartment where you killed Sergio D'Alesse. You were leaving when Audrey arrived."

"I see. And exactly *why* did I commit this crime?"

"The state doesn't have to show motive. You called, you came over, you had a disagreement, you killed him. Don't forget, in addition to being a martial artist and a private investigator, you possess a handgun and know how to use it. There's no way you can claim to be a stranger to violence."

Fairly desperate by that time, I held up my last straw. "My hands tested negative for the presence of gunpowder residue."

Maggie grimaced as she shook her head. "You washed up. You wore gloves. Who cares? Look, Phil, I don't know a lot about criminal law. I admit that. But I'm a good enough lawyer to be certain that you're in trouble. Especially if the other logical suspects have alibis."

What can I say? There are times in life when you have to surrender even your most cherished rationales. Though I had far too much experience to justify my naïveté, until that moment I'd truly believed that my innocence would protect me.

"You don't think," I said to Maggie, "the cops will settle for, 'Hey, guys, I didn't do it.' "

"You need a lawyer," she replied.

"I have a lawyer."

"You need another lawyer. A co-counsel."

"And who would that co-counsel be?"

"Maggie Santos." She sat up, spread her arms wide, cocked her head, finally turned up her palms. "Who else?"

This time I refused to be distracted. "This isn't a game," I insisted. "And you're the one who just proved it."

"I only proved that you have to take the situation seriously." She dropped down to one elbow, then stroked the stubble on my cheek. "Think of professional golfers. Just because what they *play* is generally called a *game* doesn't mean they don't take what they do seriously."

It was time for a break. Past time. I needed a moment to decide whether Maggie was the victim of some mental disease. On one level, what she offered seemed half-way reasonable. Life can certainly be played as a game. The problem was that passing even a few days in one of New York's many houses of detention was something I wanted to avoid at all costs.

I bought myself a little time by heaving myself out of bed and trotting off to the bathroom. When I returned, Maggie took my place. She was quite a long time, long enough for me to entertain the possibility that my best chance lay in uncovering D'Alesse's killer. I found the thought so depressing that it was quickly replaced by a vague hope that the killer had made some obvious mistake and the cops would put the case away. Not that I really believed it. Between John Caroll's involvement and the certainty that every potential suspect would speak to the cops only with a lawyer present, uncovering anything beyond the circumstantial evidence against Philip Beckett III would be extremely difficult. If not impossible.

THIRTEEN

I WAS GRINDING A BIT of black pepper into a pair of mushroom omelets when Maggie wandered into the kitchen. She put her arms around my waist and pressed the side of her face into my back. "I like your digs," she said.

"Thank you."

In fact, my tastes were quite conservative, and there was nothing (outside of my jade) to justify the compliment. The area rugs scattered about to add color to the dark wood floors had been machine-loomed in Belgium. The jackets of the books packed into a pair of oak bookcases added a bit more color, as did the French advertising posters I'd hung on the walls. But the furniture was as nondescript as its owner: an L-shaped leather couch, an oak coffee table that almost matched the bookcases, a butcher block table in a small alcove, a stainless steel halogen lamp that more closely resembled an industrial robot.

My bedroom was equally unimpressive. A platform bed with a quilted leather headboard and a pair of attached night tables, a double dresser and a small armoire, both modern in design and very simple. A Calder-inspired mobile (created by an artist whose name I never committed to memory) hung between the room's only windows, while a pair of braided rugs flanked the bed.

Taken altogether, they were rooms that might have been assembled in a Manhattan department store, rooms designed to reflect the tastes and pocketbooks of their clientele.

"I looked at your collection as well."

"Collection is too grand a word for it."

"Well, I can't think of another." She let me go, then drifted off to pour herself a cup of coffee. "There's one piece in there . . . you can almost get lost in it."

"And which one was that?"

"The mountain."

"Ah."

Created from a block of jade the color of spinach, the foot-high piece was indeed carved in the general shape of a mountain. On its surface, four monks climb a narrow and very steep path flanked by a minutely etched forest of pine. The monks carry offerings, which they hold above their heads as though for some god's inspection. Far away, near the mountain's summit, the path ends at a small temple where the monks, if they were ever to arrive, would leave their gifts.

Maggie took her coffee to the dining room table and sat down. A few minutes later, I carried a tray bearing the omelets and a plate of buttered toast to the table and sat alongside her. Maggie dug into the omelet with her customary gusto, while I barely picked at my eggs. I was feeling sorry for myself again. I'd put a lot of time and effort into separating myself, not only from Father and Regina, but from the ambition that drove them. I didn't want to be drawn into their orbit, but I didn't see any way out of it, and the absolute worst was that I was being drawn involuntarily.

"You're not eating."

I raised my eyes to find Maggie holding her fork aloft. Though her eyes were very serious, she was smiling a smile that deserved more than my self-pity.

"Tell me about your family," I said. "When you were a young child, what was it like growing up in the house of Emilio Santos?"

I can't recall having any particular expectations when I made the request, but Maggie (always full of surprises, especially in those early days) told a tale that accounted for much of what I'd already seen in her. She was the second of three children, all girls, each born three years apart. Because their mom (the novelist, Patricia Patterson-Santos) had spent most of the day writing in her basement office, the children had been cared for by their paternal aunt, Fulgencia Santos, who lived in the house. Fulgencia, who had a penchant for amontillado and afternoon naps that stretched into evening, pretty much left the kids to their own devices. The resulting chaos was predictable. Unlike Regina and myself, Maggie, Liz, and Cynthia had not been civilized. They'd been left to civilize themselves.

"Having a British novelist for a mother and a Spanish diplomat for a father made us different. Without doubt." Maggie leaned forward, a wicked gleam in her eye, and I knew, an instant before she spoke, that I'd been set up for a punch line. "But what really made the family odd, and what I didn't understand until a few years ago, was that my mother and father adored each other."

So much so, and so obviously, that Maggie, at one point, recalled becoming actually jealous. Emilio and Patty had presented a model for relationships that Maggie absorbed the way a plant absorbs sunlight, a model that left her unprepared for an adversarial undertone the boys she dated seemed to expect.

"And that," she concluded, "is the only conceivable reason why, at the advanced age of thirty, I'm still unwed."

I was tempted to lure her into the bedroom, then conclusively prove that she was neither old nor a maid. But it was time to get our collective butts in gear. "Are you sure," I asked as I rose to gather the dishes, "that you're ready for the Beckett family's particular corner of hell?"

"Does that mean I'm your lawyer?"

"Junior co-counsel would be a better description. And that's only if Arthur approves."

She laid her elbows on the table, then placed the tips of her index fingers on her chin. "Phil," she declared, "you couldn't be in better hands. Trust me on this. I can get you a plea bargain you can live with. In fact, I can virtually guarantee that you won't have to do more than five years hard time."

FOURTEEN

I BEGAN THE PREPARATIONS FOR my return to the family digs with a phone call to my attorney. I expected him (at the very least) to be annoyed at learning he now had a co-counsel. But Arthur proved himself more worldly than that. After I explained that Maggie worked at Exxon and her specialty was international law, he grunted, then asked, "Are we talking *girlfriend* here?"

"In a manner of speaking." I felt the need to add something, but was unsure what. Finally, I changed the subject. "Mulligan wants me to give my written statement at Father's house. Instead of the precinct."

"You spoke to Mulligan?"

"He called me at five o'clock."

"And you spoke to him?"

"Yes, I spoke to him."

"Ya know, Phil, once upon a time I used to be a pretty good lawyer. That's what everybody says. But lately I feel like I'm losing my edge. I distinctly remember telling you that unless I was physically present and gave my consent, you were not to talk about the case to *anyone*. But that's impossible, right? If I had—"

"Give it a rest, Arthur, I get the idea."

"Good, because I have another point to make before I go back to work. I spoke to the family attorney, counselor Turcotte, this morning. He tells me that when Sergio was murdered, your father was in a plane, your sister at a business meeting, and your cousin at lunch with a pair of close friends. I'll see you at eleven."

I took that bit of good news into the bedroom, where I found

Maggie fully dressed except for a pair of chocolate-brown boots that she was tugging over her feet. She looked up at me and smiled. "Caught, right?"

"Right."

She was wearing a white tank top over a straight skirt that ended two inches above her knees. The skirt was tan and matched a loosely structured jacket with large patch pockets. It was an attractive outfit, but far too casual for Exxon's legal department. If these were the clothes she'd picked up at her apartment last night, she'd never intended to go to work this morning.

"I can explain," she announced, "but I think it'd be a lot sexier if you dressed while I was doing it."

As I was naked under my robe, the process didn't take all that long. Just as well, because Maggie's story was an elaboration of a theme already explored. She'd become unhappy with the direction her life was taking long before we met. Worse yet, she imagined herself becoming increasingly bitter and angry as the years progressed. Success or failure was irrelevant here. She could not save herself by one day occupying a corner office on the thirty-seventh floor. If she hoped to avoid her fate she would have to make a clean break.

She went on to explain that her absence from work on this particular morning did *not* signal the onset of that clean break. It being Friday, and with the weekend coming, she was merely giving herself a small vacation to think things over.

"I don't want to hate every minute of my working life, but I don't want to step into something worse, either." She sighed. "And there's the money, too. It's like your trust fund. I've gotten used to the money and I don't want to give it up."

As I walked beside Maggie to a closet in the front hall, then helped her into her coat before retrieving an umbrella so large it would have been more appropriate at the beach, my only fear was that Maggie viewed me as a role model. It was one of those narcissistic moments at which I've always been especially adept and that Maggie instantly recognized.

"Look, Phil," she said as I opened the door, "I don't want you to think you're somehow responsible for me." Her eyes were very serious, her voice grave, as she succinctly defined her position. "I'm not your child. I'm not anybody's child. I'm a mean-spirited corporate lawyer with a take-no-prisoners mind-set, responsible for myself, body and soul."

It was raining hard enough outside to instantly soak my shoes, my socks, and the cuffs of my pants, and of course there were no cabs to be had. In her waterproof boots, Maggie seemed barely to notice the weather. She took my arm and tucked her head beneath the umbrella as we hoofed it to the Twenty-eighth Street subway station.

We remained silent during the ride, and during the walk north from Hunter College on Lexington Avenue. It was only as we stood on the northwestern corner of Seventy-third and Park, with the entrance to the building that housed Father's triplex apartment directly across the street, that I finally spoke.

"The ancestral homestead," I declared before consciously echoing Audrey D'Alesse. "Be it ever so homely."

The Park Avenue blocks in this section of town are divided by narrow islands planted at either end with seasonal flowers. Naturally enough, the seasonal flowers chosen by the Park Avenue Association for mid-April were tulips. Lithe as ballerinas, they danced a rain-driven dance in alternating rows of yellow and red.

"How long has your family been living here?" Maggie asked. She seemed no more eager to cross the street than I.

"My great-great-grandfather moved his family from Maine to New York in 1878. The Becketts were in the process of diversifying and he wanted to be near the action."

"Diversifying from what?"

"Abner Beckett founded Beckett Timber in 1779, under the Articles of Confederation. According to family legend, he'd made a lot of money running contraband during the Revolution, money he used to buy up vast tracts of timberland seized from war heroes unable to pay their taxes."

Maggie put her arm around my waist. "Is that something the family's proud of?"

"Steel in the heart," I responded before finally moving forward. "A concept with which the Beckett clan is very familiar."

As we stepped beneath the blue canopy in front of Father's building, a liveried doorman came out to greet us.

"Good morning, Mr. Beckett." Well into his golden years, Alexei had been opening doors and hailing cabs for more decades than I'd been alive. His deferential smile was as cold as the rain soaking my feet.

"Good morning, Alexei."

"The family's expecting you, sir." He waved us on through a small sparkling lobby and into the hands of the elevator operator, George, a newcomer with a bare twenty years experience. George dropped us at a small foyer on the sixteenth floor, wished us a good day, then went about his business.

Across from where we stood, a stout oak door that might have served to protect a battlement guarded the Beckett inner sanctum. A pair of early American portraits, one attributed to Erastus Fields, the other to Ammi Phillips, flanked the doors; beneath them, two identical Chippendale side chairs offered seats only to the terminally ill-bred. On our left, against the wall, a mahogany card table bearing the signature of Job Townsend supported a white porcelain pitcher filled with pale yellow daffodils.

"Grandfather created this foyer at the beginning of World War Two in order to demonstrate his patriotism."

Maggie's eyes swept the room. "I don't get it."

"Everything in the room is American."

She pointed at the pitcher, a curious grin beginning to show at the corners of her mouth. "And that?"

"From the Tucker Factories circa 1830."

"And the mirror?" She gestured to a gilt wood mirror on the wall above the pitcher.

"Carved by C. N. Robinson circa 1820."

"You sound like you're reciting."

"When I was four or five, someone decided that I should become familiar with the family heirlooms. The task was assigned to Father's man Calder Hallmark."

"The butler?"

"Yes." I rang the bell.

"And who taught Calder?"

The door opened before I was forced to admit that I'd never given the matter a second's thought, revealing the same Calder Hallmark. Well into his seventies, Calder suffered (according to Regina, who wanted Father to "pension the old man off") from a variety of ailments that often prevented him from carrying out his duties.

"Master Philip," he said, "it's wonderful to see you again."

"Calder, this is Magdalena Santos."

Calder bowed to Maggie, then looked down at my wet shoes. In another time, he would have fetched clean shoes and socks before letting me in the house. Finally he sighed and raised his eyes to meet mine. "It's good that you've come, sir. Your father is having a very hard time of it."

As we stepped into the ballroom, Maggie muttered an involuntary, "Wow."

And why not? The family home, roughly eight thousand square feet, covered three floors of the building. At the apex of the economic expansion following World War Two, Grandfather had removed a portion of the second floor to create a single, enormous room with a ceiling more than twenty feet above the marble floors. I won't describe the fresco on the ceiling, or the artwork on the walls, or any of the French antiques that gave the room its theme. But what made the room especially impressive was that neither Father, nor Grandfather, had purchased a stick of furniture or a work of art. Everything in the apartment, except for a single room designed by Mother, had been in the family for at least four generations.

Calder led us through the ballroom, down a corridor and into a sitting room, where we found a red-eyed Audrey D'Alesse. She started upon seeing Maggie at my side, but quickly calmed when I introduced Maggie as "My attorney, Magdalena Santos."

"I'm sorry for your trouble," Maggie said.

Audrey raised her chin on hearing Maggie's accent. "Are you related to the writer, Patricia Patterson-Santos?" she asked.

"She's my mother."

"What a small world. I met your mother and father when I was in Paris last year."

Calder interrupted with a polite clearing of his throat. "Your father," he told me, "asked that you be brought to him upon your arrival."

I nodded, then asked Audrey if Regina was in the apartment.

"Regina's with that detective and Wendell Turcotte. Giving her statement."

"Is she the first?"

"Yes. My lawyer hasn't arrived."

Though controlled, Audrey's voice carried an edge that hinted at some more powerful emotion lurking just beneath the surface. I should have understood that edge as grief, but ever mean-spirited, I assumed it was fear. It was as good a rationale as I could muster for my own voice, which offered not a hint of sympathy.

"What about Father?"

"He's in the library with Frank Pendleton."

Pendleton was Wendell Turcotte's partner at Turcotte, Pendleton, Brown. His presence, as well as Wendell Turcotte's, indicated one of two things. Either Regina and my father were unconcerned with the investigation, or they wanted the police to believe they were unconcerned. Otherwise they would have hired criminal defense attorneys.

"Who's your new lawyer?" I asked, recalling that Wendell Turcotte had represented her on the prior day.

"Claude Schweiber. He's with the firm."

I didn't bother to ask which firm she meant. Calder had already cleared his throat twice. I had either to comply or refuse outright. Since I had nothing to gain by refusing, I promised Maggie to return as soon as possible, then followed Calder up to Father's second-floor library.

* * *

When I'd told Maggie that my father had never purchased a work of art, I'd been telling the literal truth. Father wasn't interested in art per se; instead, he collected rare books, including illuminated medieval manuscripts, which he kept in his temperature- and humidity-controlled library. A true collector, he only bought and never sold.

I felt the difference in the atmosphere as soon as I came through the door that Calder, on his way out, closed behind me. It was cooler and drier, and the air, pulled by filters at either end of the room, was moving slightly. Father was sitting on one of a pair of upholstered chairs, the only furniture in the room aside from a large and very elaborately carved table. There were no chairs around the table, because the table was meant only for the exhibition of manuscripts. On that morning, perhaps in deference to the deceased, the table was empty.

"Philip," Father said in his deep baritone, "I'm glad you've come." He leaned forward to rise, moving just slowly enough to allow Frank Pendleton, sitting alongside, to beat him to it.

"Good to see you again, Philip." Pendleton nodded and smiled one of those country club smiles in which he specialized. An excessively handsome man, Pendleton administered my trust fund.

"Frank." I stepped into the room, acutely aware of the footprints left by my wet shoes on the parquet floor. "Maybe I'll see you later."

"Great." He offered me a brief handshake, told Father he'd be downstairs in case he was needed, then gently closed the door behind him.

The moment that followed was awkward. Father and I hadn't spent much time in each other's company, not enough for him to even know the boy who'd preceded the man. Now he wanted something from me and wasn't certain how to ask for it. Finally, he regained his seat and patted the arm of the chair next to him. "Sit down," he said, his voice soft enough to encourage a belief that he was giving me a choice. We both knew better. I might have the effrontery to turn his request away, but not to refuse to hear him out.

"Bad business," I said. "The worst."

"Yes," he agreed with a soft smile. "The worst."

FIFTEEN

SHORTLY AFTER I BEGAN MY freshman year at Wharton, Father invited me to a meeting of Beckett Industries' Board of Directors. I didn't think much of it, somehow imagining that I'd walk into a cozy gathering of major stockholders, the old boys' club at its most intimate. That was not the case. One of Beckett's wholly owned subsidiaries, Algonquin Paper, was in deep financial trouble and heads were about to roll. In addition to the sixteen board members, each complemented by a pair of aides, the meeting was attended by Algonquin's CEO and CFO, their aides and their attorneys, as well as a dozen attorneys from Turcotte, Pendleton, Brown.

It was a confab of warriors for which I was unprepared, and I remember feeling ill at ease while Father chatted with a fellow board member, Edgar Royce, prior to the meeting. We were in a paneled room at the Waldorf-Astoria, gathered around a table so large it was thought necessary to place a microphone before every third chair.

At some point, probably not more than a few minutes after Father and I entered the room, I noticed that a man on the other side of the table was looking our way every few seconds. Like John Caroll, he was immaculately groomed and dressed. Unlike Gaetano Carollo, he carried himself as if he'd emerged from his mother's womb in a vested Saville Row suit.

I glanced at Father, but he (or so I thought) was too deeply involved in conversation to notice. It was only when the man detached himself from the two men who flanked him, then headed in our direction, that I realized how wrong I was. Father let him come all the way around the table before demonstrating his intentions with a simple flick of his index finger. The man froze with an arm raised, a foot dangling, a smile on his lips. The blood drained from his face so quickly I thought he might faint.

The man's name was Sheldon Bannister, Algonquin Paper's CEO, the head about to roll. After the meeting convened, as the first order of business, he was told that certain accounting irregularities uncovered at Algonquin Paper were being laid at his door. He would be escorted from the building forthwith. He would scrupulously adhere to the various restrictive clauses in his contract. His health insurance and corporate credit cards would be canceled. His golden parachute would not open until the investigation was completed.

Father, of course, had been younger. His brow and jaw, which at age sixty-five thrust forward as if trying to escape his increasingly slack and papery skin, had then been merely imposing. His mustache had been darker, too, and his hair thicker. Now he had a slight curve to his shoulders, while his mouth had receded beneath a nose that drooped at the tip. It would have been enough to inspire sympathy if I wasn't certain the mind-set that produced Father's finger flick remained unchanged simply because (like Mother's enigmatic smile) he had nothing with which to replace it.

I can't be sure that Father wanted to force me to speak first, but if he did, he failed. I found myself thinking of Maggie's parents. She'd described them as intensely committed, the perfect couple, eternally in love. It seemed to me that if I could once inspire that commitment, in Maggie or anyone else, I would finally have accomplished something worthwhile.

At last, Father broke the silence. "I want you to know," he told me, "that I'm sorry about what happened to Sergio. He was a fool, but he didn't deserve to die that way."

"No, he didn't."

"Nevertheless, the man is gone."

"To his eternal rest? Or to an autopsy table where, even as we speak, a forensic pathologist is passing a steel rod through his excised brain in an effort to trace the path taken by the bullet that killed him?"

After a respectful moment of silence, Father announced, "Life goes on."

"My life," I returned, surprised by the bitterness apparent in my tone, "was going on just fine before I was dragged into this mess. Just fine."

Father shifted in his chair. I think he would have liked a prop, a glass of wine or one of those Cuban cigars he occasionally smoked, but food, alcohol and tobacco were forbidden in the library. "Philip, if I'd known that Sergio was going to be killed, I'd never have allowed Regina to call you. As you, if you'd known that Sergio was going to be killed, would not have accepted Regina's check."

It was nicely done, and I acknowledged the riposte with a smile. "So, enough bullshit. What do you want from me?"

Father bristled. He was, after all, Philip Beckett Jr. I was his son, not his equal. "Do you know who did this?" he asked.

"No, I don't."

"Could you find out?"

"I think so."

"Think?"

I turned in the chair to face him. "I suppose," I told him, "there's a possibility that Sergio D'Alesse was involved in some outside activity so awful it provided a motive for his murder. There's even a possibility that his wife and family were ignorant of that activity. But in light of Sergio's predilection for running to his in-laws whenever he was in trouble, those are two of the most unlikely possibilities I've come across in many years. And that, Father, brings it right back to the family."

As he considered my analysis, Father's expression remained neutral. Still, his gray eyes seemed distracted. Was he weighing the merits? Or was he now concentrating on some larger purpose?

Steel in the heart, I told myself. Don't look for redemption here. "You realize," I said aloud, "that I'm the only logical suspect without an alibi?"

He nodded. "Pendleton thinks that you might be arrested."

"I might."

"I don't know what to say." His hands fluttered up, then just as quickly dropped into his lap. "I really had nothing to do with it."

"You didn't know your nephew-in-law had built up a gambling debt."

"I knew that, yes."

"Did you know that he'd been threatened?"

He cut me off with a shake of his head. "When my brother came to me about the threat to Sergio, I fobbed him off on Regina. A week or two later, Regina told me that she was going to ask your advice, but she didn't offer details, and I certainly didn't know she was going to hire you."

"She didn't hire me. She asked me to do it for nothing."

Father laughed. "But you insisted on payment?"

"I did."

Before I could add a word of explanation, a discreet knock on the door was followed by Calder Hallmark's round face. Naturally, he addressed my father. "Detective Mulligan has requested that Master Philip join him in the sewing room."

"Offer the detective some refreshment, Calder, and tell him Philip will be along soon." He waited until the door closed, then tugged briefly at the crease in his trousers. "I don't think," he told me, "that you have to allow yourself to be summoned."

"I don't think I need to get Mulligan pissed off, either."

"I'll be as brief as I can." He cleared his throat and raised an already thrusting chin. I was about to be pitched. "Philip, I've spent my entire life in the service of the Beckett family. I think you know that, and I think you at least *sense* the weight of the burden you refused to bear. I'm not saying I blame you, far from it. When you declined to follow in my footsteps, it made me realize that I'd taken that route without even considering the possibility of refusal. Can you imagine? I can't remember even *dreaming* of another life."

Father was wearing a gray cardigan over a very soft flannel shirt. As he waited for me to reply, he played with the round leather buttons on the cardigan. His eyes were downcast, his smile conciliatory, the set of his jaw determined. I found myself entertaining the notion that he was speaking from the heart. As I was meant to do.

"We Becketts," Father continued when it became clear that I had nothing to say, "are not very prolific. There's only my brother and myself, and after we go, there's only Regina. Audrey . . ." He dismissed his niece with a flick of his fingers. Audrey was hopeless and would never be otherwise. "I was fortunate enough to have two children, Regina and yourself, both capable, and I thought . . . You know, Philip, your refusal to enter the family business came as a complete shock to me. Oh, I realize I'm repeating myself, but I want you to understand. I've given a great deal of thought to you over the years, and I've come to the point where I now blame my lack of understanding on the simple fact that I willingly accepted the yoke. I never thought of it as a burden when I was young. Instead, I was anxious to be considered worthy. My brother is older than I, you know, and I grew up expecting him to eventually become chairman. But he was smart enough to realize that he simply wasn't the best man for the job. In the end, it was Alfred who nominated me."

Amazing. He'd just described what must have been a tooth-and-nail battle as if it had been a competition between thoughtful academics. This time I didn't have to control my tongue. His audacity had rendered me speechless.

Suddenly he turned to me and asked, "What would you do if it simply fell onto your shoulders? Would you collapse beneath the weight?"

"Define 'it.' "

"My entire holdings in Beckett Industries, this apartment and its contents, the houses in Vail and Tuscany. Everything." He was smiling now. "What would you do?"

He'd caught me off guard, and I felt, as I often did in Regina's presence, that I'd been out-hustled. "You wouldn't consider giving me a little time to consider the question?"

"No need, Philip. It's academic, in any event. As long as Regina's shoulders are available, the obligation will never fall to your own."

The bottom line, at last. To protect my interests, I would have to protect Regina's. And Father's, of course. "Tell me what you want me to do, Father?" It was the same question I'd asked Regina. "It's not as if my sister is the one facing arrest."

"I keep forgetting." He dropped his eyes again. "Your attorney, Arthur Howell, I understand that he's very good."

"Does that mean you had him checked out?"

"You're my son, Philip. I want you to have Mr. Howell send his bills to me." His tone was gentle, as if he were invoking a time when we'd romped together on the nursery floor.

"I can't do that."

"Why?"

I delivered the same message I'd conveyed to Benny Abraham on the prior afternoon, this time more emphatically. "Because I want *my* mouth to be the *only* mouth out of which my *mouthpiece* speaks."

"Clever."

"And pertinent." I stood, walked across the room, then parted the heavy drapes covering the window. The view, to the south, looked directly into the stone and steel heart of midtown Manhattan. "What do you want me to do, Father?"

"I don't want anything to happen to you. I—"

"What do you *want* me to do?"

"Find the man who killed Sergio and tell me who it is."

"The man? Why not the woman?"

"Whomever."

I turned to him, smiling, and allowed the drapes to close. "Can I assume you want to be notified before the police?"

"Come to me first and we'll take it from there. You're not legally obliged to speak to the police."

"How about morally?"

"Morally?"

"Am I morally obliged, Father, if I learn the identity of Sergio's killer, to see that he or she is punished?"

Once again, Father was too quick for me. "That issue cannot be addressed until the individual's identity is revealed."

I let him have the last word, thinking it didn't matter all that much. I needed answers, as Father had suggested, simply to protect my own interests. If Father wished to believe I'd committed myself to his point of view, that was fine. I walked to the door and turned the knob. "I want you to instruct all interested parties to cooperate."

"I've already spoken to Audrey and Regina."

"What about Uncle Alfred and Aunt Charlotte?"

"I'll confer with them while you're with the detective. I should have done it earlier."

I opened the door, tempted to add, *And you, Father? Can I assume that you'll cooperate?* But there was nothing to be gained. Plus, the statement was too provocative for an exit line. "I'll be sending the bills for my services to your secretary," I finally told him. "Given the circumstances, I'd appreciate immediate payment."

"Consider it done."

SIXTEEN

I CAME BACK DOWNSTAIRS, TO the sitting room, where I found Audrey conferring with her parents, and her attorney, Claude Schweiber. The twenty-something Schweiber was of the new breed. He stared at me through insolent gray eyes while I greeted my aunt and uncle.

"Bad business, Philip," Alfred said. "Terrible." Shorter by several inches and a good deal heavier, Alfred was Father's polar opposite. His ample cheeks and jowls were perpetually reddened, and he was quick to display his self-deprecating humor at family gatherings. Like me, he knew his place.

Aunt Charlotte rose to give me a hug. Generally as good-natured as her husband, she'd had her face lifted once too often. As a result, her skin, when I bussed her cheek, had the texture and tension of a surgical glove. "I know you'll take care of things," she told me as she squeezed my hand. "I've always had faith in you."

"Mother, please." Audrey shook her head in disgust. She and her mother had never gotten along.

"Well, I mean it," Charlotte insisted. "I think Philip is the best of us, and I've said so before."

"Thank you, Aunt Charlotte. It's nice to know I have my supporters. I'll need them before this is over." I turned, quite deliberately, to Audrey. "Can anyone tell me where my lawyers are?"

"They're conferring in the dining room," Audrey replied.

"What about Detective Mulligan?"

"He's waiting for you in the sewing room. Regina went to work."

"Naturally," Alfred chimed in. "Where else could she possibly go?"

"Nowhere," I said. "Look, Audrey, I've got to get ready to give my statement, but I'll need to speak with you later. Do you know where you'll be around four o'clock?"

Her gaze was clearly hostile, but I couldn't know whether she had something to hide or simply resented my father's command that she cooperate. "Where would you like me to be?" she asked.

"Anywhere I can find you."

"Then I'll be sure to remain in the country."

I'd made my intentions clear, and that was enough. Within an hour or so, she'd be asking herself why I hadn't arranged to speak with Regina or with her parents. By late afternoon, her anger would be tinged with fear. I nodded again to Alfred and Charlotte, then left the room to walk down a long corridor, past a dozen sketches by a dozen Renaissance artists, to the dining room where I found Arthur and Maggie standing beneath a near-life-size portrait of my mother. Though I'd seen the portrait hundreds of times, I paused, as always, to acknowledge her presence.

Mother was exactly as I remembered her. Seated in the same Queen Anne chair before which Regina and I had acted our parts many years before, she wore a blue gown cut low enough to properly display the alternating strands of white diamonds that graced her throat and chest. All the while displaying the same enigmatic smile.

Maggie came up to me and took my arm. "It must have been hard," she said, "when your mother died."

She was right and she was wrong. It was hard for me, yes, but not because I grieved for the mother who loved me. No, with Mother gone, I'd lost the hope of winning even her approval, much less her love, and my grief has always been tinged with resentment.

"Mother was raised in a convent school," I said. "She went from there to her husband's bed."

"Was her family religious?"

"Not especially." I took her hand, pulled her to me. "The Corvascios were shoe manufacturers based in Genoa. You've probably got a pair of their shoes in your closet."

"I do. They're very expensive."

"Yes, they are. Anyway, things got very dicey for the Corvascios during World War Two. First they had to deal with Mussolini, then Hitler during the German occupation, then the Americans after the war. It was a tightrope act, or so I've been told, and they might have lost everything. My mother was born in 1939, when the family was on the move. Shortly after she began eating solid food, she was sent to the nuns for protection and education. She remained there, even after the war, until she was eighteen. Two years later, she was married and pregnant."

"You sound angry."

"It's a case of the sins of the fathers being visited on the grandchildren. Mother never learned to love, or to be loved."

Behind us, Arthur Howell rapped his knuckles on the dining room table, and I wondered if he was signaling that I'd caught a bad hand.

"Time to get this show on the road," he announced. "I've got to get back to the office."

A call to arms I could understand. After all, he was being paid by the hour and the money was coming from my very shallow pockets. "By all means. Let's find the good detective and bare our souls."

Contrary to my expectations, the interview was over almost before it began. This time accompanied by his partner, Kyle Aganda, a thick black man who never so much as glanced in my direction, Mulligan motioned me to a chair. As I complied, he restated my right to avoid self-incrimination, then offered me a standard Miranda form, which I quickly signed. Finally, he started a small tape recorder.

"Friday, April seventeenth, eleven forty-five in the morning. Present: Detectives Kyle Aganda and Kirk Mulligan. Philip Beckett the Third. Counselor Arthur Howell for Mr. Beckett. Counselor Magdalena Santos, also for Mr. Beckett." He motioned to me. "Mr. Beckett, would you describe the sequence of events that led to your presence at the D'Alesse residence yesterday afternoon?"

As I repeated the same story I'd told him the day before, I was careful to leave nothing out. I was equally careful not to embellish. Mulligan and his partner would exploit any contradiction, any variation. It's what cops do, and I had no reason to believe they weren't good at their jobs.

When I finished, Mulligan snapped off the recorder, and turned, not to Arthur, but to Maggie. My first thought was that he was tossing Arthur a dig, but he might simply have found Maggie easier to look at.

"Counselor," he said, "I'm gonna advise you here that your client is a suspect. *Officially.* I'm not gonna ask for his passport, but if I want him, I expect to find him. Understood?"

"Understood," Maggie replied.

Mulligan left without another word. When the door closed behind him, Arthur chuckled. "That boy is excellent," he said. "The way he let you go without any questions? You'd almost think he had the case wrapped up."

"Almost?"

"In theory," he explained, unintentionally echoing Maggie, "the state doesn't have to show motive. In practice, juries want to know why a given crime, especially a murder, was committed. If you don't give jurors a motive, they're half-way to reasonable doubt before they begin deliberations." He rubbed his hands together. "Damn," he declared, "I'd love to try this case. Well, gotta run."

Maggie and I watched him stride off, then returned to the sitting room. As we approached the door, I took her hand. "How did you and Arthur get along?" I asked.

"Fine." She ran her fingers over the pattern on my sweater, tracing a spiral from my waist to my throat. "Look, Arthur told me that we're page one in every newspaper, and we're the lead on the broadcast news."

"We?"

"The D'Alesse homicide."

"Was my name mentioned?"

"No, but Arthur thinks it's only a matter of time."

The count's description of his unlucky streak flashed through my mind. I found myself wondering if, somewhere along the way, I'd been infected by his karma. I'd been making stupid mistakes ever since I agreed to help him out. It was about time that I stopped.

I pulled Maggie into my arms and and kissed her. Her mouth was wondrously soft and yielding.

"You ready to kick some ass, Magdalena Santos?" I asked.

"Past ready," she declared.

"Then I think it's best we begin with a long walk, followed by a longer lunch."

"At your place or mine?"

SEVENTEEN

WE MADE OUR FAREWELLS AS brief as possible, and a few minutes later we were out the door. We walked straight down Park Avenue, past Fifty-seventh Street, and into the heart of the commercial district. The avenue was jammed with traffic, the sidewalks thick with pedestrians. It was the war of the umbrellas. The more macho among us charged forward, the tips of our umbrellas bristling like the quills of a hedgehog, while the more cautious, myself included, raised and lowered our umbrellas to avoid collisions. A middle-aged woman, wearing a raincoat that fell to her ankles, had unfurled her red and gold umbrella just far enough to protect her elaborately arranged hair. Her profile thus lowered, she slithered around oncoming pedestrians with the elusiveness of a carp in a crowded aquarium.

We walked past the headquarters of Colgate-Palmolive, Lever Brothers, Chase, and MeadWestvaco, through the Helmsley Building with its gilded facade, and into a shopping mall on the first floor of the Met Life Building. We didn't speak as we walked, and I remember drawing Maggie closer as the tension eased away.

Despite the constant press and presence of human beings, I never feel so much at home as when I'm walking the streets of Manhattan. There are moments, like the one I'm attempting to describe, when I seem to fall into myself, when the surge of traffic has the inevitability of a prairie wind, when the blowing litter might be tumbleweed careening over the high plains of Montana. By the time Maggie and I stopped long enough to decide where we were going, I was thoroughly focused on the task at hand.

We did not go back to "her place or mine." As I'd gradually calmed, I'd gradually admitted (to myself) that it was time to get to work. Convincing Maggie was a little more difficult, but not much, and a short time later we were seated on opposite sides of a booth in an Irish bar on Third Avenue. Maggie ordered shepherd's pie, while I opted for a corned beef sandwich. We both ordered pints of Guinness.

"Here's to learning from our mistakes," Maggie declared after our pints arrived.

I tapped her mug with my own. "And to profiting from the mistakes of our enemies."

"You know," she continued after sipping at her beer, "that they saw us coming?"

"They?"

"Winokur and Caroll. They were lying in ambush. And we should have known it."

"Myself," I admitted, "I just assumed that Caroll didn't challenge me because I was a Beckett."

"And I thought he was charmed by my explosive sexuality. Not to mention my quaint British accent."

But that hadn't been the case. Caroll may not have known we'd come to expose his crooked game, but he did know we were acting on the count's behalf. He knew because someone had told him. He knew about my appointment with Winokur as well.

As if aware of my thoughts, Maggie slid her mug to one side and declared, "Winokur made a mistake when he told you that Caroll threatened to kill him."

"I got under Graham's skin when I called him a thief, and he had to justify himself. As I hoped he would."

We paused to allow the waiter to place a basket of Irish soda bread on the table. I quickly buttered a slice while Maggie continued.

"Benny told us that Caroll has a violent reputation, which Graham Winokur's story confirms. But when you confronted Caroll, he was practically apologetic. What was it he said?"

"He told me that he never meant to hurt D'Alesse, that violence was bad for business."

"But he put a gun to the back of Winokur's head. Just like someone put a gun to the back of Sergio's head."

I shifted my weight so I could reach into my pocket, then removed the jagged chip given to me by the count. "This was my ticket to the club. I was supposed to show it to Caroll, but I kept it in my pocket and he never asked for it." I tossed the chip onto the table. "Caroll played me like a trout and he used my own vanity as bait."

Maggie stared at the chip for a moment, then asked, "Any other mistakes?"

"On our part, or on the part of our enemies?"

"Our enemies?"

As time passed and the threat of arrest and trial became more real for me, I was finding it easier and easier to think of my family as enemies. I sipped at my beer as Maggie chose a slice of bread, then added a thin smear of butter.

"When I saw the count, he told me not to take any risks, that things were going to get better for him, all he needed was a little time. I thought he was bluffing, but now I'm not sure."

Our lunches arrived before Maggie could respond. I remember that when she cut into her shepherd's pie with the edge of her fork, it threw up a cloud of fragrant steam that condensed, for just an instant, on her eyelashes. For the first time since finding D'Alesse's body, I was enjoying myself.

As Maggie began to speak, I opened my sandwich, spread a thin layer of mustard across the corned beef, then closed it up again. "I see two things happening at the same time," she told me. "First, D'Alesse runs up his debt to John Caroll. Second, he unintentionally creates a motive for his own murder. One has nothing to do with the other, not until he approached his family on this second matter." She paused, perhaps expecting me to challenge her. When I continued to eat, she picked up the thread of her analysis. "The individual, or individuals, with a motive for Sergio's death knew that he'd been threatened. Their best move, at that point, would have been to kill D'Alesse, then let the blame fall on Caroll. But they're people who fight their battles with money, not bullets, and they didn't have the courage to put a gun to the back of someone's head and pull the trigger. But they had a pipeline to someone who did, a pipeline opened by D'Alesse when he ran up a debt to John Caroll."

I bit down on my sandwich while I tried to imagine Regina, Audrey or Father proposing murder to Johnny the Gent, with his Armani suits, his manicured nails, his mane of red hair. Had my name come up at their first meeting, or had I been a later development? One thing sure, John Caroll would not have gone forward without protecting his flanks. Somebody had to take him off the hook.

"The rest," I said, "is history."

"And the move here," she rejoined, "is to write the denouement."

I would have toasted her remark, but I'd already consumed my Guinness. Not that Maggie was in need of affirmation. As she dug a cube of lamb from her shepherd's pie and put it into her mouth, she seemed to be perfectly satisfied.

We finished our respective lunches in silence. I can't speak for Maggie, but I was trying to concentrate on what to do next. Logic is a funny business: it gets you from X to Y to Z only by assuming that X is true. But what if X is false? What if John Caroll wasn't involved in the murder of Sergio D'Alesse? What does that say about Y and Z?

In forming any strategy, I had to take that possibility into account, and I had to proceed quietly as well. John Caroll was the proverbial sleeping dragon. Awakened, he'd execute one of a pair of options. He would come after Phil Beckett, who'd prodded him out of sleep, or he'd decide to bypass the middleman and proceed directly to the source of his problem. Somehow I couldn't see Regina, Audrey, or Father (or even Uncle Alfred or Aunt Charlotte) absorbing the full weight of the law to protect John Caroll. Faced with the prospect of a lifetime in prison, any (or all) would snitch on Mr. Caroll in a New York minute. It was a certainty that would not elude him.

We capped off our lunches with mugs of bitter, sobering coffee. Maggie's expression was so reserved that I wondered if she was having second thoughts. But when I began to speak, her eyes, as they rose to meet mine, were quick and eager.

"I'm going to take this in two directions," I explained. "First, there had to be a motive for D'Alesse's murder and I hope to uncover it by searching out his friends. That bit about things getting better for him? I don't think Sergio was the type to keep his good fortune hidden. I think he told a friend, and that friend will eventually tell me."

"And what's the second direction?"

"I'm going to get my hands on Regina's, Audrey's, and Father's phone records. John Caroll's as well. Any contact between Caroll and a member of the Beckett family would be very damning."

Maggie smiled. "I didn't know you were a computer hacker."

"I'm not."

"Then how—"

"I'm going to buy the records from a woman I know. She's a supervisor in Verizon's delinquent accounts division. For a price, she'll tell you when the mayor called his mistress."

"That's amazing. I didn't know people did that."

"People sell information every day. Knowing where to buy is just part of the business."

"The sleazy part."

"What can I say, Maggie, I'm a results-oriented guy. When I'm working."

Maggie picked up her coffee mug and used it to signal our waiter for a refill. When she turned to me, her expression was grave. "What you're doing now, it's part of that cold place you told me about. That's where you're going."

"When you told me it was a game," I explained, "I should have told you that I like to win."

"Bullshit." She leaned toward me, covering my hand with her own. Maybe she was trying to soften the blow. "You hate that place. You hate it and you fear it. That's why you're so reluctant to work."

Determined to make a point, I shook my head. "Whatever cold space I'm in now," I told her, "is tropical by comparison with the space John Caroll occupies every minute of his life. I know we've already been over this, but I need to do it again."

"Phil, I'm not afraid."

"That's not something to be proud of."

Maggie's gaze drifted to a photograph on the wall to her left. A line of six men stared back at her. With their handlebar mustaches, stiff collars and cocked derbies, they seemed reckless and defiant.

"What do you want me to do?" Maggie finally asked. "Go home and wait it out?"

"Not at all. If there's one thing I need here, it's another set of legs. A set of legs willing to commit several minor felonies."

That caught her attention. She turned back to me but didn't speak. "I want," I told her as I took her hand, "you to meet with Naomi Felder. She's the woman from Verizon. In addition to the office and home phone numbers of my father, sister, and cousin, you'll give her John Caroll's home address and the address of the club. Naomi will accept this information, along with a money-stuffed envelope, then launch into a rambling account of the latest interoffice feud at Verizon. She will, of course, be at the center of this feud, a victim of some terrible injustice, which she will describe in such great detail that you will experience a nearly overwhelming urge to interrupt. My freely offered advice is to resist. Naomi is a very sensitive woman. If slighted, she's liable to toss the envelope in your face and storm out the door. Should that happen, I'll have to spend an hour on the phone kissing her narrow ass just for the privilege of starting over again."

Maggie was smiling now. "You want me to stay away from John Caroll. That's the point."

"From Caroll and from anyone in my family who might tell Caroll that you're involved." I leaned forward. "The bottom line here, Maggie, is that if you were threatened, I'd have to back off."

"And if you back off, you might go to jail."

"Like I said, I'm a results-oriented guy."

Maggie rose from her seat to lean across the table and kiss me. "How many felonies," she asked as she fell back, "are you asking me to commit? Exactly?"

"Three. Computer trespass, unlawful duplication of computer-related material, criminal possession of computer-related material.

But don't worry, because they're only E felonies. If you're caught and convicted, you won't get more than a couple of years in prison. Plus, of course, you'll be disbarred."

It was a test, I admit it. And the results—as I read them in her eyes, in her smile, in the determined set of her shoulders—were exactly what I'd anticipated. Maggie had a reckless edge that she was now holding up for my inspection.

I have to admit that each time the curtain was pulled aside, by either of us, I experienced a moment of intense anxiety. And the fear that I would reject her was as great as the fear that she would reject me. I was in love with her, and I think, if pressed, she would have said that she loved me as well. But that didn't mean we knew each other. Or that, when we did, either of us would feel the same way.

Still, risk was something I understood, and I found Maggie's recklessness just another part of an unpredictable nature that had attracted me to her in the first place. If this was as bad as it got, we'd be together for a long time to come.

"Do you have your cellular phone with you?" I asked.

"In my purse."

"I'll try to set things up with Naomi for seven or eight. Most likely it'll be in a bar out in Sheepshead Bay, which is where she lives."

"That's on the other side of Brooklyn."

"And you're going to need the address of the San Remo and the club before you go." I proffered a set of keys to my apartment, which she accepted.

"This is beginning to sound suspiciously like work, Philip." She took the keys from my hand, then dropped them into her purse. "But you knew that, right?"

I reached for her, as she'd reached for me a moment before, but only succeeded in jamming my chest into the edge of the table between us. "We're the commanders and we're the troops," I declared as I massaged my aching ribs. "The good news is that we only have to share the glory with each other."

EIGHTEEN

I MADE A SERIES OF phone calls before I left my apartment, the first to Naomi's answering service, the second to the pager of Manny Rodriguez, a friend who'd worked for me in the past. A Dominican by birth, Manny had found his true vocation only after immigrating to New York at age eighteen. He was a bicycle messenger, an occupation that satisfied (or so he claimed) his physical, psychological, and spiritual needs.

"You know, Phil," he'd rhapsodized one night at Sharpers, "you flyin' down Broadway in the rain, and you got shit for brakes, and some cab driver, he's like comin' for your ass in a four-wheel skid, and you got a truck on the other side of you . . . Man, it's like you're lookin' into the the face of God."

I left my name and number with Naomi's answering service, and my number on Manny's beeper. Manny was the first to respond. I told him that I wanted him to shadow John Caroll. Manny had done this for me before and generally considered the work a paid vacation for the legs. He was good at the job, in part because bicycle messengers, of which there are thousands in Manhattan, are as anonymous as lampposts. At the same time, they're highly mobile, and it's no accident that small parcels in need of immediate delivery go via bicycle. Given the mid-town traffic, bicycles are by far the fastest way to get small parcels from place to place.

Manny and I discussed terms for a minute or two before he agreed to make his final delivery, then meet me at Sharpers in an hour.

I went into my bedroom and took a shoe box containing my Browning 9mm pistol from a shelf in the closet. I didn't like guns very much and rarely carried one. As a result, the unloaded automatic hadn't been touched for months and was due for a thorough cleaning. My strategy was to leave it in plain view. That way I wouldn't forget, no matter how alluring the distraction.

I was searching for my cleaning kit when Naomi got back to me. She balked, initially, when I told her that I was sending an associate, but I knew the way to her heart. "This is a complex job, Naomi," I explained, "involving a number of individuals and a client with money to burn." Naomi had three daughters, triplets, at Brandeis University. Even with Pell grants and student loans, she found it nearly impossible to meet her obligations.

Done with Naomi, I called Maggie and gave her the time and place of the meeting: eight-thirty at the Ten Pin Bar on Nostrand Avenue. Even assuming she could find a cabbie willing to carry her to Brooklyn, the trip would take an hour each way. Maggie accepted the news with good grace.

"Watch your back," she told me, her voice dropping an octave, "at all times."

I needed to make one further call, which I put off until I was in a cab headed for Sharpers. I was wearing the same clothes I'd put on that morning, but in lieu of carrying an umbrella, I'd opted for a Gore-Tex jacket with a hood. I wanted to keep my hands free.

My final call went to an art dealer, Angus Cowley, who specialized in Chinese antiques. When I told him that I might have to sell my collection, he was flabbergasted.

"Philip," he commiserated. "Philip, Philip, Philip."

"Line up some buyers, Angus."

"You'll not be gettin' the good price, lad. Ya know that, right?" He needn't have asked. Potential buyers with ready cash would react to the news that a collection was on the block (even a collection as small as mine) like crows to roadkill.

"It might not come to that," I explained, "but I want to be ready." Ready to fill Arthur Howell's wallet. Ready to pay the price for my independence.

Manny Rodriguez was standing at the bar when I walked into

Sharpers a few minutes later. I instructed him to stake out the San Remo and focus on John Caroll.

"If he goes out, follow him," I instructed. "If he doesn't show by midnight, go home, get some sleep, and come back in the morning."

"How I'm gonna know this Caroll?" he asked when I finished. "You got a picture?"

"He's got red hair, Manny. Lots and lots of red hair. You can't miss him."

I paid Manny $150 (another billable expense) to cover his first day's work, then approached Benny. It was three o'clock.

"What's up, Phil?" he asked as I slid into the booth.

I detailed my conversations with Father and Arthur Howell, including Howell's belief that I might well be arrested. As there was nothing much to be said about the latter, Benny unhesitatingly cut to the chase. "You gonna deliver for the old man?"

"Assuming he isn't the bad guy?"

Benny smiled. "Yeah, let's say he's not involved."

"My primary goal, if I discover who killed D'Alesse before the cops do, or before I'm arrested, is to protect myself. After that, I don't know."

"Good, good. That's the way I'd play it, too."

We paused as Luisa Czernowitz approached with a cup of tea I hadn't ordered, and that I wouldn't have time to drink before heading out to meet Audrey. Luisa wanted to talk about Maggie, but I put her off. "I'm working," I told her, "and I only have a few minutes." I watched Luisa walk away, then returned to Benny. "What's the word on Caroll?" I asked.

"Good news. Caroll's not a made guy."

It was, indeed, good news, because it meant that in the event of John Caroll's demise, the mob would not be obliged to avenge him. The Italian mob has taken some heavy hits over the past ten years, but they were still too big for the likes of Phil Beckett.

For a moment, I said nothing, content to play with the idea that it was now strictly between Gaetano and me. "It's a relief," I finally admitted. "It's a definite relief."

"But it don't mean," Benny instantly rejoined, "that you should relax. Caroll's still a rough guy, and he's got a kid on his crew who I heard is a born shooter. His name's Tony Farelli."

"Are you talking about the security guard?" I pictured the skinny, lantern-jawed kid who'd held the door for me. It didn't seem possible.

"Look, Phil, what you see, when you walk into the club, it's a performance." Benny shifted his weight as he sought the right words. Finally he said, "You should think of a crew, in a setup like this, as if it were the cast of some play where the audience participates. Whatever this kid does at the club, it's part of a show. When the show's over, he ain't the same kid. None of them are."

Fair warning being fair warning, I wouldn't have disputed the point, even if I'd disagreed.

"Anyway," Benny continued, "I called Johnny the Gent this afternoon and I told him if something bad happened to you, I'd have to take it personally."

"Was he impressed?" I attempted to make a joke of it, but the truth is that I was moved by the gesture. Benny had been inching toward the legitimate world for some time. He owned six or seven small businesses I knew about, including Sharpers, and he expected to sell the bookmaking operation to his nephew by the end of the year. Benny's father had died in prison, a fate Benny was determined to avoid. No matter how nonchalant his manner, he was putting his future on the line.

"He told me to go fuck myself, which is about what you'd expect. But he's gotta be thinkin' about it."

I squeezed lemon into my tea, added a packet of sugar, then took a sip. It was time for me to be on my way. "I'm grateful, Benny," I said, "for the risk you're taking. But I want you to lay off." I set the cup in its saucer and raised my eyes. Benny's expression was carefully neutral, but his small black eyes had lost their glitter. He would listen now, but decide later. "My overall strategy here is to find D'Alesse's killer without upsetting John Caroll. I want him to think I'm spinning my wheels, getting nowhere."

Benny took a cigar from his pocket and rolled it between his fingers.

Behind me, I heard the clink of bottles as one of the bartenders filled the beer coolers. It was three-thirty on a weekday afternoon, and Sharpers was nearly deserted.

"You tellin' me you're not pissed off?" He pointed the cigar in my direction, then gave it a shake. "These people made you into a patsy, and they're gonna come after you if you don't take it lying down. It's not right, Phil. You gotta do something about it."

"Nobody's come after me," I pointed out, "and nobody's *threatened* to come after me. For now, my story virtually absolves Caroll. Why would he want me any way other than healthy?"

"For now."

I conceded the last word on the subject to Benny and left Sharpers a few minutes later, stepping into a brisk April wind. The rain had stopped while I was inside and the clouds overhead were tearing apart like cotton candy in the hands of a greedy child. Across the street, an orange school bus pulled to the curb and a pair of bearded Hasidim wearing poorly tailored black suits climbed aboard. Anxious to bear its passengers home to Brooklyn prior to the onset of Shabbes, the bus, which bore the notice MOISIACH IS COMING, edged back into the evening traffic on Hudson Street.

It's never difficult to find an empty cab in a residential area of Manhattan during the afternoon rush, and I was headed uptown within a couple of minutes. I felt satisfied. If not in a row, my ducks were at least shaping up, and I was confident that I could put the case away in a few days. There are hundreds of books and movies in which super-wealthy individuals command armies of thugs. But they all miss the point. The rich, as Maggie suggested, protect themselves with money, not guns, with the civil code, not the penal code. They don't need thugs, because, in the last analysis, the cops and the military, the biggest, baddest gangs of all, exist to preserve their interests.

I retrieved my cell phone. Punching in Father's number, I recalled the months of culture shock that followed my joining Fisher Security. It had seemed to me as if the world I'd entered was wholly divorced from the world I'd left, as if there was no point of intersection. And though I'd very quickly come to realize that the same deadly sins applied to both cultures, the rules of engagement had eluded me for longer than I care to admit. My family, of course, wouldn't know those rules at all.

I expected Calder Hallmark to answer the phone, but got his wife, Frieda, instead. In addition to preparing most of Father's meals, Frieda managed the household's day-to-day affairs.

Frieda put me through to Audrey, who agreed to see me as soon as I could get there. "Where can I go?" she explained. "The police won't let me return to my apartment."

"Your home is a crime scene," I told her. "The police don't want anyone in there until they've had a chance to go through the place."

"I know that, Phil. And I don't think it's right. It's not as if we're like . . ."

She left the metaphor dangling and I hung up a moment later. The cab was standing in traffic near Penn Station, at Thirty-fourth Street. Ahead of us, the Lincoln Tunnel, the Port Authority Bus Terminal, and the whole congested mass of midtown awaited. I would have made far better time on the subway, but I wasn't in a hurry. My intention was to interrogate Audrey, and I needed a few minutes to rid myself of any residual sympathy I may have had for her recently widowed status. Audrey might or might not have loved her husband. We weren't close enough for me to have an opinion. But either way, the count was still the surprise she'd found in the bottom of the Cracker Jack box, and her marriage had provided a psychological independence that she would now have to surrender. The family was about to reclaim her.

Maybe, I told myself, if she hadn't lied about the door being unlocked, I'd be more understanding. But I wasn't absolutely certain that she'd lied. Yes, I remembered the snap of the retracting bolt, and I could visualize Audrey turning the key in the lock. The problem was that I hadn't been paying any particular attention to the operation. My memories were after the fact, and there was at least the chance I was recalling only what I expected to see and hear, not what had actually happened.

But none of that mattered. Even if Audrey was completely

innocent, I was going to have to make her very uncomfortable, as I would eventually make all of them uncomfortable. Regina had accused me of being crude and I intended to live up to her expectations. I couldn't afford to observe the proprieties, or to have any consideration for Audrey D'Alesse.

NINETEEN

I FOUND AUDREY WATCHING TELEVISION in an upstairs bedroom. The large room was furnished in a minimalist style that made it seem larger still. A queen-size platform bed with a plain, low headboard was flanked by matching night tables, each supporting a stainless steel reading lamp. A pair of featureless double dressers rested against opposite walls, while a set of three canvas sling chairs were arranged before a television encased by a wood cabinet. The chairs were pale green, as was the bedspread and a George Inniss landscape on the wall over the bed.

Mother had created this room sometime in the late 1950s. I can't, of course, speak with any certainty to what she had on her mind, but the decor, despite its quality, was so out of keeping with the age-related furnishings in the rest of the apartment that I'd long ago concluded the design was as near as she could bring herself to an act of deliberate rebellion.

Audrey was seated on the edge of the bed when I entered the room, her attention riveted to a promo for the upcoming evening news. On the screen, her husband's earnest features appeared in a box to the left of an attractive middle-aged anchorwoman.

"Twenty years ago," the anchorwoman informed her audience, "the marriage of Count Sergio D'Alesse to Audrey Beckett was described as a union of European and American royalty. Now . . ."

When the set went blank, Audrey turned to find me holding the remote control in my hand. She removed a tissue from a box in her lap and swiped at her tear-streaked face.

"Well," she asked, her sarcasm apparent, "have you *cracked* the case?"

"Do you want me to?" I walked past her to the opposite wall and sat, not in one of the sling chairs but on the dresser, where she would have to look up at me.

"That question doesn't deserve an answer."

"Then let's try another. Was Sergio insured?"

I've known very plain women who were nevertheless attractive. At the risk of sounding like the host of an afternoon talk show, I'd say they projected an inner beauty so powerfully felt that it became visible. They liked themselves and it was obvious. As it was obvious that Audrey did not like herself. I could see it in her pinched features, her mottled neck, the angry defiance in her eyes. She had the look of a child perpetually under attack, a child who compensated with a vigilance bordering on paranoia.

"Yes," she admitted after a long pause, "my husband has been insured for twenty years. Somehow, despite our difficulties, we managed to pay the premiums. Does that make me a suspect?"

For the time being, I decided to ignore her question. "What's the payout on the policy?"

"That's not your business."

"How much?" I insisted. "What's the bottom line?"

"I'm not going to tell you."

We'd gotten down to it early in the conversation. Just as well, because I was certain we'd eventually reach this point and I'd prepared my response. "You're not going to get away with that," I said.

"Don't . . ."

I waved her off. "Enough bullshit, Audrey. You promised your father, and mine, to cooperate. If you've now decided that cooperation is no longer in your best interests, then go to your father, and mine, and tell them so."

Her glare was so filled with rage that I nearly laughed. Audrey would, I think, have given a great deal to have the charismatic presence so utterly natural to Father and Regina. Unfortunately, Audrey was far too open and honest, far too wounded.

"Audrey, listen to me for a minute." I softened my tone, then smiled. "You asked me if you were a suspect and maybe I should have answered sooner. Yes, the spouse is always a suspect, especially if there's money involved. Do you really think you can keep the details of Sergio's life insurance from the police? Or from . . ." I flipped my hand at the television. "Or from *them*?"

"Four million," she muttered. "My husband was insured for four million dollars."

"Is there a double-indemnity clause that applies here?"

"Yes."

"And how long has the policy been in effect?"

"As I said, for twenty years."

"Has the bottom line remained in place for all that time? Has it been raised or lowered?"

She smiled a bitter smile. "You were always the smartest," she told me. "You're smarter than your father and smarter than your sister."

"That's not an answer."

"Approximately eight months ago, the face amount on my husband's life insurance policy was raised from one million to four million dollars. I don't recall the exact date."

Satisfied with the progress we'd already made, I leaned against the wall, then abruptly changed course. "Do you know," I casually asked, "why your husband was murdered?"

The question caught Audrey off guard, as it was meant to do. "He was threatened," she told me, inflecting the last word so that it sounded more like a question than a statement of fact.

"John Caroll wanted to collect a debt. He had nothing to gain from killing the debtor. So I ask again: do you know why your husband was murdered?"

She shook her head, then declared, like an actor suddenly recalling her lines, "You were there, Phil. Maybe you should tell me."

"Please, Audrey, just answer the question. Do you know why Sergio was killed?"

"I don't."

The lie was so apparent, I didn't feel a need to prolong the agony. "Was that so hard?" I asked.

"Don't patronize me."

"You want to throw off the proprieties, do you?" I watched her rise to the balls of her feet, then settle back on the bed. For reasons of her own, she was unprepared to defy our respective fathers. "I want you to help me create a list of Sergio's close friends," I told her.

"Why?"

"Because the sooner I discover why he was killed, the sooner I discover who killed him."

For the first time, I saw fear in her eyes. "I don't," she told me, "know very much about my husband's—"

"Why don't you say his name, Audrey? Instead of 'my husband'? And why don't you stop lying to me? It's pitiful."

"I'm not lying."

"No? You not only lied about the door being unlocked, you deliberately put my ass on the line." Though I wasn't angry, I allowed my tone to gradually sharpen. "Tell me what there is about me that makes you think it's all right to put me in prison for the next fifteen years? Do you expect me to accept my part graciously? Maybe sit in my cell waiting for you to send a box of cookies and a fifty-dollar money order? All in the spirit of family unity?"

We were both standing by the time I ground to a halt, staring at each other from a distance of less than ten feet.

"The door was unlocked," Audrey insisted. "As you know."

"And how would I know?"

"Because your hand was on the knob."

I laughed in her face. "Audrey, you can tell the cops my hand was on the knob, and you can tell our parents that my hand was on the knob, but you and I both know differently."

"You were closing the door," she insisted. "I saw you."

She slapped her palm against her thigh, once, then twice. I let her have her tantrum, in part because I couldn't remember exactly where my hand was at the time she emerged from the elevator. I was certain I'd rung the bell at least twice, and it was possible that my hand was close to the knob when the elevator doors opened. But I was not touching the knob.

Still, there was nowhere to go on this particular topic. Audrey wouldn't be moved from her position by anything smaller than a hand grenade, while I, unfortunately, had none to throw. Thus I allowed my tone to moderate as I again shifted the conversation.

"Did you ever love him, Audrey?" I asked. "I always thought you did, at least in the beginning, but now I find myself uncertain. When I hear you say 'my husband,' I think you could be saying 'my piano,' or 'my pre-Columbian artifacts which I was forced to sell in order to pay my husband's debts.' I mean, it sounds—and you should think about this before you talk to the cops—like Sergio was just another worn-out possession in need of disposal. Cops, they're very attuned to that sort of cue. If Mulligan adds 'wife doesn't give a shit' to 'four-million-dollar life insurance policy,' he's gonna be all over you."

Audrey's face went pale. I recognized a grief in her eyes so profound that I knew, without even considering the question, that she'd been sheltering her sorrow for a very long time. I knew also that her anger would not protect her, that it had failed her before.

"Why are you doing this?" she asked. "Why?"

I felt that cold place in me grow colder still. Knowing that my cousin would now do almost anything to be rid of me.

"You might as well give me that list of Sergio's friends," I said after a moment. "Because I'm not going to leave here without it."

TWENTY

ARMED WITH A SHORT LIST (shorter than I would have liked) of Sergio's friends, I was half-way through the ballroom when Father called to me from behind.

"Philip," he said, the single word enough to freeze me in my tracks.

"Father?" Noting that he hadn't dispatched a servant to fetch me, I turned to face him.

"We're sitting down to supper. I wonder if you'd care to join us?" He looked small to me, dwarfed by the great room and the fabulous possessions he'd once dominated.

"I've got work to do," I told him. "*Your* work."

"Please, Philip. You needn't stay, but there's been a development." He extended his arm toward the hallway leading to the dining room. As I dutifully stepped forward to precede him, I admitted to myself that our little scene had been crafted brilliantly. By appearing in person, Father had made a concession. By insisting that I go first, he'd put me right back in my place. Any doubts I may have had about our relative status had been neatly erased. Nevertheless, there was more to come.

The dining room table was set for five: my father and sister, my aunt, uncle, and cousin. The setting was formal, the cutlery sterling silver (though not the best Father owned). The elaborately painted service plates were Chinese and old enough to have enjoyed the appreciation of a succession of emperors. The dominant color of the plates was red, the motif floral, complementing a centerpiece of red roses. A pair of candelabra was already lit.

Father's position, of course, was at the head of the table. He assumed it immediately upon entering the room, then smiled at his daughter, who was seated to his right. The other places were empty.

"What have you done to Audrey?" Regina asked. "She's furious."

"Furious?" It wasn't what I would have predicted.

"Do I have to repeat myself?"

"No, you don't." I walked to the table, but did not sit. "Father," I said to my client, "you told me that we had something important to discuss."

"And you told me you were in a hurry."

"I'm still in a hurry." I might have added something like, *After all, it's not as if you backed up your invitation by setting a place for me at your table.* But it didn't seem worth the effort.

Father looked from Regina to me. He was smiling. "I have friends," he told me, "in city government. They're helping me track the police investigation. Not that I intend to influence the investigation, mind you, but I feel we have a right to be informed." A right not granted to the great mass of Americans, a right appropriate to his station. "Sergio's autopsy was conducted early this morning, at my insistence. As you would expect, the family wishes his body released for burial as soon as possible. Audrey deserves closure, as do we all." He paused long enough to grin impishly at his use of the New Age buzzword. "In any event, I'm told the medical examiner's report will specifically mention the possibility of suicide. And why not? We know that Sergio was deeply in debt and we know that his marriage was failing. Without Audrey, he had no ability to support himself, and even less ability to deal with the consequences of poverty."

"Well, that's good news for me." As indeed it was. Arthur Howell was being handed an alternative explanation for the count's death. If worse came to worst, he would offer it to a jury with the reverence of a priest offering the Communion host. "But, of course, it's impossible. Sergio was holding a cup in his right hand when Audrey and I found him. Even if he was left-handed, and I'm almost certain he wasn't, he would have put the cup down before pulling the trigger."

"Interesting," Father admitted, "but we thought you'd want to know."

After a momentary pause during which I glanced from Father to Regina, I turned to leave. Regina's voice brought me back to attention.

"There's something else, Philip," she declared. "Something else you need to know."

"Yes?"

"I'm pregnant."

Without doubt, I was shocked. But not so terribly shocked that I didn't search Regina's face for some indication of her basic motive in choosing this particular moment to reveal her condition. I found her expression serene, the planes of her face unmarked by even the hint of a blush, her eyes suffused with Beckett pride. As performances go, it was magnificent.

"Two months ago, at a clinic in Lisbon, I had myself artificially inseminated with sperm from an anonymous donor." Her words were coming a little more rapidly now. "It wasn't an easy decision. I just . . . I wanted my child to be a Beckett. There wasn't any other way to accomplish both ends."

I glanced at Father and found him composed. Somewhere along the way, assuming it wasn't his idea in the first place, he'd given his consent. "A long-term investment," I said, "for an iffy return. Suppose . . ." I was going to ask Regina what she'd do if her offspring chose a path similar to my own, but halted in midsentence as an infinitely more amusing series of questions hopped into my mind, playful as kittens.

"Did you get to choose your sperm?" I asked.

"I would hardly allow someone else to choose for me."

"What about eye color? Did you pick the color of your child's eyes?"

"Blue."

"And the color of your child's hair?"

"Darker than mine."

"And your child's height? And intelligence? And race?"

"I don't see where this is going."

"And your child's gender? Did you choose the sex of your child?"
She nodded, then smiled. One for me. "A boy," she said. "I'm going to have a boy."

I spent the remainder of the evening and a good part of the night working hard but accomplishing very little. I had four names on my list of Sergio's friends, names lacking addresses and phone numbers. Without access to her husband's Rolodex, Audrey had been able to supply only the boroughs or neighborhoods in which these gentlemen lived. Thus John Simone from Brooklyn, Carlos Mogollon from TriBeCa, Hugh Wallace from Astoria, and Ilya Romanov from the Riverside Chess Club near Columbia University.

Though my body was screaming for exercise, and I needed a quiet space in which to think, instead of walking home, I returned to my own apartment via taxi. If I wanted to reach any of Sergio's friends before the night was done, I'd have to find him first.

Simone, Wallace, and Romanov were each listed in the five-borough phone directory stored in my computer. I had their phone numbers and addresses within minutes. Mogollon proved a bit more difficult. I had to run his name through an on-line database called TRACKDOWN before I got results. Mogollon had recently filed an application for a credit card, supplying his address and phone number in the process. This information had then been sold to TRACKDOWN by the bank issuing the card. Though ugly in the extreme, the transfer of header information is quite legal and done many thousands of times each day.

I made calls to each of the four men, not in an effort to interview them on the telephone, but only to make sure they were at home. None were, and I found myself relieved. I would take care of business on the following morning, with Sergio's friends recovered from their weekly labors and presumably eager to cooperate.

I was tempted to call it a day, to involve myself in preparing a supper for Maggie when she returned. Ripe fruit, a rich pâté and two varieties of runny Brie (with herbs and without), a crisp French bread, and chocolate-dipped strawberries for dessert. In fact, I found myself thinking, I could break out the fondue pot stored on a closet shelf and create the ultimate aphrodisiac. Viagra may work effectively, but unlike dark chocolate, you cannot lick it off your lover's fingers.

Though I might have extended my daydream indefinitely, it lasted for only a few minutes. According to Audrey, the count spent at least two nights each week at the Riverside Chess Club, and had been doing so for many years. The other members would know him, some perhaps well enough to point me in the right direction. Even if Ilya Romanov wasn't there, I had to make the trip.

I went into the bedroom to change my coffee-stained sweater, only to find my pistol lying on the bed. I don't know what I'd been thinking when I put it there, but it was more than obvious that if Maggie returned to the apartment before me, the presence of a weapon on the bed would send an unintended (if not entirely predictable) message.

I carried the Browning into the kitchen, where I gave it a thorough cleaning, then loaded it with 9mm Remington hollow points. As I fed bullets into the clip, then slid the clip into the butt of the automatic, then jacked a round into the chamber, I found myself wishing that I'd overcome my dislike of guns, and spent more time at the firing range. Even under practice conditions, I was a mediocre shot. There was no reason to believe that under combat conditions, conditions entirely unknown to me, I'd fare any better.

If you're more than thirty feet away, I told myself as I fumbled through the foyer closet, what you'll do is run. Maybe the jerk aiming at you can't shoot, either.

In the back of the closet I found a long-unused, soft-sided briefcase specially designed to accommodate a Browning Hi-Power automatic. The case was divided into three compartments and came with a shoulder strap so it could be carried with both hands free. The inner compartment was actually a holster designed to secure and conceal a handgun.

I'd bought the case on impulse some years before, and carried it once or twice. Now I eased the Browning inside, set the briefcase in the hall closet, then went back into the bedroom where I exchanged my sweater for a navy turtleneck. At the door, I added a light gray, three-quarter wool coat before I finally left the apartment. I didn't take the gun because I felt I was in no physical danger. I felt it was too early for that.

TWENTY-ONE

MY TRIP TO THE RIVERSIDE Chess Club brought me no closer to the motive for Sergio's death. I spoke to six or seven members (excluding Ilya Romanov, who was competing in an out-of-state tournament and wouldn't return until the following day) and learned that Sergio D'Alesse was a great guy, quick with an anecdote, and friendly even to the impoverished Romanian who ran the club and who smelled like a homeless schizophrenic. One member, Clark Zenda, described both the count and his chess game with a single word: whimsical. Another, Wendon Kufo, declared, "The boy lacked the killer instinct. He didn't understand the game. It was like a woods-for-the-trees thing. Like a learning disability."

Later, both Kufo and Zenda told me that Sergio had bragged to them of his improving fortunes. "Yeah, I remember that," Kufo declared. "He told me he was movin' up big-time."

I stayed for an hour without encountering anybody who failed to get along with D'Alesse. One and all, they were sorry to lose him and wished to attend his wake. Their greatest fear was that his family would be offended if they presented themselves. But as a member of that family, I was quick to reassure. Certainly, they would be welcome.

It was a bit after ten o'clock (late enough to call it a night without arousing a pang of guilt) when I found a cab on Broadway and headed downtown. As we cruised through the Upper West Side and into Times Square, my thoughts were focused neither on the count, nor on the gaudy billboards and marquees that leered at me from both sides of the street, but entirely on Maggie Santos. I wanted to please her, and I ordered the cabbie to drive me to a greengrocer on Third Avenue near Seventeenth Street. The shop was well known for its quality produce as well as its late hours, and its strawberries were fresh, ripe, and succulent. I chose a package carefully, added a wedge of feta cheese, a half-dozen stuffed grape leaves, a container of bitter black olives, and a loaf of seeded Italian bread. Then I paid the bill and walked to my apartment a mile away.

It was eleven when I got home. Except for a dim glow emanating from the bedroom door at the end of the hall, the apartment was dark. I laid my package on the dining room table, draped my coat over a chair, and tiptoed into the bedroom, where I found the candles on the bureau lit, and Maggie Santos asleep.

By accident or design, the quilt and sheet, instead of covering her naked body, were gathered at her waist, leading me to conclude that sleep had not been her intention when she'd first gotten into bed. Encouraged by this bit of reasoning, I cleared my throat, an inconsiderate act that produced no discernible result. Still hoping, I then sat on the edge of the bed to remove my shoes and socks, but when she again failed to respond, I left the bedroom to put the groceries in the refrigerator.

When I returned, Maggie was still asleep. This time I made no attempt to awaken her. Instead, I stood alongside the bed and simply looked at her. I traced the inverted curve at the juncture of her neck and shoulders. I followed the loose waves of her black hair as it flowed onto her back. I counted the shadowy dimples between her vertebrae. I watched the rise and fall of her chest, and the movement of her eyes beneath her closed lids. I stared at her until I felt I could see the blood surging through the pale blue veins running the length of her throat.

I did not touch her, not even after I blew out the candles and climbed into bed, not even when she stirred in her sleep and moved closer to me, not even when I became aware of the faint commingled odors of her shampoo, and her perfume, and her flesh. Though I was a long time getting to sleep, I was neither frustrated, nor even terribly aroused. It was miracle enough for me that she was there.

* * *

I was roused the next morning, shortly after sunrise, by a sharp pain that I only gradually localized in my right earlobe. Even longer in coming was the realization that my suffering had been caused by Maggie's incisors. In fact, I might never have reached that point of enlightenment if she hadn't bitten me again.

"Rise and shine, sleepy-head," she ordered.

"I need to use the bathroom first," I mumbled.

"Pardon?"

"Before I rise."

"Then by all means . . ."

An hour later, I took a call from Arthur Howell. "Hey, buddy," he told me, "I have some news for you."

"Good or bad?"

"Depends on whether you have an alibi." He chuckled before adding, "Graham Winokur was murdered last night."

I sighed, thinking that only a lawyer could find homicide amusing, then signaled Maggie to pick up the extension in the kitchen. "It's started already," I told Arthur. "The weak links are being cut."

"But not by you?"

"No, Arthur, not by me."

"Good, because I want to set up a polygraph for early next week, and I want to invite the cops to attend."

"Do it."

"Speaking of the cops, Mulligan invites you to come into the precinct at ten o'clock tomorrow morning. He's hoping you'll account for your movements last night."

"And if I don't show up?"

"Look, Phil, the police investigation might be focused on you, or it might be going in an entirely different direction. There's no way to know. But if it's focused on you, and you don't come in voluntarily, Mulligan will likely conclude that you have something to hide. At the least, he'll be anxious to get you off the street before you kill somebody else. Remember you were seen in the hallway outside the count's apartment a few minutes after he was murdered. If you weren't a Beckett, you'd be in jail awaiting trial."

A not unreasonable position, I was forced to admit. "So what's your best advice?"

"Don't cooperate unless you have an unbreakable alibi," Howell replied. "Remember, you're stuck with anything you put on the record."

"How can I know if I have an alibi if I don't know the time of death?"

"Mulligan wants to make sure you don't concoct a story. He'll try to make you account for as broad a period of time as possible."

I took a moment to think, a moment in which I decided that a moment wasn't enough. "I'm going to have to call you back. Where are you?"

"I'm on my way out to breakfast."

"Are you taking your cell phone?"

He gave me the number, then hung up. I joined Maggie in the kitchen, noting her hands on her hips and the firm set of her jaw.

"When did you come home last night?"

"Around eleven."

"Then tell Mulligan that I was waiting for you. Tell him we discussed your case for the next two hours until we went to bed. That makes the conversation privileged."

The lie was brilliantly conceived. Alibis provided by spouses, lovers, close friends, and relatives are routinely disbelieved by investigators, public or private. To break these alibis, the smart interrogator separates the parties, then takes each over the details of the accounted-for time. What did you do? Describe the conversation. Was the television on? The radio? The stereo? Were there any phone calls? Who from? How long were they? At time of trial, disparities are used by prosecutors to impeach the alibi witnesses. But if the conversation was a privileged communication between attorney and client, I had every legal right to withhold the details.

I wanted to take Maggie in my arms and thank her. Instead I growled, "That's it? Another felony?"

"I'm not giving you up."

The phone rang before I could respond. It was from Manny Rodriguez, who told me that John Caroll had yet to leave his apartment. I told Manny to stick with it, then turned my attention to Maggie.

"I'm going to take a bath," I announced. "I need to think."

"About what, Phil?"

"About what I'm going to do next."

That caught her attention, and a few minutes later we were facing each other across three feet of hot, soapy water. Our conversation began with Regina's pregnancy. Maggie persisted in her belief that my sister's revelation was somehow connected to the D'Alesse homicide. My own feeling was that the scene had been orchestrated by my father (certainly it could not have occurred without his permission) simply to provide me with an additional reason to protect the family honor.

"If you're thinking," I told Maggie at one point, "that my sister had an affair with Count Sergio D'Alesse, and that she's making up this artificial-insemination business, put it out of your mind. The process of deciding to have herself inseminated, then of finding the appropriate doctors and hospitals, then of choosing a donor, must have taken many months. With Father approving every detail."

The water in the tub was rapidly cooling when I finally got to the point. I remember that Maggie's wet hair clung to her shoulders and that her breasts, half in and half out of the soapy water, seemed to be floating. Her smile was expectant, but it disappeared when I told her that we wouldn't be seeing each other for a while.

"Caroll's decided to cut his losses," I told her. "I could be next and I can't put you at risk. There's no need for it."

"And you're going out there alone? You're going to play macho man while I sit at home? Maybe I can knit you a pair of socks."

"If you do," I said as I struggled to rise, "don't mail them, because I won't be coming back here." I helped Maggie up, pulled the drain plug, then turned on the shower. "My goal is to survive, and I think I've a better shot if I make myself hard to find."

My little speech sobered her up and she agreed, finally, to keep a

Sunday brunch appointment with Naomi Felder, then analyze whatever records Naomi produced. We would stay in touch by cellular phone.

"Tell me," I asked her as we dressed. "Do you still think it's an adventure?"

She slapped me then, square in the face, a blow so unexpected I simply stood there, mouth agape, while I struggled to understand exactly what had happened.

"Don't you do that to me," she declared. "Don't you even try."

Genuinely baffled, I asked, "Do what?"

Maggie said nothing. She held her fist beneath her jaw, her eyes very wide and very dark. Her weight shifted to the balls of her feet and for a moment I thought she was going to hit me again.

I raised my arm to block the side of my face, but finally realized that she was simply afraid, and she'd been afraid for some time. "All for a fish," I said.

"A fish?"

"A yellow dragon-fish leaping from a yellow sea, carved in jade by an unknown Chinese artist in the last decades of the eighteenth century. If I didn't want the fish, I wouldn't have agreed to work for Regina. If I hadn't agreed to work for Regina . . ." I took her hand. "Just because I don't have a choice doesn't mean it can't be an adventure. It's all a matter of attitude, right?"

Maggie touched my cheek and smiled a guilt-free smile. "I'm sorry I hit you," she said.

"I accept your apology," I told her as I pulled on a pair of charcoal trousers. The trousers, wool and roomy in the legs, offered me considerable freedom of movement. The shoes I chose, a pair of black oxfords, had a very hard toe, and were also designed to play a dual role. I didn't explain this to Maggie, nor did I show her the gun when I eventually pulled the briefcase containing the Browning over my shoulder. I didn't even tell her that I was prepared to defend myself. But I felt that I was, and any doubts I might have entertained were gone before I reached the curb outside the building.

TWENTY-TWO

IT WAS A BEAUTIFUL DAY. Sunny, windy, brisk. A perfect day for a long walk, or to listen to a free zydeco concert in the plaza of the World Financial Center, or to face up to a skinny, lantern-jawed creep named Tony Farelli.

Wearing a black leather coat so absurdly padded in the shoulders it made him look even thinner, Tony smiled the same obsequious smile he'd worn at the club.

"Hi," he said as I came through the door. "I'm Tony. You remember me?"

As I listened to his reedy, high-pitched voice, I found myself flashing from the whimsical Sergio D'Alesse to the chubby Graham Winokur. Had Tony, I asked myself, been the designated assassin in both cases? Had he enjoyed his work enough to go to dinner afterward? Or to celebrate with a hooker and an eight-ball of powder cocaine? Or did he go home to a family tucked safely away in some corner of Staten Island, maybe give the kiddies a lecture on family values?

"Mr. Caroll would like to speak to you." Tony's smile was unchanged, but his brown eyes had become mocking. You'd refuse, they told me, if you had the balls. "Just for a minute."

He gestured to a Mercedes sedan parked at the curb. I couldn't see past the car's smoked windows, but a glance up and down the block left me pretty sure Caroll wasn't inside. Manny Rodriguez was nowhere in sight.

"What does he want?"

"A talk. No big deal." He took hold of my left arm. "C'mon."

"You're not gonna hurt me," I said. "Are you?"

"Phil, please . . ."

He was finished before the smile left his face. I hooked his right arm with my left hand, pulled him forward and down, then slammed my cupped palm into his ear. His dark eyes rolled in his head, loose as marbles. His legs, when I let him go, dropped out from under him as though I'd severed his spine. I had just enough time to pull his gun from the holster beneath his arm before he hit the pavement.

The gun was heavy, a .45-caliber Colt Commander. Like the leather coat, it was much too big for Tony Farelli. I shoved it under my jacket, shielding it from passersby as I stared into the darkened windows of the Mercedes. The doors remained closed, even when I raised my chin and smiled. Even when I began to laugh.

Tony Farelli rose onto his hands and knees, then fell, then forced himself up again. The blow to his ear had robbed him of his sense of balance and I was sure he was wondering when (or if) it would return. Still, he managed to suck up his resolve, then declare, rather predictably, "I'm gonna kill you."

I rejected a number of pithy rejoinders before settling on the appropriate response, a snap kick to his good ear. Tony dropped onto his forehead, balanced his weight for a moment, then slid down and onto his back. His mouth opened, then closed as he stared up at the small swift clouds running at a diagonal between the buildings on either side of the street. He looked like he wanted to scream but couldn't remember how.

As my attention returned to the Mercedes, I slid my index finger beneath the Colt's trigger guard. I think if the doors had opened at that moment, I would have killed the first man to climb out of the car. Fortunately, the back window rolled down instead, and I managed to control myself as I stared into the eyes of the house dealer at the club who'd fed Sergio D'Alesse so many winning hands. According to the count, his name was Carlo and he was a hell of a nice guy.

"You gonna kill Tony?" Carlo had a soft round face and a tiny nose with tilted nostrils that wriggled as if searching for the origin of an offensive odor.

"Would that be a problem?"

"For Christ's sake, man, we just wanna talk to you." He shook his head in disgust. "We were *told* you were someone we could talk to. We were fuckin' *told*."

"By anybody I know?"

I didn't expect an answer and I didn't get one. The window rolled up and I was left to stare at my own reflection as I realized, for the first time, that Tony and I had company. A number of pedestrians had gathered to observe the festivities. Visibly frightened, they parted when I strolled past, then closed ranks as if seeking each other's solace. I slid the Colt beneath the waistband of my trousers, and repressed a smile as I made my way to Lexington Avenue.

I turned north, against the traffic, and walked for a couple of blocks before I found a quiet moment to kneel by a parked car at the curb and toss the Colt into a storm drain. I even remembered to wipe the pistol first.

I continued up Lexington Avenue, with the burnished crown of the Chrysler Building in sight, while I made three short phone calls. The first went to Arthur Howell. I let him know I wasn't going to speak to Detective Mulligan, then gave him the number of Maggie's cellular phone in case he needed to reach me. The second call went to Benny Abraham, who took it in his bedroom. I apologized for calling so early, then filled him in, beginning with Audrey's interview. He listened patiently, offering no more than an occasional grunt, until I described my confrontation with Tony Farelli.

"What were you thinkin', Phil? You just gave away your hole card."

"The rational explanation," I told him, "is that once Farelli put his hand on my arm, violence was my only option. He was telling me that I *had* to get into that car." As I continued north into the midtown area, a middle-aged man wearing a pinstriped power suit bore down on me. He plucked at his salt-and-pepper crew cut as he came, a cell phone pressed to his ear. "Sergio D'Alesse," I told Benny as I dodged to the left, "and Graham Winokur both trusted John Caroll. Now they're both dead."

"Phil, I think you took it too far. Most likely Caroll just wanted a talk."

"Most likely isn't good enough when the consequence of a hasty judgment is permanent death."

"All right," he finally agreed, "that's the rational explanation. What's the irrational?"

"I get off on confrontation," I told him. "Which is something you knew when you signed on."

"Yeah, I did," he admitted, remembering, perhaps, the dozen times we'd touched on the subject. At one point he'd told me that unpredictability was part of my charm. "So, what's next?"

"I want to vanish for the next few days and I need a place to sleep at night."

"Call me back in a couple of hours."

"Thanks, Benny."

By the time I hung up, I'd calmed sufficiently to become aware of the angled spring sun washing over the office towers on the west side of Lexington Avenue. I've never cared much for unbroken lines of curtain wall construction. I find these sheets of glass and metal, despite their imposing bulk, not only inhuman, but also monotonous. Their one virtue, however, brought to the fore on perfect spring days, is their ability to reflect light. I took a moment to watch the sun-drenched towers on the east side of the street ripple through a thousand panes of glass on the west, as tantalizing as fog.

Despite it being a Saturday, there were pedestrians on the street. Young people, mostly, clutching briefcases as they scurried into one or another of the towers in search of that sixty square feet of space they could reasonably claim for their own. About the size of a prison cell.

As I punched Father's number into the phone, the last of the tension dropped away. I was in it now and there was no turning back. Somehow I found the idea comforting.

Calder Hallmark answered on the third ring and I asked him if Regina had slept over.

"She did," Calder responded. "She's in her room."

"Asleep?"

"I believe your sister is awake. Shall I summon her to the phone?"

"No. I want you to tell her that I'll be there in fifteen minutes and that I need to speak to her."

Calder drew a wheezy breath. This was not the kind of message he was anxious to deliver. "Master Philip . . ."

"All right," I relented. "Apologize to Regina for my crass behavior, explain that I'm pressed for time, then tell her I'd like to speak with her in fifteen minutes if it isn't too inconvenient."

It still wasn't the bottom line Calder hoped for, but he wasn't prepared to demand that I speak directly to Regina. Calder was, after all, a servant. He couldn't reasonably expect each and every service he performed to be palatable.

"Yes, sir," he said as I rang off. "I'll see that she gets your message."

TWENTY-THREE

I FOUND REGINA IN THE billiard room, bent over a table with carved rails and legs that our great-grandfather had acquired on a visit to London in 1926. A pair of worn leather sofas rested against the walls on either side of the table. Above them, and on the adjoining walls, simply framed oils (purchased on the same trip) depicted every aspect of a British fox hunt, from the anticipatory breakfast to the triumphant display of the carcass.

Regina's choice of the billiard room for our meeting was quite deliberate. At twelve years of age, I'd been sent off to Choate, a lonely child made lonelier by the effort to find a place among my very competitive peers. I don't know which was worse, Father's silent home, in which any echoing sound felt intrusive, or the carnivorous atmosphere that hung, thick as blood, over the dormitory at Choate. Eventually I'd rejected both, proving, I suppose, that I'd learned to live with neither.

Nevertheless, the first years at Choate were very difficult, and when I returned to the home of my parents on holidays and in the summer, I sought out the only readily available company, my sister. Regina and I, especially in those first years, spent many hours together in the billiard room. We were self-taught fumblers, the pair of us, but nevertheless competitive. Or, at least, we were competitive until it became clear to me that Regina was the far better player. I was never going to beat her.

As I eventually became friendly with several schoolmates from New York (and became old enough to be allowed on the streets of Manhattan unattended), the time I spent with Regina gradually diminished. It was callous of me, I suppose, though Regina never complained. Instead, she continued to practice when I wasn't around, as she'd been practicing all along. By the time I graduated from Choate, I wasn't fit to chalk her cue.

"Still at it?" I asked from the doorway. Regina was wearing a man-tailored white shirt over a pair of black pants made from a synthetic fabric that stretched when she bent over the table. She was trim and sexy, and I remembered that as a student at the Dalton School, then at Princeton, she'd gone from boyfriend to boyfriend as if the supply of available males was infinite.

"It's my escape," she said.

"From what?"

"From my obligations."

Another reproach. "Yes," I told her, "I can understand how your obligations might seem burdensome at the moment. There's nothing like murder and pregnancy to add a bit of stress to one's already stressful life. A kind of camel's straw effect."

"Are you implying that I was involved in Sergio's murder?" Holding the cue across her chest with both hands, she turned to face me. Her voice was quite steady when she pronounced the word *murder.* Too steady.

"I believe we're discussing obligations, Regina." I walked all the way into the room. After my long hike from Twenty-seventh Street, the sofa on my right seemed downright alluring, but I wasn't about to spend the remainder of the conversation staring up at Regina. My sister was imposing enough without that. "For example, what are my obligations should I uncover the individuals who conspired to murder our cousin's dearly beloved spouse? The question, I don't mind telling you, troubles me greatly."

"You're going to carry the identity of those individuals to the family, Philip. The family will decide what to do with it."

"That's my obligation?"

"You know it is."

I think Regina meant what she said, the idea of family obligation having been pounded into her throughout her entire life. Nevertheless, she was full of shit. "You claim," I said, "that because I'm a Beckett, I'm obliged to consult the Beckett family before acting in my own interest, that all Becketts share this obligation. You make this claim even though your definition of family excludes me, as it probably excludes Audrey and her parents."

"Nobody's excluding you."

"Then why won't you tell me what you know about the motive for Sergio D'Alesse's murder?"

Regina continued to hold her cue as if preparing to defend herself. Her featureless blue eyes never left my own. "If you think," she calmly informed me, "that I'm going to respond to your accusations, you're mistaken."

I stepped around her and walked to the far end of the room. "In that case, allow me to rephrase." A wooden chandelier, its individual lamps focused on the playing surface and the area immediately surrounding the table, provided the only light in the room. With the drapes closed, I was standing in deep shadow. "Is there anything you haven't told me about the murder of Audrey Beckett's husband? Anything at all?"

She stared at me for a moment, then swung back to face the open door. "Father," she said, "is such a fool to trust you."

"Well, at least you didn't lie to me."

"Lie?" She threw up her hands. "Philip, you've got to stop this."

I shook my head. "The sad truth is that you not only don't know me at all, you don't know that you don't know me at all. For you, we're still the older brother and younger sister competing for Mother's approval and Father's fortune. It's pathetic."

She sniffed twice, a sure sign she was regaining her composure. "I told Father you couldn't be trusted."

"It wasn't Father who lured me into this mess. It was you."

"Lured you?"

"The count's gambling debt was never the issue."

Ready, apparently, to face me without a weapon, Regina laid the cue on the table. "If you won't consider me, and you won't consider Father, might you at least consider the child?"

"The one hundred percent pure Beckett you're presently incubating?"

"My son, Philip. Your nephew."

"And the heir apparent. Perhaps I should fall to my knees, or attend the birth with gifts of frankincense and myrrh."

She sighed, then folded her arms across her chest. She'd had enough. "I'd like to know if you're aware of the morality clause in your trust fund."

"Damn," I said as I prepared to make my exit. "For a moment there I thought I was going to win one."

In fact, I did remember a loosely worded clause that allowed my trust fund to be taken from me if I proved to be an individual of dubious moral character. Although no precise definitions were offered in the formal document, a charge of murder would more than qualify. Regina's problem was that any effort to invoke this clause would have to be initiated by Father, the trust's executor.

I crossed the room to the doorway, then, without turning, said, "Last chance, Regina. Do you want to cooperate with me, or take your chances with Gaetano Carollo?"

"Father," she said for the second time, "is such a fool." Then, before I could leave, as if she'd made a last-minute decision, she added, her voice tight with the effort to get the words out, "You won't be convicted of any crime. I promise you. That's just not a consideration."

"For a Beckett?" I waited for her to respond, but she held her peace. "I have no alibi, and our cousin, the victim's wife, who just happens to have an unbreakable alibi, not only told the police that the door was unlocked, she told them my hand was on the knob. If Mulligan doesn't come up with another suspect in the very near future, he's *obliged* to arrest me."

"It's a long way," she countered, "from arrest to conviction."

"And that way, Regina, is either called 'out on bail,' or 'incarcerated defendant awaiting trial a year down the line.' Tell me, would you feel safer with your big brother on the street or confined to Rikers Island? Which would better serve the interests of the family?"

Back on her game, Regina tapped the sole of her foot against the massive leg of the pool table. "I realize that you're frightened," she told me, "but you're being overly dramatic. Nothing—"

"Do you know that Graham Winokur is dead?"

"Who?"

"Graham Winokur. He was a tubby, red-face investment counselor who thought he could deal with John Caroll. Sometime last night he was murdered."

TWENTY-FOUR

I WAS IN A CAB, half-way to the Riverside Chess Club, before I finally calmed sufficiently to do something I should have done long before. I began, no surprise, with a call to Maggie.

She was at home when I phoned, in the process of creating a grocery list. "It's only been a couple of hours," she told me, "and I miss you already."

"Work," I answered, "is the most effective remedy for loneliness."

"Well, live and learn, right?"

"Right."

"And speaking of live and learn, Graham Winokur's murder was featured on this morning's news. Last night, at around midnight, he was stabbed to death on East Sixty-third Street. His wallet and watch are missing."

As I only had a few moments, I filed the information away for later, then got down to business. "Are you on the Internet?"

"Yes, but I only use it for e-mail."

"Don't worry, this is going to be a little more complicated, but not much. Do you have a pen?"

I wanted Maggie to run the names of seven individuals, and three corporations, through TRACKDOWN's database of periodicals. Though simple enough in execution, the job would not only take many hours, it would be tedious in the extreme. Maggie, however, didn't comment as she wrote down my password and TRACK-DOWN's Internet address.

"Choose *periodicals* from the main menu," I instructed. "You'll get a sub-menu offering a number of categories. Choose *all*, then *run*."

"Got it," she said. "Anything else?"

The cab was passing through Central Park on the Ninety-sixth Street transverse. The road was sunken here, and the massive stone walls on either side were gray with a century of dust and soot. On the sidewalk to my right, a ragged hump that I only belatedly recognized as a man dozed in the shadows.

"Be sure to use first and last names. If you try to search with a last name only, you'll get too many hits. As it is, you'll still have to cull out the irrelevant data."

"Got it," she repeated. "Anything else?"

"Yes. This research—would the results by any chance fall under the general heading of client confidentiality?"

"Darling, they couldn't get it out of me with torture."

On a whim, I bought a half-dozen bagels, a half-pound of lox, a tub of cream cheese, and a quart of grapefruit juice, then carried the groceries into the Riverside Chess Club. Ilya Romanov seemed both pleased and surprised by the gesture.

He was a short man, shorter than Benny, but just as broad across the chest. He and Benny shared a heavy-boned skull and wide brow as well, but whereas Benny's features, especially his eyes, were small and pinched, Romanov's eyes were as large and round as a deer's. His nose was full and fleshy, his lips, in those rare moments when they weren't moving, actually succulent.

I was hungry enough to let Ilya recite his family history while I took my time with an onion bagel. His family, he told me, was distantly related to Czar Nicholas. After the Bolshevik Revolution they'd lived under constant threat. His grandfather had been arrested twice, his father and himself as well, yet they'd avoided the dreaded gulags and the firing squads until he, Ilya, had defected to the United States in 1973 while on tour with the Soviet chess team.

Ilya's accent was very pronounced. He seemed to wrestle the words out of his mouth, his cheeks swelling with the effort. "See what they have do to me?" he explained as he shuffled over to the coffeemaker on stiff legs. "In Lubyanka prison. KGB."

It seemed unlikely to me that the KGB would allow a man they'd half crippled to tour the United States, but I didn't interrupt. The brutality of the Soviet Union's internal security apparatus wasn't Ilya's point, anyway. His point was that he and Count Sergio D'Alesse were drawn to each other because royal blood flowed through both their veins.

"We are greatest friends," he told me. "I did not even mind that his chess is like baby's."

I finished the last of my bagel and wiped my fingers. "When I spoke to Sergio," I said, "the day before he was killed, he told me that he expected his fortunes to improve. I—"

"As well," Ilya interrupted, "Sergio has said this to me. But he does not say to me the details."

"Do you think he was telling the truth?"

"Why you are asking me this?"

"Because I want to find his killer."

"*Da.*" He picked up his right leg with both hands and draped it across his left. "See what they have do to me," he repeated before looking up to add, "I have never know Sergio to be bullshit. Always, he is honest man."

"Did you know about his debt?"

"The gambling. Yes, I know this. Forty thousand dollars to men who are threatening to hurt him." He looked down at his hands for a moment, then addressed my next question without my having to ask it. "Very strange, *da?* Owing so much money to men such as these, but he tells me that soon everything is fixed. No more problem with money."

"That's why I asked if he was telling the truth. Some people, they just like to brag."

"*Nyet.*" His right hand sliced the air between us. "This is not Sergio. He is not liar."

"I believe you, Ilya, but that doesn't make Sergio look any better. He had no resources and he wasn't going to get a job. So if he expected his fortunes to improve, and he was unwilling to tell you how, he must have been up to no good. Maybe the kind of no good that gets you killed."

There was nothing for Ilya to do but agree. After all, we were discussing a hypothetical. For me, on the other hand, the conversation had already proved useful. If D'Alesse confided his gambling problems to Ilya, they'd been close enough to validate Ilya's belief in Sergio's basically honest nature. The count had expected to come into money.

I decided to take a chance before I moved on, a chance based not only on Sergio's character, as I viewed it, but on many centuries of Old World tradition.

"The family," I began, coughing into my hand as if embarrassed by my lack of manners, "has long known that Sergio had . . ." I sighed, smiled apologetically, then delivered the bluff. "We've known that Sergio was . . . seeing a woman. On the side."

It was a good thing Ilya's game of choice was chess and not poker. His eyes widened, his jaw dropped, his eyes jerked quickly away.

"It's all right," I said. "I understand these things. After all, to the best of my knowledge, nobody's contemplating a divorce."

Though he smiled, it occurred to me that what I'd said wasn't strictly true. We were, of course, well past the time for legal separation, but Audrey, according to Regina, had been contemplating divorce for some time.

I leaned forward to tap Ilya's hand. "Men, you know, they sometimes have loose tongues after . . . You understand, I'm sure. I must have the name of Sergio's lover."

Ilya tried to pull his hand away. When I grabbed it and held on, he stared at me for a moment, then allowed his hand to relax. "This woman, she is my friend. Without permission, I cannot give her name."

"If you don't," I told him as I finally released him, "the police will be talking to you before the day is through. This is about murder, Ilya. Laudable as they may be under ordinary circumstances, your chivalrous instincts don't apply here. I want her name and address, and I don't want you to call her when I leave."

Another long pause, followed by a deep sigh. I'd worked Ilya pretty well, jumping from topic to topic and mood to mood as I played both ends of the good cop–bad cop paradigm. Now it was time to play my last card.

"Look, Ilya," I said, allowing my tone to soften, "Sergio had other good friends. The information could have come from any of them. There's no reason for your name to be mentioned. Just tell me who she is."

I found myself happy as I subwayed south toward Battery Park City in lower Manhattan. Armed with a vivid description of Ms. Vivian Walpole, and with her phone number, I was fairly certain I'd gain her cooperation. According to Ilya, Vivian was Sergio's lover, not his mistress, and they'd been together for many years. I would appeal to her sense of justice, to the dearly departed's need for vengeance. It would—or so I supposed as the 1 train roared through a graffiti-scarred tunnel between Times Square and Penn Station—be easy.

Ten minutes later, I rose from the depths. The day was brisk, its sharpness a last reminder of the passing winter, and the humidity was very low. With the engines of commerce shut down on a Sunday, the air was free of soot and the harbor sparkled in the early afternoon sun. There were sailboats out on the water, the first I'd seen this year, and I briefly watched a yacht with a blazing red sail cut through the wake of the Liberty Island ferry before I set myself back to work.

Forty years ago, the land on which the condominium complex known as Battery Park City rests was part of the Hudson River. It was only as the many subbasements of the World Trade Center's four buildings were dug, and the earth dumped in the river, that the acreage for the World Financial Center, as well as for Battery Park City, emerged from the waters. The housing subsequently erected, a mix of featureless high- and low-rise buildings, were (and are) pricey.

The World Trade Center is gone, of course. And for a time, so was Battery Park City. The residents, except for a few who simply refused to leave their homes, were evacuated after 9/11. Many chose not to return. The memories were too painful. But others, driven by a housing crisis more than a century old, came in to replace them. Today the complex is fully occupied.

I phoned Vivian Walpole for the second time as I approached her building. The first call had been made only to determine that she was at home. I'd hung up at the sound of a woman's voice. Now, when she answered, I quickly introduced myself.

"Vivian Walpole?"

"Who is this?"

"My name is Philip Beckett. I'm—"

"I know who you are. What do you want?" Though her reply was confrontational, her tone was quite calm.

"I'm investigating Sergio's murder, Ms. Walpole, and I believe that you can help me. If you can just give me a few minutes of your time."

She hung up without saying good-bye, and I settled down to wait. A few minutes later, she walked through the outer door, took three steps onto the sidewalk, then saw me standing there, blocking her path with my arms folded, and came to an abrupt halt.

Though she was exactly as Ilya had described her, I found it hard to imagine Vivvy Walpole and Count Sergio D'Alesse sharing the sidewalk, much less the connubial bed. Walpole was taller than I, and one of those overweight women who carries the extra pounds between her breasts and her thighs. Not that I could see all that much of her figure beneath the gold and black muumuu flowing from her throat to her ankles. The muumuu was decorated with alternating rows of geometric figures. Over it she wore an unbuttoned, sky-blue coat, the collar trimmed with white faux fur. The contrast between the gold and the blue was so pronounced I wanted to close my eyes.

She put her hands on her hips when she saw me, but the glare she attempted never really came off. After a moment she smiled, then grinned, then started to laugh.

"The count," she told me, "approved of you."

"Is that what you called him? The count?"

"That's what his in-laws called him. It was kind of a joke between us."

I smiled, and nodded encouragement. "Are you going to talk to me?"

"Perhaps," she said, as she led me away. "It depends on you."

TWENTY-FIVE

I TRAILED VIVIAN WALPOLE'S BROAD shoulders east to a booth in a nondescript coffeehouse on Rector Street. Neither of us apparently in a hurry, we stared across the table at each other for some time without speaking. Vivian's features, once I got past the feathered earrings (two to an ear), were quite regular. Her brown eyes, though bloodshot and underlined by sooty crescents, were large and warm, her prominent nose perfectly sculpted. Her hair was blond and very thick. Pulled tight along the sides, it was held against the back of her head by a mother-of-pearl comb. From there it fell in broad waves to the middle of her back.

"Somehow," I told her after we ordered coffee, "I'm having difficulty picturing you and Sergio together." Ilya had told me that Vivian had two careers. She was a life counselor (a title that allowed her to offer psychological therapy without the petty annoyances of an education or a license), and she designed New Age posters. On the way down, I'd turned these facts over in my head, finally deciding that if she chose to lie, she'd be very accomplished at the art.

"The count was a great lover," she explained without changing expression. "As am I."

"Do you miss him?"

I'd hoped to break through her calm, but she was at least a step ahead of me. "Sergio liked you," she told me. "He thought you were brave."

"Brave?"

"To break with your family. He didn't have the balls, and he knew it."

"He didn't have a trust fund, either."

"Yes, he did. He had Audrey's. He just couldn't live on it."

I conceded the point with a nod. "Speaking of Audrey, did she know about you?"

Instead of answering, Vivian went into an enormous shoulder bag to extract an oversized deck of cards, which she held up for my inspection. Dutifully, I read, *THOTH TAROT DECK*, then below, *Aleister Crowley*.

"Did you know that Aleister Crowley was once considered the most evil man on Earth?" she asked.

"I didn't, actually."

"Well, this is the tarot deck he designed. It's good for unmasking dark impulses." She shuffled the cards and offered them to me. "Cut with your left hand."

I did as I was told before returning the pack. She laid a card in the middle of the table, then surrounded it with four additional cards. The card in the center, I recall, bore the legend "Fortune," which meant so little to me that I barely glanced at the others. Vivian, on the other hand, stared at them for several minutes, long enough for the waitress to return with our coffees, before looking up at me.

"You didn't kill him," she told me.

As there's nothing I care for less than New Age mumbo jumbo, my first considered response was sarcastic. I restrained myself with some effort. "The cards," I asked, "don't by chance tell you who *did* kill him?"

"Sorry."

I added a teaspoon of sugar and a dollop of half-and-half to my coffee, then stirred judiciously. "Sergio told me, on the day before he was killed, that he expected his fortunes to improve. He told his friends the same thing. The problem is that nobody knows how."

She looked down at the cards, then up at me, then changed the subject. "The cards also tell me that you can't be trusted."

"To do what?" I waved off her reply. "I'm in a very peculiar situation, Vivian. I'm a suspect here, and I need answers."

"You want them so you can save yourself."

"What does that mean? That my heart isn't pure? That I'm not worthy?"

"It means that you can't be trusted."

"To do what?"

"To do what's necessary."

"And what is that?"

She picked up one of the cards and offered it for my inspection. Dutifully (although not hopefully) I studied the card, a mounted figure clad in black armor staring into a flaming orange sky.

"This is the Knight of Discs and represents the fiery part of Earth. On the scale of the planet, he is the agent of eruptions and earthquakes." She returned the cards to the table. "You should think about what he might represent on the human scale."

We went around for another ten minutes (during which Vivian made it very clear that she could help me, but wouldn't) before I packed it in. "The cops'll be around before long," I told her as I paid for the coffee. "You play games with them and they'll make you pay for it."

"I've dealt with the police before."

I walked back to the waterfront but was too pissed off to enjoy the scenery. I kept telling myself to move on to Carlos Mogollon, another of the count's friends. Mogollon lived in TriBeCa, one neighborhood to the north and within easy walking distance. But I couldn't leave it alone, and twenty minutes later I found myself returning to Battery Park City.

The outer door of Vivian's building was propped open by a mover's dolly loaded with boxes, and I had no trouble getting to her apartment on the sixth floor. My strategy here was to demand that Vivian cooperate. If she refused, I would pound on her neighbors' doors, beginning with the one closest to her own. I would tell her neighbors that I was investigating the murder of Vivian Walpole's lover, then ask for an interview. Whether I got an interview was, of course, beside the point.

I took a moment to gear myself up, then rang the bell. I was prepared to be forceful and determined, prepared to counter all resistance, prepared for anything but the appearance of Detective Kirk Mulligan in the doorway. Ten feet behind him, Vivian Walpole stood before a low sofa covered with a violet throw. She smiled at me, then waved.

"Well, hello there," Mulligan said. "Fancy meeting you in a place like this."

I stared into his sad blue eyes, thinking that the son of a bitch was smarter than he looked. "We're not supposed to talk," I said. "At all."

He put his hand over his mouth. "Oh, I forgot. You won't tell on me, will ya?"

Of course, I should have turned away. I knew that. But again prodded by the ludicrous belief that my innocence would protect me, I said, "Last night, when Graham Winokur was killed, I was in bed with my girlfriend."

Mulligan's smile, though friendly, betrayed his eagerness. "Awake? Asleep?"

"Awake."

"And what did you talk about?"

"My girlfriend is also my attorney. We were discussing my legal situation. Our conversation is privileged."

"Okay," he said, "I can accept that. So, is it true what they say? Once you go black, you never go back?"

"What are you talking about?"

"Didn't you just tell me that Arthur Howell is your girlfriend?"

His laughter followed me all the way to the loft apartment of Carlos Mogollon on Duane Street in TriBeCa. What I didn't consider, not until I was standing on the corner of Duane and Greenwich, was that Mulligan hadn't detained me. At least for the present, I had nothing to fear from the police, and it was still possible that Mulligan would uncover the killer's motive without my help. But somehow I didn't like the idea very much.

Mogollon's loft was on the top floor of a converted nineteenth-century warehouse. I rode up in an ancient freight elevator that slammed back and forth against its housing as if trying to escape before it finally stopped four inches below the concrete slab fronting his door. The buzzer, when I rang it, was loud enough to double as an air raid siren. It rasped in the barren space like a swarm of maddened African bees.

When Mogollon finally appeared, he was shirtless beneath paint-stained coveralls, his left palm smeared with so many colors I had to believe he was using it for a palette. I apologized for interrupting, then introduced myself. Like Vivian Walpole, Mogollon knew who I was. Like Ilya Romanov, he also knew that D'Alesse was expecting his fortunes to improve but was ignorant of the details.

"I asked," Mogollon said, "but he wouldn't talk about it."

"Do you know anyone he might have told?"

"Who have you tried?"

"His entire family, plus Ilya Romanov and Vivian Walpole."

"You met Vivian?"

"A dead end."

"Huh." As he pondered the information, he rubbed his paint-stained palm over his forehead, depositing a virtual rainbow in the process. "How about John Simone?"

"From Brooklyn."

"That's him. He's a lawyer, works for Smith, Barney, but he used to help Sergio out with his creditors. You know, give him advice." Mogollon laughed. "Sergio was a great guy, but there was always somebody after him for money."

John Simone lived on Eighty-fourth Street in the Bay Ridge section of Brooklyn, a good forty-five-minute drive that no cab driver in his right mind would want to make. It was now well after six. The shoppers were on their way home, while the day trippers were just arriving at the bus and train stations. A run to Brooklyn would require the driver to come back empty, a definite financial hardship on a night when relatively few people came out to party. Tough shit.

I stationed myself on Hudson Street, which runs north toward the heart of Manhattan, then hopped into the first cab that stopped and demanded to be taken east, over the Brooklyn Bridge. The driver, a turbaned Sikh, began a predictable spiel almost before I'd given the address.

"I am very sorry," he told me. "But I must return the cab to the garage in Queens. I would—"

"There's only two possibilities here," I interrupted. "Either you take me to Brooklyn, or we meet again in a Taxi and Limousine Commission hearing room on Forty-first Street. Understand?"

As the minimum fine for a refusal is two hundred dollars, more than a cabbie makes on his best day, we were off to Brooklyn without further ado.

By the time we reached the bridge, I was on the phone with Maggie. Detective Mulligan, she told me, had already called. "When I told him that the details of our conversation were privileged, he didn't argue."

"I hope you don't think he believed you."

"I'm an officer of the court. He has to take me seriously."

There was no point in arguing, and I quickly changed the subject. "How's the research going?"

"At this rate, I'll be at it all night. The individual searches are taking forever."

"TRACKDOWN's database includes virtually every newspaper, magazine and journal printed in the United States and Canada. It's slower than most of the other services, but you don't have to worry about missing something important."

"Well, I did find one item that caught my attention. Did you know that there's an ongoing proxy fight for control of Beckett Industries?"

To say that I was surprised would be to understate the matter to a considerable degree. "I didn't," I finally admitted. "I had no idea."

Maggie took a minute to fetch a copy of an article which had appeared in the February 16 edition of the *Wall Street Journal*. When she returned, she read directly from the text. " 'A group of investors led by Mercer Fredricks threw down the gauntlet at a press conference yesterday, accusing the Beckett family, which has controlled the family business since its inception, of gross mis-management.

Although the Beckett family owns thirty-eight percent of the voting shares, Fredricks predicts victory when the battle is joined at the annual shareholders' meeting of Beckett Industries on the last weekend in May.' "

There was really nothing for me to add. Although losing control of Beckett Industries wouldn't necessarily have any impact on the family fortune, it would leave a pretty big hole in the working days of Father, Regina and Uncle Alfred. It would leave a pretty big hole in their egos as well.

"Do you think it means anything?" Maggie asked.

"If Fredricks' challenge is genuine, any scandal, personal or professional, could tip the scales. Without doubt, if the Becketts have something to hide, they're ripe for blackmail."

"Is that what D'Alesse was up to? Blackmail?"

"I can't think of any other way his fortunes could improve. And believe me, I've been trying. He must have had something on somebody in the family."

"Then why did the family refuse to pay his gambling debt?"

"Maybe he hadn't gotten around to making any demands."

"Then why have him killed?"

Asking the right question at the right time is at the heart of the detecting business. Most often, when it happens, it's a matter of pure luck, the right guess as much as the right question. In this case, I hadn't even been astute enough to do the guessing.

TWENTY-SIX

THE PHONE RANG BEFORE I could return it to the briefcase. It was Manny Rodriguez calling to tell me that John Caroll had emerged from the San Remo three hours before and was now holed up in an apartment on Tenth Avenue.

"He jumped into a cab, and like the dude was flyin', man. I hadda hitch onto a truck bumper to keep up."

I dutifully thanked him for making the effort, then asked, "You didn't get the apartment number, did you?"

"No, but I seen him in the window. Third floor front, on the south side of the buildin'. He's up there with a woman."

"A girlfriend?" I was thinking out loud.

"Not unless he's some kind of a freak. The broad is like old enough to be his mother."

"Anybody hanging around the building? Besides you."

"You mean like from Caroll's crew?"

"Exactly."

"Uh-uh. It's quiet."

I made a decision, then, clearing a conscience that had been nagging at me since I'd learned of Winokur's death. It was getting very rough out there and I didn't want Manny hurt. "You're done," I told him. "Take a ride down to Sharpers, have a couple of beers, tell Luisa to put them on my tab. If Benny's around, he'll pay you off for the time you worked."

We were approaching the merger of the Brooklyn-Queens and the Gowanus expressways, a perennial choke point narrowed still more by a construction zone. I was glad for the delay (and oblivious to the muttered obscenities of my driver) as bits and pieces of the last few days drifted through my mind. Why, Maggie had asked, if Sergio had meant to blackmail the family, did he lack for the forty grand to pay off John Caroll? And if he hadn't made any demands, why was he killed?

The answer to that was not only simple, it had the added virtue of getting Father off the hook. The individual to whom Sergio had made his demands—demands for a great deal more than forty thousand dollars—could not approach the individual who refused to pay the count's gambling debt without revealing the facts underlying the blackmail attempt. Nor, for the same reason, could this individual—or individuals—meet those demands.

The proxy fight for Beckett Industries added another layer of pressure to the mix. Beckett Industries belonged to the Beckett family. It had always belonged to the Beckett family, as much a possession as the manuscripts in Father's library. It could not be surrendered, as Sergio D'Alesse could not be allowed to make his sordid tale public.

Of course, I had no specifics regarding that tale, and no physical proof that it existed. But I was certain, as I'd been certain all along, that I would find it, especially now that I was finally beginning to ask the right questions. For example, the question that should have jumped out at me on first learning the news of Winokur's death finally took shape. Except for the subject, it was the same question Maggie had asked. Why was Graham Winokur killed?

Because he was a shill in a bustout poker game? Because he carried a videotape to John Caroll, more than likely at Caroll's behest? Or because Winokur had performed a service that could not become public knowledge? A service that Caroll, who never expected Winokur's name to be associated with his own, knew the chubby stockbroker would reveal if the cops began to pressure him.

I returned to my original scenario. A member of the Beckett family hears of Caroll's threat, then approaches Caroll with a business proposition. In business, something of value (usually money) is exchanged for something else of value. I say "usually" because there are times when a transfer of cash would be extremely inconvenient, not to mention incriminating. In that case, another medium of exchange must be found, and I was pretty sure I knew what that medium was. If I was right, it would only be a matter of time until I could prove it.

I raised my head and looked around as we finally accelerated into moving traffic on the elevated Gowanus Expressway. We were riding above a heavily industrialized section of south Brooklyn. Rows of abandoned factories, as stolid and implacable as gravestones, dominated the skyline. It wasn't the most attractive view the city had to offer, but I didn't have all that much time to inspect the broken windows or the grimy brick facades. Finally released, my cabbie was now careening through traffic at a speed that precluded contemplation of anything short of my imminent demise. I buckled up and braced myself, all fear of Gaetano Carollo now banished to some unexplored corner of my subconscious.

My driver saved the best for last. At Eighty-sixth Street, our exit, he cut across three lanes of traffic onto the off-ramp. I heard a squeal of brakes and instinctively glanced through the rear window at the vehicles we'd cut off. But instead of an angry driver displaying the customary upthrust finger, I saw a brown Toyota take the same path we'd taken an instant before. I was being tailed.

Good guys or bad guys or gangsters? In all conscience, I couldn't lead the Taurus to John Simone's door until I found out. With the killing of Graham Winokur, Caroll had made his intentions clear. He would eliminate anybody who threatened him. And why not? Under New York State law, D'Alesse's contract murder qualified his murderer for the death penalty.

As we turned onto Eighty-sixth Street, I spotted the golden arches of a McDonald's restaurant a couple of blocks ahead and told the driver to enter the parking lot and leave me by the door. I paid the fare, then strode directly into the crowded restaurant before turning to watch a familiar figure back the Taurus into a parking space. The last time I'd seen the woman tailing me, she'd been serving drinks to a horde of excited gamblers in an East Fifty-seventh Street town house.

I waited a moment, until I was sure the woman wasn't going to follow me into the restaurant, then ordered a supersized Happy Meal and carried it to a table. As I ate, I imagined the sauce on my Big Mac drawn from my stomach into my bloodstream, thence to be deposited on the arteries feeding my heart. The resulting guilt made the meal even tastier. As I wiped my lips, then reached for the cell phone, I remember thinking that Mother, if she could have known, would have been horrified. I'd thrown off centuries of good breeding and surrendered to a culture geared entirely to the lowest common denominator.

John Simone answered his phone on the third ring, whereupon I launched into a spiel worthy of a boiler-room pitchman. After identifying myself and my mission, I told him that Sergio had spoken of him so many times, I almost felt that I knew him. I told him that he was welcome to come to Sergio's funeral. I told him I was terribly sorry for bothering him on a Saturday night and that I was being unforgivably rude by conducting the interview on the telephone. I told him that I'd already spoken to Ilya Romanov, Vivian Walpole, and Carlos Mogollon, and while they were eager to cooperate, they were unable to help me. I even told him that I'd partaken of the biscotti he'd so thoughtfully carried to his friend in Manhattan.

I have a prodigious memory, an entirely unearned attribute that has aided me again and again. In this case, it cut through John Simone's misgivings. I could almost see his smile as he said, "From the Villabate Pasticceria on Eighteenth Avenue. The greatest Italian cheesecake on the planet."

"And not the greatest biscotti?" I managed a companionable chuckle as I awaited his response.

"The biscotti is excellent," he told me, "but the cheesecake is divine. So, how can I help you?"

I breathed a sigh of relief. Nobody in the investigation business conducts unannounced interviews over the telephone. It's far easier to hang up on a caller than to slam a door in someone's face.

"Sergio told me that he hoped to reverse his financial situation in the near future. He told his friends as well. The problem is that he didn't tell anybody how."

"I'm afraid he didn't tell me, either."

"But you knew about his expectations."

"I knew, yes."

"Well, what do you think?" It was the kind of open-ended question that only gets asked when an interview reaches a dead end.

Simone took a moment to gather his thoughts, then finally drew a breath and said, "Did Sergio tell you that I did a stint with the Brooklyn D.A.'s office?"

"I vaguely remember him mentioning it."

"This was right out of school. At the time, I believed the only real law was practiced in a courtroom." He laughed, perhaps in contemplation of his naïveté. "I lasted three years and hated every minute. Still, I learned to think like an investigator. Hell, I still think that way. My wife says I'm the most suspicious man on Earth."

I ignored the last bit as I turned him back to the topic at hand. "And where did your thinking lead you?"

"Well . . . this is all pretty vague. Understood?"

"Understood."

"Going back a few months, Sergio was really depressed. It wasn't like him, Phil, and that's probably why I remember. Despite his many problems, Sergio always wore a smile. He was the one who cheered *me* up. Not the other way round."

D'Alesse, of course, like any other child of his class, had been trained to regard displays of intensely felt emotion as vulgar. It was part of the civilizing process. "I—"

Simone cut me off as if I'd been the one prolonging the conversation. "I've gotta get off the phone. My wife and I have reservations and we're already late. Let me just say what I have to say."

"Go ahead."

"Like I told you, Sergio was really depressed for a few weeks, but I couldn't get him to talk about it. Then, out of the blue, he asked me if I could recommend a good doctor. A couple of weeks later, he was his old self and he was talking about how things were looking up for him."

"And when did all this come to a head?"

"About two weeks ago."

"That would be after John Caroll began to threaten him."

"John Caroll?"

"Over his gambling debts."

"Right, right. But the point is that Sergio had his own doctor. Why did he come to me? I'm insured by a health maintenance organization. For all I know, the doctor I recommended couldn't diagnose a case of hemorrhoids."

I held him on the phone long enough to get the name and address of the physician he'd recommended, then thanked him profusely before hanging up. Then I gathered my tray and dutifully carried it through the crowd fronting the counter to a refuse can bearing a happy face. From there, it was only a few yards to a door facing away from the parking lot.

TWENTY-SEVEN

I CIRCLED THE BUILDING, HALF running, and came up behind the Taurus. As I'd hoped, my tail's attention was trained on the restaurant's huge windows in an attempt to pick me out of the crowd. It was a mistake, a mistake compounded by her leaving the car's window down, as she fully realized when I pushed the Browning's barrel into the side of her head.

"How's Tony Farelli doin'?" I asked.

"He's fucked," she said without turning. "Just like me."

"Now, now. Nobody said anything about sex." When my little witticism failed to produce so much as a disdainful glance, I sobered up. "What's your name?"

"Zoe."

"Well, here it is, Zoe. Being as you interfered with my business in Brooklyn, I think the least you can do is give me a ride back to Manhattan. How about it?"

"No problem, sport." Her voice was low-pitched and very hoarse. "Anything you want."

"I'm glad you feel that way. Why don't you shut off the ignition, then hand me the keys."

It was her last best chance to escape. Though I was using my body and my briefcase to keep the Browning out of sight, the parking lot was crowded. Even assuming that I meant to kill her, would I have the *cojones* to pull the trigger if she threw the car into gear and stepped on the gas?

I watched her shoulders relax and her tongue dart across her lips as she checked her own reservoir of courage and found it empty.

Still, her tone was casual as she handed me the keys. "Here ya go, sport."

"Now toss your purse into the back and unlock the rear doors." I quickly scanned the front seat as I returned the Browning to its place in my briefcase, but found nothing resembling a weapon. Then I got into the car and positioned myself directly behind her before returning the keys.

"I want you to take me to Hudson and Perry streets. Use the Battery Tunnel, then go up the West Side Highway." I waited for a nod before adding, "No quick moves, Zoe. Just stay in the right lane and follow the traffic."

The bag she tossed into the back was large enough to conceal a rottweiler, but I wasn't shocked, when I dumped its contents onto the seat, to find a very tiny gun, a .22 automatic. No, what surprised me was the attached silencer. Zoe wasn't carrying the weapon to protect herself. She'd been sent to kill me.

"Did you benefit, Zoe?"

"Benefit?"

"From the murder of Count Sergio D'Alesse?"

"I didn't kill him."

"But did you benefit?"

She tapped her thumb against the steering wheel. "I know where you're goin', okay?"

"Do you know where *you're* going?" I took her wallet from the purse, located her driver's license, then committed her address to memory.

"No, where am I going?" She was a tall girl, and fairly nondescript except for her dark hair, which looked as if it'd gone from her pillow directly to a can of superhold spray. No more than three inches long, it flew off in all directions and was dyed vermilion at the ends.

"Contract murder is a crime punishable by death," I explained. "The minimum sentence is life without the possibility of parole."

"Tell me you're not a social worker. Please."

I let it slide for the moment. It was dark now, and the interior of the car seemed nearly protective, a cocoon ensuring a necessary metamorphosis. There were no lines anymore, and I had to accept the fact. John Caroll intended to see me dead.

I again asked, "Did you benefit?"

"How long are ya gonna keep askin' me that?"

"Until you answer."

Zoe was angry enough to spit. Never mind that she intended to kill me. Who was I to annoy her with my questions? "No," she finally admitted, "I didn't benefit."

"Then why are you protecting John Caroll's interests?" I watched her adjust the rearview mirror until we could see each other's faces. "I'm in touch with the cops," I told her, "through Arthur Howell, my lawyer, and I'm feeding them information as I go. Within a day, two at the most, your boss will be arrested and charged with murder. Where does that leave you, Zoe? Caroll was handsomely compensated for killing D'Alesse; he can mount a vigorous defense against any charge. How much are you prepared to spend?"

Afraid that if I told another lie my nose would begin to grow, I lapsed into silence. There was nothing more to be said anyway. If she hadn't gotten the message by now, she'd never get it.

We pulled up in front of Sharpers twenty minutes later. By that time I'd unloaded the .22 and put it back in her purse.

"This is it?" she said. "You're just gonna let me go?"

"What can I say? You seem like a nice person. That's why I'm giving you this parting word of advice. Get out while you have the chance, Zoe. Because if I see you again, I'm going to kill you."

I wasn't halfway through the tale of my encounter with Zoe before Benny lost his temper. He'd told Caroll that a threat to my life would be countered, so now he'd have to make good. Or so he thought until I once again told him to stay out of it.

"It's like you never grew up," he complained. "You wanna shoot it out on Main Street at high noon. When are you gonna get that it ain't like the movies?"

"And when are you going to realize that you've been away from the muscle end of the business for too long?"

"You don't think—"

"Who do you intend to dispatch? You've only got one man on your payroll under fifty, and that's your nephew. Are you going to send Paulie? You think that'll help me?" When he didn't answer, I finished describing my conversation with Zoe. "It's all up for John Caroll's little crew. Their basic scam is gone, and it's not coming back. My educated guess is the payoff for killing Sergio, though it wasn't made in cash, runs into the middle six figures. If Caroll didn't pass that money around, there's no good reason for the rats to remain with the ship."

I stayed long enough to drain a frosted mug of Bass Ale, then rose to leave. Benny tossed me a set of keys, then rattled off the address of an Upper West Side apartment, a safe house.

"You've got this thing in you," he told me, "this little voice that tells you it's some kinda noble thing to die in battle. That's bullshit, Phil. Dead is forever. You don't get to re-shoot the scene."

Well meant and well said. But if I didn't want to underestimate John Caroll, I didn't want to overestimate him, either. He wasn't anybody's godfather. Nor was he a supervillain out of a Hollywood movie. Gaetano was a tough guy, cool enough to operate an elaborate con over the long term. But he also was a greedy fool who'd involved himself in an unfamiliar business: contract murder. In light of Winokur's demise, I had to respect Caroll. I had to respect him, but I didn't have to fear him.

I made one stop on the way uptown, at the building on Tenth Avenue to which Manny Rodriguez had trailed John Caroll earlier in the day. According to the register, an A. Carollo occupied apartment 3F.

Fifteen minutes later, I was safely tucked inside a veritable fortress on the Upper West Side. Benny had chosen well. The one-bedroom apartment was in the basement of a town house. Not only did it have its own entrance, thus ensuring privacy, but every window was barred to prevent burglaries.

Of course, I wasn't expecting to have to fight it out. Caroll had no way to find me, and that's the way it would remain as long as I didn't tell anyone in my family where I was. Still, I found the fortifications comforting.

I settled down in the living room, on a sofa covered with some greasy fabric that vaguely resembled suede. Like the rest of the furnishings, it had come out of one of New York's many discount furniture shops.

As a matter of conscience, I called my father first. Calder initially told me that Father had retired for the night, but when I insisted, he put me through.

"Philip," Father said, his tone so businesslike I was certain I hadn't interrupted his rest. "I'm glad you called."

"Why's that?"

"Surely you know there's an element of danger in what you're attempting." It was as close as he would come to admitting that he worried about me.

"Worry about yourself, Father. Yourself and your family. John Caroll is cutting his losses. Think of it as the ultimate proxy fight."

Predictably, Father ignored the jibe. "You think the entire family is in danger?"

"Just the one—or *ones*—who conspired to kill Sergio D'Alesse."

"And you don't know who that is?"

"I'm only sure that it isn't you." Actually, I was not certain that Father was entirely innocent. Even if he hadn't been the one to hire Caroll, he might very well be trying to cover it up. Still, a bit of deflection never hurts. "Look, you need to keep everyone behind closed doors for the next few days. Don't let anybody leave for any reason."

"I'm not their jailer," he protested. "I can only advise. But at least everyone's here. Sergio's body is being released tomorrow and we've been discussing the funeral."

"Put the funeral off for a few days. By that time it'll be all over."

I left him to consider the repercussions, then called Maggie. I needed to review the data she'd collected, and I needed to get my hands on a computer. The problem was how to get either from her apartment to my hideaway.

"I hope your evening," she told me, "was more amusing than mine."

"Was it that bad?" I commiserated.

Her day was, she explained, more than two hundred printed pages long, with not a single paragraph seeming pertinent. I told her I was sure I'd find a nugget or two, then asked if her computer was by any chance a laptop. When she answered in the affirmative, I said, "Well, I need to borrow it."

"Do you want me to bring it to you?"

"No, Maggie, I don't." I went on to describe my encounter with Zoe, including the lie I'd told about my being in contact with the police.

"That's clever," she conceded after a moment's reflection. "But I think it would have been better if you'd just killed her." When I let that pass, she said, "How do I get the computer to you?"

"Pack the computer and the printouts in a small suitcase, then place the small suitcase in a larger suitcase. Catch a cab on Seventh Avenue and tell the driver to drop you at Grand Central Station on the Vanderbilt Avenue side. While you're in the cab, unpack the smaller suitcase, then offer the driver fifty dollars to bring it to me. If he accepts, which he will, write down his name and license number, and make sure that he sees you do it. Finally, when you reach Grand Central, walk straight through the terminal. You shouldn't have any trouble finding a cab on Lexington Avenue."

"Do you really think I'm being watched?"

"Caroll's getting information from inside the Beckett family. You and I were together in Father's apartment. Caroll is very, very desperate."

"That last part is what I don't understand." she said. "Why should Caroll be so worried? What do you have on him?"

"Killing Graham Winokur was an act of pure desperation."

I hadn't really answered the questions, but Maggie chose not to pursue it, perhaps because she had something else in mind. "I'm going to need your address," she told me.

With no real choice, I gave it to her, then asked if she could leave right away.

"I'll be out of here," she promised, "within five minutes."

TWENTY-EIGHT

I WON'T SAY THAT I heard some clue in Maggie's voice, or even that I secretly hoped she'd ignore my instructions. What I do say is that shortly after hanging up, I quit the apartment to cross the street, then stationed myself behind a customized Ford van. The weather had turned from cool to out-and-out cold. I felt my body tighten as I pulled my briefcase against my body. A hundred yards down the block, a pair of dog walkers conversed while their pets tugged in opposite directions. A window rattled up behind me, and I turned to find a middle-aged woman staring at me from the second floor. "Don't hurt the fuckin' car," she said before closing the curtains. "I'm watchin' ya."

I turned my attention to Amsterdam Avenue a hundred yards away. All west-bound traffic entering the one-way street on which I waited had to come from that direction. Occasionally, vehicles turned onto the block, among them a few cabs, but it was a good ten minutes before the cab I awaited, the one with Maggie in the backseat, finally arrived. I watched her pay the fare, then get out, then approach the door to the town house just as a Lincoln Town Car made the left from Amsterdam and parked a few feet from where I stood.

Maggie had started to ring the bell when she glanced over her shoulder and realized that she'd been followed. I don't know what she was thinking, but her attention was so tightly focused on Tony Farelli, who sat behind the wheel of the Lincoln, that she failed to see me at all. The same can be said of Tony. His eyes jumped back and forth between Maggie and the cell phone he was attempting to dial.

I suppose I might have pulled off something similar to the move I made on Zoe that afternoon, even though the Town Car's windows were rolled up. But I was angrier this time around, at myself for not issuing a stronger warning to Maggie, at Maggie for playing the game by her own rules, and at Tony Farelli merely for existing. I picked up a metal garbage can, one of six arranged along a wrought-iron fence, then took three steps forward and drove it through the window.

The can was too big to pass through the opening, or I think I might have killed him. As it was, hit only by the leading edge of the can, Farelli's head snapped toward the far end of the seat. An instant later, his body followed.

Somehow avoiding the shards of glass remaining in the frame, I reached through the broken window, unlocked the door, and pulled Tony into a sitting position. His scalp was cut over his left ear and his blood was running freely, a sight that cheered me.

"You fuck," he groaned. "You bastard fuck."

"Words," I observed as I disarmed him for the second time, "unlike garbage cans, do not break bones."

I yanked him out of the Lincoln and tossed him onto the side-walk. He was very light, probably under a 150 pounds, and driven as I was by a flood of adrenaline, seemed almost weightless. "The word out there is that you pulled the trigger on D'Alesse," I told him as I dumped him onto the sidewalk. "You know what that means?"

"Fuck you."

"Tony, you need to work on your vocabulary, maybe look up the meaning of the words 'cooperating witness.' " Without taking my eyes off Tony, I signaled Maggie to join us. When she was standing by my side, I told her to brush as much glass as she could from the Lincoln's front seat while I kept an eye on Farelli. Though I had no clear idea where we were going, it was definitely time to leave. The few pedestrians on the block had recovered from their initial shock and were moving toward us. There were people coming from Amsterdam Avenue as well.

"I gotta go," I told the still-prone Farelli, "but I want you to think about what I said. Remember, you've been proven an incompetent punk on two separate occasions. There's no reason to think your boss'll give you a third chance to redeem yourself. Find a good lawyer, go to the cops."

I managed to rid the window frame of glass by the time we reached Eighty-sixth Street, opening several minor cuts in the process. Maggie said nothing; she was holding a green leather suitcase in her lap and her chin was resting on the handles. We were riding on Broadway, heading downtown.

"I'm glad to see you." Having cooled down a bit, I was able to admit the truth.

"Then you're not angry?"

"I feel guilty."

"You think you lured me in?"

"I had other options."

"Like?"

"There are a dozen 24/7 messenger services in Manhattan. I could have had any one of them pick up the package without giving you my address." What I told her was true enough, though I hadn't thought of it until just that moment.

"That wouldn't have prevented Tony from getting to you."

"No, but it would have kept you out of it." I paused long enough to reach for her, but found only a handful of suitcase. "What I'm trying to say is that I have what I really wanted."

"Which is what?"

"Which is you in my bed tonight."

Maggie shook her head. "Your idea, to switch suitcases in the cab, would have worked. Tony wouldn't have found you." Maggie finally tossed the suitcase into the back, then moved closer to me. "I was in control, Phil. I made the choice, not you."

An hour later, after ditching the Lincoln, we checked into the Holiday Inn on Thirty-third Street near Penn Station. The room was decorated in a motif that can only be described as hotel ugly, but the king-size bed to which we immediately retired was both firm and odor-free. Our lovemaking was adrenaline-driven and close to violent in its intensity. Nevertheless, the prevailing mood of the moment, at least for me, was joyous. We were united now, for better or for worse, and all we had to do, to realize the better, was survive.

Like many hotel rooms in New York, our room had a phone jack dedicated to computer use, and I got Maggie's IBM up and running while she went out in search of coffee and a few doughnuts for later. It was already past twelve, and it figured to be a very long night. Again, I accessed the TRACKDOWN Web site, this time in search of the first name and phone number of A. Carollo. It took me seconds to learn both, then another few moments to add her Social Security number. But when I tried to connect Angelina Carollo to John Caroll, I had no luck. Caroll's mother's name (which, somewhere along the line, he'd listed on an account for purposes of identification) was Grace Carollo, née Zarega, and she was deceased.

I put the information to one side, then removed the stack of printouts from the suitcase. There were five stories on the proxy fight for Beckett Industries, including the one printed in the *Wall Street Journal* from which Maggie had quoted. I picked these off the larger pile and settled into an armchair covered in burnt-orange Naugahyde.

I was working my way through the second article when Maggie returned. She set out the refreshments, then picked up the notes I'd made on Angelina Carollo.

"What's this?" she asked.

As I explained, a malicious grin slowly advanced to claim her mouth, then her eyes. "Let's call," she urged once I'd finished.

"For what reason?"

"You've been turning up the heat all day. What's another ten or fifteen degrees?"

"If Angelina isn't involved, the net effect of calling her will be to lower the temperature, not raise it." The statement was true enough on its face, but I already suspected that Angelina had played a vital part in the death of Count Sergio D'Alesse, even if she'd never heard his name.

I dialed Angelina's number and was greeted by a familiar gravelly voice. "Zoe," I said, "it's Phil Beckett. How's it going?"

"It's goin' good, sport." Zoe's voice held only its natural quaver. If she was upset by my knowledge of Caroll's Tenth Avenue hideaway, she wasn't showing it. "By the way, thanks for not killing me this afternoon."

"No problem. Say, is your boss around?"

"He's in the other room with his aunt."

"Would that be Angelina?"

"Sure would, sport. You want I should get him?"

"Will you tell him I called?"

"I'm not sure. I'd have to think it over."

"Sounds like you're getting the picture."

"Sounds like."

"Say, you hear from Tony yet?"

She laughed deep in her chest. "Were you cruel to him again?"

"Perhaps a little too cruel. He should have been able to call by now." I gave her an instant to absorb the implications, then added, "Well, I gotta go. If you decide to consult your boss, tell him I dumped the Lincoln on East Thirty-ninth Street near First Avenue. Most likely it's already been towed."

I laid the phone on the table and looked up at Maggie, who was sitting on my lap with her ear glued to the receiver. "Satisfied?" I asked.

She straightened up, shook out her hair, and rose to her feet. "You like her," she accused as she sat on the bed and folded her arms across her chest.

"Who?"

"Zoe."

"Zoe?"

"Zoe."

It was the sort of accusation that lacks a reply that doesn't immediately seem defensive. Even the truth, as I told it, sounded false. "I like her as much I can like anyone who'd kill me without thinking twice about it. She definitely has style."

"Is that why you let her go this afternoon?"

"I let her go, Magdalena Santos, because unlike Zoe, and her employers, and her coworkers, I'm not a killer." I again hefted the stack of printouts. "I think it's time I got to work."

"You don't want me to tell you what's in there?"

"Let me go through it by myself, then we'll compare notes."

"Are you dismissing me?"

Though I was on the verge of becoming angry, I got up and sat beside her on the bed. It was the first time I'd seen her demonstrate anything resembling insecurity. "I need to work," I told her.

She put her hands behind my head and pulled me into a ferocious kiss. "Just remember," she told me after a breathless moment, "you have to share. I'm your partner. If you treat me like an employee, I'm going to get in your face. *¿Comprende?*"

"Permission granted." I wanted to take her in my arms but was afraid that if I did, it'd be another forty minutes before I got back to work. "But you've read the material and I haven't. Let me get even, then we'll talk about it until we're both bored."

TWENTY-NINE

UNFORTUNATELY, BY THE TIME "THEN" rolled around, nearly three hours later, Maggie was sound asleep. I remember that it was warm in the room and she was wearing a long T-shirt over a pair of wispy red panties, and that the T-shirt had ridden up to her hips while the bedding had slipped down to her knees. It was a beautiful sight, made even more beautiful by the fact that I was so tired that I could appreciate it without becoming unduly aroused.

I undressed, turned out the light, and got into bed. I wanted rest; I needed rest. My workday had been long and difficult, and tomorrow promised to be equally arduous. Unfortunately, the analytical aspect of my mind, pitifully small as it was and is, refused to shut down. Seconds after turning out the lights, I found myself working familiar ground.

The proxy fight for control of Beckett Industries was much more intense than the short paragraph Maggie had read to me indicated. A story in *Fortune* was especially hard-hitting. According to informed sources, Mercer Fredricks was at the heart of a whispering campaign alleging financial improprieties (and a continuing cover-up) by the Beckett family. Another story, published a month later in *Money*, blamed a 10 percent drop in the price of Beckett Industries' common stock directly on the rumors. The author, Seth Inman, while he felt the Becketts would survive the challenge should it come to a vote of the shareholders, also felt the chairman of the board, Philip Beckett Jr., was taking a serious beating. If the stock continued to drop, rumor had it that Philip would resign in favor of his daughter.

In fact, I already knew that the Becketts engaged in financial improprieties. I knew because Regina had explained it to me (in an effort, I suspect, to again illustrate the extent of my foolishness) years before. For example, both she and Father were paid consultants to a number of Beckett Industries' subsidiaries. As consultants, they offered only the sort of advice they, as Beckett Industry board members, would have offered free of charge.

And why not? The maintenance costs for Father's Manhattan co-op ran fifteen thousand dollars per month, the mortgage another eight thousand dollars. And there were the properties in Tuscany and Vail to keep up, and the expense of the servants. Then there was the cost of cleaning the paintings in the apartment, an incredibly expensive task that had to be performed every ten years if the family's priceless masterpieces were not to deteriorate.

A fleet of chauffeur-driven cars, and a pair of Learjets, and a power wardrobe, and the mandatory social giving, and all of Regina's expenses, and Uncle Alfred's, and Aunt Charlotte's. Somehow it not only had to be paid for, there had to be enough left over to bid on illuminated medieval manuscripts.

There's no life so filled with wealth that more cannot be imagined, and it was Regina who'd devised a plan to greatly increase the family's disposable income. She, Father, and Uncle Alfred (or so she'd bragged) would purchase a privately owned company with a shaky balance sheet, provide an infusion of Beckett cash and Beckett prestige, then take the company public. The first offering of the stock in such a company is referred to as an initial public offering, or an IPO. Though the offering price of IPO stock varies, a market value of twenty dollars for shares originally worth a dollar is common enough.

I realize that I'm not only greatly oversimplifying the process, I'm also making the transition from private to public appear to have a guaranteed positive outcome. In fact, the business of initial public offerings is risky for any number of reasons. For example, even the most carefully scouted businesses sometimes underperform, despite infusions of cash. Then there are bear markets, which simply do not support IPOs, and the potential for an ill-timed family scandal to taint the company.

But the risks and rewards of my family's investment strategy are beside the point. The point is that when I'd demanded a fee for my services, Regina had paid me with a check drawn on Halstead Financial Services, a company I'd never heard of before and whose name I remembered when I'd drawn up the list of individuals and business entities I wanted Maggie to research.

The inclusion of Halstead had been an afterthought, a shot in the dark, a wing and a prayer, but it had paid off handsomely. I'd finally asked the right question.

Wholly owned by Father, Regina, and Uncle Alfred, according to the *Wall Street Journal*, Halstead was to be offered to the public in early September at a price in the twenty-five-dollar range. The offer was being underwritten by the very prestigious Salomon Brothers, with a number of equally prestigious firms placing the company on their buy lists.

Farther on, I'd run across a photo published in the *New York Times* of Regina Beckett, Halstead's CEO, and Alfred Beckett, Halstead's CFO, shaking hands with a Salomon Brothers vice president. In the body of the text, the deal was twice referred to as "a blockbuster."

Maggie groaned in her sleep and rolled onto her back. Behind me, on the night table, the numerals of a digital clock threw an eerie green light across her face. All we have to do, I reminded myself as I turned her pillow to the dry side, is survive. Though I didn't find the words especially convincing, they at least broke my train of thought. A few minutes later, I fell asleep.

In the morning, over breakfast, we discussed the material as if preparing a doctoral thesis. Maggie was quick to grasp the IPO angle, but less certain that investigating Audrey D'Alesse was the way to proceed. She, herself, would be tied up with Naomi Felder in the morning, then, armed with the phone numbers of Audrey,

Father, Regina, John Caroll, and Angelina Carollo, would spend the afternoon cross-checking the data Naomi provided.

"If we can prove that Caroll had contact with someone in the family," I told her, thinking out loud, "I'm going to wrap it up."

"By doing what?"

"That's the part I don't know yet." I expected Maggie to offer an opinion, but she continued to study me from across the table without speaking. It was, after all, my family's reputation on the line, not hers. "I should," I reluctantly added, "take what I have to the police. They can put together all the relevant documents in a couple of days."

But there was one set of records, I explained, that I would acquire on my own: Angelina Carollo's credit records. All it would take was an hour on the computer and the claim that I had a legitimate need to know. Unfortunately, I wasn't going to get that hour, not right away, because I had to pursue a more important line of inquiry. I had to ride up to 116th Street on the East Side, to a drug treatment center where Countess Audrey D'Alesse, according to a gossipy story on the People pages of the *Daily News*, volunteered her time on a regular basis. In addition to energetic fund-raising (which had allowed Project Rehab to expand its client base from fewer than twenty to more than a hundred), Audrey chaired the advisory board and was involved in day-to-day operations.

Maggie's cell phone rang as a waiter in a sparkling white shirt poured our second cups of coffee. It was Arthur Howell, and what he had to say cut through our burgeoning confidence with the efficiency of a surgeon's knife through a disfiguring wart. Vivian Walpole, the count's lover, had been murdered around midnight, shot eight times through her own door as she (presumably) responded to a visitor. Mulligan had remained at the crime scene long enough to set an investigation in motion, then come searching for the man he'd seen there earlier in the afternoon, Philip Beckett. Not finding Beckett at home, Mulligan had proceeded to the abode of his admitted lover, Magdalena Santos. Not finding her at home—by this time it was nearly six o'clock—he'd retired to his desk and drawn up a warrant charging Philip Beckett with the murder of Sergio D'Alesse. The warrant was currently being reviewed by an assistant district attorney, after which it would be taken to a judge for signing. After which, if Philip Beckett didn't surrender voluntarily, he would become a fugitive.

"The cops are demanding that I produce my client, Maggie, and I have to ask if you know where he is." Arthur's voice, though tinny, was audible as I leaned an ear to the receiver.

"I don't, but I can tell you that he was with me last night."

Howell chuckled. "The question here," he patiently explained, "is where Phil was at the time D'Alesse was killed. He hasn't been charged with any other crime."

"I understand."

"Good, because it doesn't get any better. If Phil doesn't come in today, the fugitive squad will go out looking for him. As far as they're concerned, he's just another murderer who needs to be taken off the street. If they confront him and he makes a mistake, they'll shoot first and worry about violating his civil rights later."

"What about the media?" As usual, Maggie jumped from the fearful to the practical. "How long until we see Phil's face on the little screen?"

"His name will be released to the press by midafternoon. At the latest."

"And the circus will begin on the evening news."

As I watched Maggie return the phone to her purse, I recalled Vivian Walpole in her muumuu and her feathers and knew that I'd led Caroll to her, that Zoe had been following me all day. Why hadn't I spotted her? Because my ego had gotten in the way? Because I'd assumed that I was so good that I didn't have to be good? I could just *assume* I was good?

Maggie reached out to take my hand. The consoling gesture did nothing to clear away the guilt. But at least she didn't tell me that I wasn't responsible.

We sat in silence for a few minutes, a few minutes we didn't have, then she let go of my hand and said, "We can't stay here."

I shook my head. "I'm not going to run. Not from a crime I didn't commit. If I can't put it together by this afternoon, this evening at the latest, I'm going to surrender."

"For what it's worth, I don't see you being convicted."

"You're right. I won't be convicted. But I can certainly be murdered in jail. Which, from John Caroll's point of view, is even better."

THIRTY

IT SHOULD HAVE BEEN AN exit line, but knowing that I might soon be forced to gaze upon Maggie's fair countenance through a spit-stained Plexiglas partition, I couldn't bring myself to walk away. Instead, I followed her upstairs and stationed myself on the edge of the bed while she took a shower. As I listened to the hiss and spatter of the shower through the closed bathroom door, I told myself that I could wrap it up by late afternoon, that it was possible, even probable, that it was a near certainty. All I needed to do was confirm the motive for the count's murder, which (or so I believed) could be found on 116th Street, just four miles north of where I sat. How hard could that be? Especially given Project Rehab's known point of vulnerability.

Project Rehab, the charitable enterprise to which Audrey gave so much of her time and energy, is what's known in the drug rehab business as a residential treatment center. The conditions within are demanding by design. Only the most trusted clients, after months and months of work, are allowed day passes or a weekend with the family. The rest (motivated in the main by a judge ordering the stay in lieu of a prison sentence) not only endure endless therapy sessions, group and private, their personal labor keeps the center up and running. They do everything from preparing meals, to stocking shelves, to answering telephones, to cleaning toilets.

From my point of view, the clients were useless, as were the managerial and medical staffs. The clients because they were locked inside and I had no way to get to them. The staff because they'd be unlikely to speak freely about a peer.

There was, however, one group of employees who might be persuaded to open up by the rustle of money, if not the power of argument. As I mentioned, most clients in residential treatment centers accept the harsh conditions only because the alternative is a prison sentence. Nothing about their presence is voluntary, at least not initially, and there's nothing many of them would like more than to sneak out and catch a toke on the old crack pipe. Or better still, find a way to smuggle drugs into the center itself.

The common solution to client negativity is, at best, a mixed blessing. Security guards, usually supplied by private agencies, control all exits and entrances. They are there to challenge visitors, to check day passes, and to manage clients driven to violent expression by the pressure cooker atmosphere. All for eight or nine dollars an hour, barely minimum wage in New York City.

I knew all this because a friend of mine, Karen Berne, spent fourteen months in an RTC trying to kick a heroin addiction that had already cost her a husband, a child, and a job at CBS. Karen had volunteered for the treatment, stuck it out, stayed clean for a year, then finally relapsed. The cops had found her dead one January morning in a vacant lot on the Lower East Side, a supercilious smirk literally frozen to her face.

I knew about the smirk because my number had been found in her wallet and the cops had asked me to identify the body.

For the first six months of Karen's stay at the Second Chance Rehabilitation Center, she had not been allowed to communicate with the outside world. No letters, no calls, no visitors. Then one evening she phoned me to announce that she'd at last earned the privilege of an hour's visit by a close friend. I went up to see her on the following day, then continued to visit until she was finally released. In the course of those visits, I got to know the staff fairly well, including a security guard named Ahmed, who was arrested for smuggling contraband into the center. If I could find Project Rehab's Ahmed . . .

My concentration was broken, at that moment, when the shower abruptly stopped. A minute later, a cloud of steam billowed into the room as Maggie flung open the bathroom door. She favored me with a quick smile, then turned to the mirror and wiped it down before she picked up a tiny hair dryer. I watched her without speaking, watched the small sure movements of her hands as she worked from the center of her scalp to the very tips of her hair, as she curled the ends slightly inward, as she turned a critical eye to the mirror. She'd yet to put on her makeup and I noted the faint laugh lines at the corners of her eyes (wondering if she, in her darker moments, thought of them as crow's feet), and the almost childlike set of her mouth as she focused her concentration.

She was wearing a thin cotton robe that clung to her damp body, leaning forward with her weight on the balls of her feet so that her breasts quivered with each stroke of the brush. The muscles in her calves were bunched, her legs slightly apart. Every so often she shook out her hair, then turned her head to the right or left as she measured her progress.

I felt as if I could have watched her forever, that just having her there, a few feet away, would be enough for me. But there's no forever to it, not for Maggie, not for me, not for anybody. It was a lesson I'd learned when Mother died, the sort of lesson that can't be unlearned. Like it or not, we were going to have to move on.

Nevertheless, I didn't speak, or even shift my weight on the bed, and it was Maggie who finally broke the spell. She tossed the hairbrush on a shelf, walked up to me, then pushed me onto my back. "I'm not leaving you today," she said as she straddled my waist. "If you have to deal with the police, you'll want your lawyer present. Everybody knows that."

"What about Naomi?"

She took my wrists and pinned them to the bed. "Let Naomi analyze the phone logs. I'm sure she'll be great at it. Or let her hold on to them. I don't give a damn. I'm not leaving you." She leaned forward to place her weight on her hands. "And I'm not letting you go until you say 'I give up.'"

I had sense enough to surrender, then to roll her onto her back and rise to my feet. As I reached for the telephone, she sat up, a wicked and triumphant smile creasing the lower part of her face.

"Men," she announced, "have little pride and no self-control. They're pitiful."

Though initially annoyed at being awakened early on a Sunday morning, Naomi agreed to perform the extra service without undue protest. We did haggle a bit over the cost, but it was mostly pro forma. The job was to establish telephone contact between Father, Regina, or Audrey, either from home or from the office, and John Caroll, either at his residence, his club, or his aunt Angelina's. It could be completed, I maintained, in an hour or two. Naomi, on the other hand, was certain it would take all day, then stretch into the night. Eventually we compromised on four hours at a hundred dollars per.

"Thanks a lot," I finally told her after dictating Angelina's phone number and address. "I really appreciate what you're doing for me here."

"Anything," she grandly replied, "for a friend."

Maggie and I were still grinning forty-five minutes later as we exited the subway at 116th Street, a major commercial street in the neighborhood called Spanish Harlem, and began to walk east from Lexington Avenue. It was relatively quiet on that Sunday morning. The knuckleheads were sleeping, and the sidewalks had been reclaimed by families on their way to the many churches in the area. The little girls, I remember, were dressed in brightly colored, frilly dresses, the little boys in white shirts and clip-on ties. There was a sprinkling of elderly widows in black, and old men in Kangol caps and spit-shined shoes. In front of La Casa de Dios, a storefront Pentecostal church, a van unloaded a trio of wheelchair-bound worshipers, while a small wiry man in a black suit and narrow black tie supervised the operation.

It was much warmer this morning, and the sun was high enough in a cloudless sky to bathe the north side of 116th Street, six lanes wide, in a celebratory light appropriate to a day of worship. There were no high-rise buildings on the street, only tenements of brick painted red and orange and yellow and white and blue. The brick glowed with an inner warmth, as did the sculpted cornices at the roof lines, and the small architectural details: a cupid blowing his horn above a doorway, a sloping mansard roof faced with slate, a row of arched upper-story windows separated by columns, an elaborate wrought-iron fire escape.

Though the neighborhood was tough and poor, and had been from the time these tenements were raised, each structure carried some bit of costly ornamentation that distinguished it from its neighbors. I could easily imagine, as I slid my arm around Maggie's waist and drew her close, the pride that had driven the landlords to include the unnecessary expense. No matter how humble, each building was as much a personal expression of the man who'd commissioned it as the suit he wore, the car he drove, the furniture in his home.

"What are you thinking about?" Maggie asked as we approached Second Avenue. "You seem a million miles away."

"Light on stone," I replied. "The Grand Canyon."

My cryptic answer deserved a sarcastic reply and Maggie was up to the task. "Brick," she corrected, "is not stone, and the Colorado River isn't dotted with piles of dog shit, either."

"Party pooper," I shot back.

We turned left on Second Avenue and made our way to a small auto rental company operating from a garage on 117th Street, where we rented a two-year-old Buick sedan with a creased quarter panel on the driver's side. The choice of car was quite deliberate. Though Maggie might have passed for a Spanish Harlem resident, I was definitely out of place, an anomaly in a neighborhood where anomalies are carefully evaluated. Within a few hours, these sidewalks would be crowded. The knuckleheads and the dopers would be out, and the gangs, with their proprietary sense of turf, would become active as well. Though I was well armed (and thus unafraid), I might have to spend a number of hours parked near Project Rehab, and the last thing I needed was a confrontation.

Fortunately, there was a common persona to which we could both aspire—a persona to cover all bases, to satisfy the curious and hold at bay the hostile—and that persona was cop. Two thirty-somethings, well dressed if slightly rumpled, sitting in a beat-up sedan on a Sunday morning in a ghetto neighborhood? What else could we be?

"What you want to do," I explained to an attentive Maggie, "is evaluate every citizen over the age of ten. Make your look frankly evaluating but not overtly hostile. You might not be here for them, but you're a member of the largest gang in New York. You're to be respected."

We were parked on the south side of 116th Street, across the street and slightly west of the five-story tenement occupied by Project Rehab. Maggie was sitting behind the wheel and she had to face me in order to eyeball passing citizens. I watched her eyes widen slightly as she fixed a paunchy middle-aged man with the appraising stare of an infant. The man standing in front of a doorway leading to the upper floors of the tenement behind him wasn't doing much of anything, and it took him a moment to realize that he was being studied. His eyes flicked to Maggie's, his glance at first curious, then cautious. Finally he took a set of keys from his pocket, opened the door behind him, then vanished.

"This," Maggie told me, not for the first time in our relationship, "is fun."

THIRTY-ONE

MAGGIE WAS RIGHT. FOR THE first half hour or so, it *was* fun. But as time passed, as morning progressed into afternoon, as the temperature and humidity rose, it became apparent that our Buick's cooling system and air conditioning were feuding, and the game wore thin.

Inevitably, the sidewalks slowly filled with pedestrians. The discount furniture and clothing stores raised their shutters and opened for business, and the shoppers followed. The air was filled with a commingling of Spanish and English. Twenty feet away, a boom box shredded the air with the pounding rhythms of the Caribbean islands. A gathering of neighbors, perched on sagging lawn chairs, drank Budweiser beer from pint cans while two adolescent girls wearing identical pink tank tops fumbled their way through an up-tempo *meringue*. After a moment, another couple rose to join them, then another.

"Do you think," Maggie asked, "we'd blow our cover if we got out and danced?"

Across the street, the door leading to Project Rehab remained shut. It had not opened, to admit or release a single soul, at any time during our watch.

"I think," I told her, "that I'd do just about anything to be out of this car."

My efforts, when we began a moment later, were predictably clumsy. Maggie, on the other hand, executed a series of steps that drew exclamations of appreciation.

"Huepaaaaa."

"Ayyyyyyyy."

I backed away to lean against the Buick as the music came to an abrupt halt. A man with coppery skin and a prominent scar on his forehead approached, his manner polite. He introduced himself (to both of us) as Juan Fuentes, then asked Maggie, in Spanish, if she cared to dance. Fuentes' eyes widened at her response. Maggie's Spanish, learned at the knee of her Aunt Fulgencia, was purely Castilian, a dialect rarely heard in New York City.

A conversation followed, a conversation beyond my schoolboy abilities, as they began to samba. A few seconds into their dance, the other dancers stopped in their tracks. Passersby stopped as well, even a trio of knuckleheads in hooded sweatshirts and baggy shorts that hung below their knees.

It was as if Maggie and Juan had been partners for years. They flowed from one move to the next with an assurance I found shocking. I knew, of course, that dancing was Maggie's passion, that she'd studied ballet and modern dance as a child, but I had no idea how good she was. Nor had I been aware of the extent to which she'd humbled herself to accommodate my limited skills the single time we'd gone dancing.

After the music stopped, Maggie and Juan extended their conversation long enough to arouse a pang of jealousy in my usually tolerant soul. Maggie looked at me from time to time, her eyes conveying an unfathomable message. Finally, she and Fuentes walked to where I was standing.

"This is Juan Fuentes," Maggie said, as if Juan hadn't already introduced himself. "Juan, this is Phil Beckett."

"Hey, man," Fuentes said as we shook hands. "How you doin'?" His English was slightly accented with the extended vowels of the dialect generally called Nuyurican.

"Juan knows someone who works in Project Rehab."

"Tino Colón," Juan said. "From my social club. He's a security guard."

A message to warm the cockles of my heart. "How long has he been working there?" I asked.

"Since it opened. What? Eight years ago? Tino, he's got a big family."

The next cut on the tape in the boom box started up, a blast of trumpets driven to near frenzy by a battalion of conga drums. "Juan asked us to move the Buick down a block. He'll take care of the rest."

Juan nodded to me but kept his gaze fixed on Maggie. "I'll call Tino," he said. "No problem." He took Maggie's hand, then bowed and kissed it. *"Vaya con Dios, señorita."*

Leaving Juan to nurse his broken heart, we moved to the east of Pleasant Avenue, to a space beside a fire hydrant. A block away, FDR Drive was packed, and an unbroken stream of traffic was deserting the highway in search of easier going. Beyond the Drive, on the East River, a white tugboat dragged a barge loaded to the waterline toward the Triborough Bridge. The sun was dropping by that time, and the elongated shadows of the buildings closest to the water rippled in the currents.

We watched in silence for a moment, then Maggie laid her elbow on the steering wheel, producing a small chirp from the horn, which she ignored. "I'm not going back to Exxon," she told me, her tone defiant. "Never."

"Good."

"Good?"

"I hate the idea of you returning five times a week to a place you don't want to be. Just as I hate the idea of you doing what you don't want to do with people you don't want to be with."

Maggie, apparently, was expecting me to play the parent. When I didn't, she was forced to take on the job herself. "But I have to make a living."

"I have a trust fund," I told her. "We'll make out."

Neither of us was able to continue the conversation. For myself, I was struck dumb by the implications of my assurance. And Maggie, when I finally plucked up the courage to look at her, was silently crying. I watched her swipe at her eyes with the back of her hand, then fumble for the tissues in her purse, thinking that I'd been waiting all my life for her and that I could not be happy if she was unhappy. It was really that simple.

Tino Colón showed up ten minutes later. By that time Maggie's eyes were dry and I'd recovered my tongue. Colón was a large man with very thick eyebrows and a pronounced underbite, which he made even more conspicuous by sucking on his lower lip. He was wearing a tan uniform with sergeant's stripes pinned to the sleeves of his blouse. A can of Mace and a set of plastic restraints hung from his belt.

I reached behind me to unlock the back door, and Colón slid inside. He grunted at me, then addressed Maggie in rapid-fire Spanish. Though I couldn't understand what she said, her response, measured and formal, underlined the differences in their use of the language. Colón seemed impressed, in spite of himself.

"We need to speak English," I interrupted.

"Tino wants to know what this is all about," Maggie replied.

I looked Tino in the eye. There was no getting around the truth. "It's about money and information," I said. "I have one. You have the other." I took a roll of twenties from my pocket (I would have preferred fifties, but the banks had been closed and I'd had to settle for whatever emerged from the bowels of an ATM), then counted off ten bills.

Colón examined the cash with greedy eyes. "What you wanna know abou'?" he asked, his accent considerably thicker than that of Juan Fuentes.

"Audrey D'Alesse."

He leaned back in the seat and lit a cigarette. To his credit, he didn't reach for the money in my hand. "Audrey, man," he said as I rolled down the window, "she's like . . . you know, man . . . like okay." He said something to Maggie in Spanish, but she merely shrugged and gestured to me. It was my show.

"I'm not here for a character reference," I explained. "I can get a character reference for nothing."

Tino stared at the tip of his cigarette, as if the decision he sought was concealed in the rising smoke. His first response made it clear that he liked Audrey, while his reluctance to speak meant that he knew something about her that she wouldn't want revealed. The question was whether he'd sell her out.

I counted off another five bills, bringing the total on the betrayal side of the scales to three hundred dollars. That was as much as he made, after taxes, in a week.

"Wha you wanna know?" he finally asked.

"I want to know who she was fucking."

Tino sighed, the question apparently not unexpected. "Her old man," he said, "don't treat her right. And she was like, you know, lonely and shit."

"The name, Tino. Let's start with his name."

Again he hesitated, a decent man making a hard choice, but in the end he took the money from my hand. "Marcus Packard," he said. "He was doin' her."

"And what's Packard's job at the center?" I asked.

"He's the social worker."

"How well do you know him?"

"No too good."

"Is he inside today?"

Tino's look was contemptuous. "On Sunday? No way, man There's only us an' them."

I paused long enough to get my bearings. Though fully anticipated, Tino's sordid tale was getting to me. It was my family he was talking about. My sordid little family. Finally I said, "You know about Audrey's husband?"

"I hear somebody kill him."

"Have the cops been around?"

"I ain't seen no one."

Bad news. I had to assume that the trail, for Detective Mulligan, stopped at Vivian Walpole's apartment. Maggie and I were on our own.

"You know where I can find Marcus Packard?" I asked.

"Like, tomorrow, man, he'll be comin' to work."

"I need to reach him now, Tino. I can't wait until tomorrow." Irrespective of the need for haste, I didn't want to confront Packard at the rehab center, where he'd be supported by friends and colleagues.

"I don' know where he's livin', man. I already tol' you we ain't friendly."

"His home address is on file, Tino, and what I figure, given the stripes on your sleeve and its being a Sunday, you can get into the office. It won't take more than a couple of minutes."

Tino tried to dodge the bullet by claiming that he couldn't leave the center again, that he'd already taken a large risk. I offered the number of my cell phone, but he again demurred.

"C'mon, man, like I already done enough to her. Audrey, she only wants people to be likin' her. She's like sad, man. She din' do nothin' wrong."

True enough. Unless one considers it a crime to cheat on the philandering husband who'd subjected her to one humiliation after another for the better part of twenty years, Audrey D'Alesse, lonely and hapless, had done the right thing at every turn.

I counted off another five bills. "Sooner or later, I'll find Marcus Packard. It's not like he's going to disappear. All I'm asking you to do is make it sooner."

"Oh, man," Tino said as he snatched the money, then opened the door. "This is gonna make like a lotta trouble for a lotta people. It's fucked up."

Maggie watched him as he walked back toward the center. "Do you think," she asked, her tone sincere, "that it's sinful to corrupt another human being?"

"Not when it's done for the greater good."

"But how does that help him?"

"Who?"

"Tino. When he tries to go to sleep tonight."

"He's a poor man with a big family and he can't afford to be fastidious."

"As you can't afford to be ethical?"

I touched her shoulder and she turned toward me. "Invading people's privacy? Bribing otherwise decent men and women? Naomi Felder? Tino Colón? It's called private investigation, and outside of cashing trust fund checks, it's the only thing I know how to do.

"But you like the game," she said.

"What can I say? I keep promising myself I'm gonna stop playing, but here I am."

It was the wrong time and place for this discussion, but I knew that somewhere down the line I'd learn how she felt about breaking and entering. I found myself looking forward to it as we settled down to wait.

The phone in Maggie's briefcase rang at that moment. It was Arthur Howell calling to offer a deal. "If I guarantee Phil's surrender tomorrow morning," Howell explained, "Mulligan will shelve the warrant until then. But I have to guarantee it, Maggie. No last-minute change of mind. So if you should hear from Phil, tell him to call me within the next twenty minutes."

Two minutes later I phoned back to accept the deal. "And I promise," I concluded, "not to murder anybody else before then."

"Well, I'm really glad to hear that," he said, "because if you do, better start with me. I called in a lot of favors to buy this time. If you fuck me here, I'll have to kill you myself."

THIRTY-TWO

THE ADDRESS TINO GAVE ME when he phoned in a few minutes later was almost directly across Manhattan, on 120th Street near Columbia University. It was after four o'clock, but Maggie and I took the time to run the Buick to the garage before heading crosstown in a gypsy cab. I instructed the driver to cruise past Marcus Packard's building, then circle the block before dropping us at the corner of 120th and Amsterdam. There was nothing suspicious about the empty vehicles lining either side of the road, or about the pedestrians who drifted along the sidewalks.

"Is something wrong?" Maggie asked.

"Marcus Packard is a logical target for John Caroll."

"You think Caroll knows about Packard?"

"Maybe."

"That would mean Audrey told him."

"Audrey's never laid eyes on John Caroll."

"Are you sure?"

"I'm sure."

"Then how would Caroll get to Packard?"

"I'm not saying Audrey didn't tell anyone about Packard."

"But she didn't tell John Caroll."

"No, she didn't."

Maggie took my arm and smiled. "You think Audrey loved her husband, right?"

"Yes, despite everything."

"Even her own infidelity?"

"Even that."

We were standing a block from the heart of the Columbia University campus, staring east along 120th Street toward Morningside Drive. There were people about, mostly students who brought to the scene a vivacity entirely natural to their young, unmarried status. They traveled in groups, and their loud voices and sharp laughter projected their enthusiasm for the great adventure of life. By contrast, Maggie and I, though we shared a certain intensity, were huddled together, our voices tightly controlled. We were old enough to know that adventures can end badly.

I took out my cell phone and punched in Packard's number, which Tino had been good enough to supply. When a man answered on the third ring, I asked if he was Marcus Packard, and he grunted in assent.

"My name," I said, pleased to find him at home, "is Philip Beckett, and I'm representing the Beckett family. I'm in the neighborhood and I need to speak to you."

"Sure," he unhesitatingly replied. "Come on up."

"See you in about fifteen minutes."

As I returned the cell phone to my briefcase, I pulled Maggie close to me so she could view the handgun lying next to it. It was the weapon I'd taken from Tony, a .32-caliber Seecamp automatic.

"It's got an internal safety," I explained. "All you have to do is point it, then pull the trigger."

I wasn't surprised when Maggie slid the tiny gun from my briefcase to her purse. I just knew I didn't want to leave her standing there without any protection. Tony Farelli, after all, would recognize her if he should happen to come by.

"I'm going up alone," I told her. "If I don't phone you within ten minutes, get the police in there as fast as possible. Tell them anything, but get them inside."

Maggie put a restraining arm on my shoulder. "Why do you have to go up at all? Why not wait until he comes out?"

"I have to go up," I told her, "because I know that Marcus Packard is alive and I want to keep him that way." I put my hands on her shoulders. "Maybe I'm getting jumpy because I'm so close to the end. But I'd feel better if Packard had at least put up a token argument."

"He didn't even ask what you wanted?"

"No, he didn't. But he knows what I'm after, and he's had plenty of time to consider what to do if he's confronted. Maybe he simply decided to cooperate. Maybe when I called, I confirmed the wisdom of that decision. I'll know soon enough."

I kissed her, then opened the compartment on my briefcase that held the Browning as I strode west along a block of handsome town houses and low-rise apartment buildings. There were pedestrians about, as there are always pedestrians about in Manhattan. Most of them were on the move, but a cluster of older men chatted at the foot of a high cement stoop, and a youngish woman in a red beret walked a small dog at the curb. The city was rapidly cooling now that sunset was near. It was a perfect evening for a stroll.

I glanced around as I stepped between a pair of marble columns flanking a glass door. The door was open and led to a small foyer closed off by a second door, this one locked. I turned my attention to the little name tags next to the intercom buzzers. They were barely legible and I had to look closely for a moment to find the one for apartment 3F. It's the only excuse I have for allowing Zoe to come up behind me.

"Hey, sport," she said, "took you long enough."

"Zoe." I turned to face her, smiling despite the gun that she held in her right hand and that the coat folded over her forearm concealed from passersby. Next to her, an exceptionally ugly mutt dragged its leash along the sidewalk. "I was expecting Tony, but I'm delighted to see you."

"You smashed Tony's cheekbone." The red tips of her hair, I noted, had been re-dyed a uniform black. Her hair was neatly brushed as well, and covered almost completely by the beret. "Johnny asked me to stand in."

"And a wonderful job you've done." I let my hands drift away from my body. Maggie was already coming up the street and I didn't want to do anything to alarm Zoe. "What's with the dog?"

"The dog belongs to Packard. We've been up there all afternoon and the dog had to go out."

"All afternoon?"

"You should check your answering machine more often, sport. Packard's left a dozen messages." She smiled. "But I gotta admit that I'm impressed with you getting here on your own. Now push the buzzer."

Though my lips were as dry as sandpaper, I managed an apologetic smile. "Well, see, that's a problem. Ordinarily I'm an accommodating sort, but in this case I'm fairly certain that a very bad thing will happen to me if I do what you're asking."

"You don't press that buzzer, something bad's gonna happen to you right now."

"And then what?"

"And then I'll have the satisfaction of seeing you dead."

"Which you'll carry into a prison cell for the rest of your life."

"There's that, sport," she admitted. "But a girl's gotta do what a girl's gotta do."

"Can't you see," Maggie said as she came up behind Zoe, "that Zoe's in love with him?"

"With John Caroll?" Though I was incredulous, neither Zoe's attention, nor the gun in her hand, wavered in the slightest. "I don't believe it."

"Believe it," Maggie said. "It's the only reasonable explanation for her behavior."

" 'For her behavior?' " Zoe responded. "What am I? A guinea pig? A fucking lab rat?"

Maggie pressed the nose of the Seecamp into Zoe's lower back. "What you *are* is irrelevant, Zoe, because if you hurt the man *I* love, I'm going to shoot you."

Myself, I found Maggie's emphatic statement thoroughly convincing, but Zoe, apparently, had fewer options. I could see her waver as she considered them. Maggie was standing right behind her, standing too close. If Zoe turned quickly, she could, without doubt, knock Maggie's arm away before Maggie could pull the trigger. I knew that because I'd spent time in the gym learning to defend against armed attackers. I think Zoe knew it as well. The problem was that she wouldn't have time to shoot me, *then* turn on Maggie. It was an either-or situation.

"You have to get out now," I told Zoe. "This is your last chance, and you're smart enough to know it." I let my hands drop to my sides and kept my posture as casual as possible. My heart was beating very fast, the urge to jerk my body away from that gun barrel nearly overpowering. "I see that you changed your hair style and color. Why'd you do that, Zoe?"

"Just seemed like the right time, Phil."

"The right time to make yourself less conspicuous? In case you have to run?" I watched her shrug. "Tell me who's upstairs. Besides Johnny the Gent."

That brought a smile. "Nobody," she replied.

"Is that because the rest of the crew took off?"

"That's why."

"But you stayed."

"I stayed."

I shook my head. "Admirable on the surface, I admit, but do you know that Johnny was paid fifty thousand shares of common stock in a company named Halstead Financial Services to murder Sergio D'Alesse? Do you know the potential value of that stock a month down the line is two million dollars?" I was guessing, of course, but the mere fact that I'd found Vivian Walpole, Angelina Carollo, and Marcus Packard lent credence to my statement. "How many shares are in your name, Zoe? What's in it for you? Why would you risk your life and liberty for a fool and a thief?"

Zoe's head jerked back as though I'd slapped her. She opened her mouth, then closed it as Maggie began to speak.

"And besides," Maggie said, in the tone of a Roman executioner driving in the last nail, "the bastard is married."

"He doesn't love her." Zoe's reply was reflexive and rapid-fire, as if she had to get it out before her brain kicked into gear.

"But he hasn't left her, either."

There was nowhere to go with that one, so we stood in silence for a moment before Zoe finally made up her mind. "I didn't have anything to do with D'Alesse," she said. "Not with Walpole, either."

"We believe you," Maggie said. "We've believed you from the beginning."

Zoe took a step to the left, then another, then a third, until she was out on the sidewalk, the gun still trained on my chest. Preserving the stand-off, Maggie turned with her while I edged my right hand toward the briefcase and the Browning. Zoe was out of reach now. If she turned on Maggie I wanted to be prepared.

"You know," Maggie said, her British accent lending a surreal patina to the conversation, "there is one more thing you can do for your lover. If you still feel you owe him anything."

"What's that?"

Zoe finally let the barrel of her weapon drop. She was ten feet away by then, and her attention was drifting toward Maggie. I continued to inch my hand closer to my briefcase.

"Well," Maggie said, "Johnny's upstairs in 3F, holding Marcus Packard against his will. That about right?"

"Keep goin'."

"Now, we both know this is a dangerous situation, for Packard *and* for Johnny. There's only one way out of that apartment, and—"

"Three ways," Zoe corrected.

Maggie's smile was innocent, the widening of her eyes inquisitive. "Three ways?"

"There's a fire escape in the back and the roofs connect all the way down the block."

"This is a hostage situation, Zoe. That means cops in the hall, cops in the alleys, snipers on the rooftops." Maggie shook her head. "Johnny's facing life without parole or lethal injection and he knows it. Hell, Zoe, by taking Packard hostage, then attempting to lure Phil to the apartment, he's virtually admitting that he was involved in the D'Alesse, Walpole, and Winokur murders. Put yourself in his place? What will he do when the cops knock on the door? One thing certain, if he puts up any resistance, the cops will kill him without hesitation."

I had the Browning in my hand now, and Zoe's gun was pointing down. She was facing Maggie, an amused smile playing on her lips. "I heard you're a lawyer. Is that right?"

"Yes," Maggie admitted.

"Well, you're pretty good, but you could take some lessons from Sport over here. I mean, Johnny got two million dollars. You know what I got? I got to give him a blow job. Toodleoo."

I pulled the Browning as Zoe turned to walk away. She was faster than I expected, swinging back to face me, her eyes narrowing, but I had the advantage of surprise. I grabbed her wrist with my left hand, pressed the muzzle of the Browning into her belly, and twisted down until she released her hold on the automatic and it clattered to the sidewalk. Then, as Maggie bent to retrieve the gun and an elderly pedestrian pushing a shopping cart broke into a gallop, I locked Zoe's arm behind her back.

"You're a very bad girl, Zoe. I can't just let you walk away."

"What's that supposed to mean?"

"That you fingered Vivian Walpole."

"I never . . ."

"Don't bullshit me. You were staking out Walpole when I showed up yesterday. You saw us walking together, then you followed me to Brooklyn, then you went back and told your boyfriend. The rest, as they say, is homicide."

Zoe continued to protest. "I didn't know what Johnny was gonna do."

"Just like you didn't know what was supposed to happen to Marcus Packard? And to me, if I took the bait? Maybe I'm being overly dramatic here, but that sort of behavior simply cannot be rewarded. I mean, it threatens the social fabric that binds us together. Don't you think so?"

THIRTY-THREE

IT WAS A FINE DECLARATION, as declarations go, but it left me with a limited course of action. I couldn't possibly control Zoe and at the same time subdue John Caroll. I would either have to leave Zoe in Maggie's hands or bring in the cops and hope for the best.

"Call Mulligan," Maggie said. "Get it over with." Something in my expression brought a smile to her face. "I know you want the glory for yourself," she added, "but if you leave Zoe with me, I'm not going to shoot her if she tries to get away."

"Maybe you can subdue her with brute force," I suggested.

"Sorry," she apologized. "When it comes to fistfighting, I'm definitely testosterone-challenged. Call it a genetic defect."

The subject of our exchange, perhaps upset at again being discussed as if she were not present, twisted in my grip, then struck me in the chest with her fist. The blow itself, though it stung, wasn't much. It certainly wouldn't have been sufficient to affect her release if Marcus Packard's little mutt, which had been racing about our feet, didn't choose that moment to sink its teeth into my unsuspecting ankle. I'd like to claim that it was shock that caused me to jump back and let go, that I was bewildered, or feared attack from an unseen adversary. But the truth is that the animal's teeth were not only needle-sharp and very painful, it simply refused to let go. Meanwhile, fleet as a panicked gazelle, Zoe took off for Amsterdam Avenue.

Maggie waited until Zoe rounded the corner, then turned her attention to me. "Do you think Zoe's going to warn him?" she asked.

Before I could even consider a reply, the dog, which I'd finally shaken off, renewed its attack. This time the beast fastened its jaws to the right cuff of my Brooks Brothers slacks. I dropped to my left knee, prepared to seriously damage the animal, when I felt Maggie's hand on my shoulder.

"Can't you be serious?" she asked. "Whatever we're going to do, we have to do it right away."

"Tell it to the mutt."

"He just wants to play." She scooped the animal into her arms, whereupon it emitted a series of squeaks more appropriate to a rodent before licking her face. "Now, can we get down to business?"

I took a moment to examine my frayed cuff, then gathered my dignity, and finally rose. "I think," I said, "that Zoe will try to warn her lover."

"And then what?"

"If he has time, he'll run."

"Without killing Marcus Packard?"

Well, that was the question. Reality was closing down on Gaetano Carollo, aka John Caroll, aka Johnny the Gent. No more svelte club, no more San Remo, no more wife and family, no more girlfriend, no more tailored wardrobe or manicured fingernails or perfectly barbered hair. Even should he escape the death penalty, he would remain in prison for the rest of his life. He would grow old in prison. He would grow sick in prison. He would die in a prison hospital. It's the kind of scenario that excites the more impulsive elements of the human personality.

"Given a warning, I'm sure he'll run," I said. "Beyond that . . . We can't help Marcus Packard, Maggie. There's no way to get into the apartment."

In fact, there are only two ways in—or out—of a low-rise New York apartment, the front door and a window leading to the fire escape. By regulation, the front door is constructed of steel to prevent the spread of fire. By necessity, it is secured with a minimum of two dead-bolt locks. The window leading to the fire escape is also protected, usually by a padlocked folding gate. There are no exceptions in a city that includes ten thousand drug addicts among its residents.

There was good news for Caroll in this arrangement. He could not, after all, be taken by surprise, not by me or by the cops. On the other hand, any fortress can become a trap. If the cops showed up before he had a chance to flee, his choices would be reduced to surrender, or a battle he could not win.

"Why would Caroll harm Packard?" Maggie asked. "He has nothing to gain and he can't get away with it."

"He's already kidnapped the man. He could get twenty-five to life for that alone." I shook my head, then added, "It's probably better if Caroll has a chance to run. Better for Packard. The cops would trap both of them in the apartment, and that would only turn up the pressure."

Maggie glanced at the door as if expecting Caroll to emerge. It was too early for that. Zoe wouldn't stop long enough to warn her lover until she was well away. If she stopped at all.

"I want you to go up to Morningside Drive, then contact Mulligan from there. Do you have his card?" I waited for her confirming nod, then added, "Mulligan's home and beeper numbers are on the card, but if you can't reach him, call 911. After you have the cops committed, take the handgun I gave you and ditch it in the park. I got it from Tony Farelli and I don't know its history. Keep Zoe's gun. Hopefully it'll have her fingerprints on it."

Maggie nodded at every point. "You know," she said, "if Packard's dead and Caroll gets away, you'll be the logical suspect."

It made sense, though I hadn't thought of it before. Still, I wasn't worried about the police. The simple fact that Caroll had targeted Packard, and that he'd used Packard in an effort to get to me, confirmed my suspicions. Over time, even if Packard didn't survive, the truth would also become clear to Kirk Mulligan.

"The cops are not the problem," I said. "Not even close." When she didn't reply, I added, "I'm going to go around to the back, where I can watch the fire escape and the back door."

Maggie stared at me through obviously fearful eyes, but she didn't dispute our respective roles. We were both doing jobs that had to be done. "I love you," she told me. "I love you to pieces."

"I'll be careful," I promised. "It took me thirty years to find you, and I'm not about to lose you in the next thirty minutes."

It was another of those perfect moments, and as I leaned forward, eyes closed, for my farewell kiss, I was certain I'd retain the memory as long as I lived. I was right. The mutt's teeth missed the tip of my nose by a millimeter.

The head of the downward-sloping path leading to the rear of Packard's building was blocked by a wrought-iron fence, which I climbed without difficulty. Though I could see a light fixture at the end of the building farthest from me, it was unlit, and I assumed the bulb was out. It was only when I turned the corner that it became apparent that the whole line was out. I was now at the head of a second, very dark alley, this one perhaps forty feet wide and a hundred yards long, which ran the length of three buildings to a chain-link fence. There was a fence behind me as well, each fence separating the apartment buildings from a pair of much smaller town houses to the east and west.

Zoe had bragged that the rooftops extended from one end of the block to the other, but she'd been exaggerating. If Caroll went from Packard's apartment to the roof, he'd have only a hundred yards with which to work. The drop to either town house roof was more than twenty feet.

A narrow path, maybe twenty yards away, offered John Caroll's best hope of escape. It separated two apartment houses and led to 121st Street. From there it was only a short distance to Amsterdam Avenue and a host of gypsy and medallion cabs.

I was a floor below the front entrance now, standing next to a locked door that led to the service area of Packard's building, the boiler rooms, the trash compactors, the gas and electric meters. On a weekday or Saturday, I would likely be challenged by the maintenance staff. But it was Sunday evening and I was able to cross the alley and squeeze myself behind a wall of discarded gas stoves without being seen. The stoves were piled, one atop the other, before the wall of a building that faced 121st Street.

I took the Browning from its holster in my briefcase, then dropped the briefcase to the ground. Again, I found myself wishing

I'd been to a shooting range sometime within recent memory. Instead, after buying the gun, I'd practiced only until I was good enough to place a round near the center of a paper target twenty feet away before dumping the weapon on a closet shelf. Not only is twenty feet the length of an average New York living room, paper targets don't shoot back, an important distinction that I was only beginning to appreciate.

It was very quiet in my little den, the traffic noise and the blare of a distant siren no more intrusive to me than wind through the canopy of a forest to a lumberjack. Above me, a foreshortened rectangle of night sky seemed flush with the roofs of the surrounding buildings. Not even the flashing red lights of a passing jetliner dispelled the illusion.

A cat jumped the fence behind me, walked to within six feet, then fell to its haunches and stared up into my eyes for a few seconds before moving on. I dropped from a squat to my knees just as a window rattled up in the building directly across the alley. A moment later, John Caroll's large head appeared in the opening. The light was on in the room behind him and his now unkempt red hair seemed garish and intrusive against the surrounding shadows.

Caroll looked right, then left, then twisted his neck until he was staring up at the rooftop. His desperation was apparent in his jerky movements, and in his voice when he called to someone behind him.

"Just stay where I can fuckin' see ya."

Marcus Packard was alive.

A moment later, Caroll withdrew his head, and the window crashed down. As predicted, Zoe had stopped long enough to make a phone call. She'd told Caroll that we were out front, and that we were armed, and that we'd called the police. Bad news for Johnny the Gent.

Suddenly I found myself eager for the confrontation I was certain would follow. I'd begun haunting Johnny Caroll when I walked into the club intending to expose his scam. He'd been trying to shake me ever since, and without doubt he hated me simply because I refused to go away. That was fine. In fact, that was great. The man had tried to kill me twice, and I was prepared to return his anger in equal measure. At that moment, any emotion was better than fear.

My eyes were moving from the doorways, to the fire escapes, to the roofline, and it was only by luck that I saw the tiny strip of illumination visible beneath the door closest to me suddenly vanish. Somebody had turned out the light inside. I steadied my wrists on the stove in front of me, then trained my Browning on the door as it opened to emit a short, wiry black man. The man took several pigeon-toed steps away from the building, then looked right and left. His eyes swept the piled stoves, but if he saw me, he gave no sign.

"That's far enough, Packard." Though I couldn't see him, the voice belonged to John Caroll.

"There's nobody out here," Packard replied. His tone was calm, his manner relaxed, and I could see why Audrey had been attracted to him. He was very dark, and his finely chiseled African features had a haughty quality. Though he was a prisoner, he was not imprisoned.

"You better be right," Caroll said. "Cause if you ain't right, bro, you're gonna be fuckin' dead."

Packard didn't answer, nor did his expression change. A moment later Gaetano Carollo emerged. No longer Johnny the Gent, his jacket and trousers were rumpled, his tie hung askew, his hair tumbled over his forehead. He swept the alley in a series of sharp jerks, then barked, "We're goin' left." His jaw was so tightly clenched that the words popped out of his mouth in a series of little explosions, as if they'd piled up behind his teeth and were now taking this one opportunity to escape. "Nice and slow. No mistakes. You understand that, you diseased motherfucker?"

As I watched Caroll and Packard move away from me and into the heart of the alley, I remembered Maggie when she'd pushed her gun into Zoe's back. It had been a mistake getting that close, an amateur's mistake and not one John Caroll was prepared to make. Packard was a good ten feet into the alley before Caroll began to move.

Wondering if I should let them go, I waited until Caroll's back was fully turned. In all likelihood, I told myself, Caroll would release

Packard once they reached 121st Street. If I intervened at this point, I'd have to shoot Caroll without warning. Otherwise Marcus Packard stood a good chance of taking the first bullet.

I checked myself again, my pulse and breathing, and decided that I was still calm, that my calculations were not driven by rage or fear. Then I rose to my feet and steadied my hands on the stove in front of me as I locked the Browning's sights on John Caroll's spine. If I was going to move, I would have to do it soon, before Caroll got too far away. I would have to do it now.

My finger refused to tighten, to squeeze, or even to yank. I couldn't bring myself to kill a man in this way, that was the certainty. The question was whether I could bring myself to kill a man under any conditions.

"Awright," Caroll said, "that's far enough." He waited for Packard to halt before adding, "*Adíos*, nigger."

"Don't do it." Despite all my efforts, I found myself running on instinct. I couldn't let Caroll shoot Packard, and I couldn't shoot Caroll in the back. All I could do was shoot off my big mouth.

Caroll whirled. "You," he shouted as he began to pull the trigger of the semi-automatic in his hand. "You *fuck*."

The gray concrete of the alley and the glazed white brick of the surrounding buildings jumped into stark relief, then into shadowy afterimage, illuminated by tongues of flame that leaped from the barrel of the gun as if in search of a host. A hundred unlit windows reflected the glare and for a moment I felt I was being attacked by an army. In the stone confines of that back alley, the shots were frighteningly loud, the tearing metal, as bullets pounded into the stove that protected me, more terrifying still. My hands were shaking now, from a burst of hormone unleashed by an adrenal gland that simply would not listen to reason. I told myself that I had every advantage. All I had to do was make sure I hit him with the first shot. As he wasn't moving and only a bit farther away than the paper targets on which I'd practiced, how hard could that be?

Caroll pulled the trigger eight or nine times in quick succession, then abruptly stopped. For a few seconds, seconds so long they stretched toward infinity, I was blind. I imagined Caroll running toward me, imagined him only inches away, the image carrying the certainty of a vision, and still I didn't pull the trigger. Still.

The white curtain in front of my eyes faded to light gray, then into overlapping shadows. The process was slowed because I couldn't stop looking for John Caroll's gun, which I still imagined to be a few feet away. But Johnny the Gent, though he'd changed his position, was no closer to me than he'd been when he'd stopped shooting. The difference was that he was now lying prone, with Marcus Packard on his back. Pounding his head into the concrete.

Packard had seen his chance and taken it, and what I felt, as I pondered my own failure to act, was overwhelmingly relieved. Caroll was down and I hadn't fired a shot. I was saved.

I knew that my reaction was that of a child escaping a punishment, but I couldn't control it any more than I'd been able to control my trembling hands a moment before. Meanwhile, Packard had dropped Caroll into a spreading pool of his own blood and was retrieving Caroll's gun.

"You the cousin?" Packard's voice, though far from relaxed, was under control.

"Yeah." I came out from behind the stoves and approached Caroll. He lay without moving, absolutely silent, though he was still breathing.

"Audrey said you'd be coming by. She thought . . ." He shook his head as if forcing water from his ears. "Audrey liked you, man. She thought you were good people."

"Right up until the time she decided that I killed her husband?"

"Yeah, well, everybody makes mistakes. That why they give rulers to nuns."

In the distance, I heard the rush of oncoming sirens. I put my gun on the concrete, then stepped back. "You might want to do the same thing," I said, "before the cops arrive and draw the wrong conclusions."

He tossed the automatic away, the gesture careless. "I left some messages for you," he said, "on your machine. He made me do it."

"I know all about that, Marcus, but at the moment, I don't give a shit." I waited for him to turn around, to meet my eyes. "I need to know what you gave Audrey. What disease."

I remember hoping against hope that it was hepatitis C, or resistant tuberculosis, or anything except what it was.

"HIV," he said. "I gave her HIV. I didn't know I had it until a couple of months ago when I couldn't shake an infection. I told her right away, man. I swear." Once Packard got started, he couldn't stop. He led me through a convoluted tale about a former girlfriend, now deceased. The girlfriend, Ramona, was an occasional abuser of heroin, a weekend warrior who'd kept her dirty little secret to herself until she'd become too sick to carry the deception forward.

"Audrey was okay," he declared as if the issue were in dispute. "She didn't deserve what she got. You know what I'm sayin', man? Her family, her husband . . . she didn't deserve any of it."

With nothing to add, I quickly recovered my briefcase, then removed my cell phone. The sirens were closer now, but I had one more thing to do before the cops arrived. "When the police show up," I told Packard as I dialed Naomi Felder's number, "do yourself a favor. Keep it simple. Tell them you stopped pounding Caroll's head into the concrete as soon as he released the gun. It's what they'll want to hear."

I had only one question for Naomi and her answer was succinct. Neither Father, Regina, nor Audrey had contacted Caroll at any of the locations I'd supplied.

As I shut the phone off, Packard's dog shot into the alley, followed by Maggie. The dog spotted its master and began to wriggle with joy. Though somewhat less demonstrative, Maggie was obviously relieved to find me standing. She returned Zoe's gun to her purse, then took my hand.

"I think it's time to grant my father his wish," I said.

"His wish?"

"Father wants to be the first to know, Maggie, and what Father wants, Father gets. After all, he *is* my client."

THIRTY-FOUR

WE GATHERED IN THE DINING ROOM, two generations of Becketts (three if you count Regina's developing fetus) watched over by seven generations of Becketts. The forebears observed from within gilded frames, grandfather and great-grandfathers stretching back to Abner Isaiah Beckett, war profiteer and patriarch of the Beckett clan. With a single exception, the portraits were formal and quite professional. Only Abner's portrait, composed before he made his fortune, was crude, the work of an itinerant artist. As family lore would have it, this unidentified artist strolled into the town of Yaphet Mills in the summer of 1783, bartered his talents for a gallon of rum, then returned to the great wilderness from which he'd emerged forty-eight hours earlier.

I was seated at the end of the table, in the position Mother once routinely occupied, staring at Father and at Father's portrait, which graced the wall behind him. Father had demurred, initially, when I'd asked him to gather the troops. He clearly wanted to be the first to hear the bad news, and his lips curled into the tiniest of tiny frowns at my request.

As my client, Father had the right to be first, a right he didn't claim. He glanced at Maggie instead, then sighed. "May I assume," he asked, "that anything said here will remain confidential?"

Another rebuke. To me for including an outsider, and to Maggie for being an outsider.

"For as long," Maggie replied, "as my client wishes."

Father didn't argue the point. He was far too smart for that. Not so, Regina. The first to respond after Father dispatched Calder to fetch the gang, she looked at Maggie, then at me. "I assume, Philip," she declared, "that you're here to discuss a family matter."

"That's right."

"Then I suggest we keep the matter in the family."

"Maggie *is* family," I snapped. "Accept it."

"I won't be abused by you."

"You can leave anytime you want, Regina. Right now, I'm too tired to care one way or the other."

I knew, of course, that Regina wasn't going anywhere, not without hearing what I had to say. Still, if she didn't want to bear the brunt of my temper, she had an option: she could keep her mouth shut. I glanced at Maggie and found her features composed. The look in her eyes was intensely curious, yet devoid of compassion. On the way over, though our hands remained joined, we'd barely spoken.

Uncle Alfred chose that moment to enter the dining room. Five years older than Father, he showed every day of his nearly seventy years. The sooty pouches beneath his eyes had the look of rotting lace, while the deep wrinkles on his neck might have been gouged from wet clay. Despite its being Sunday, he was wearing a white shirt over a pair of pleated brown slacks.

"Good news?" Uncle Alfred's narrow lips expanded into an obsequious smile with which everybody, save Maggie, was quite familiar. He'd been playing second fiddle for a long time.

"John Caroll's in custody," I said. "The cops have him." True enough, but as he'd yet to regain consciousness, there was a decent chance that he'd either die or be so neurologically damaged he'd no longer remember his name. I left that part out. "But that's not what I'm here for."

"And what exactly *are* you here for?" Predictably, the question was asked by Regina.

"I'm here to reveal which member of my family conspired with John Caroll to murder Sergio D'Alesse."

"Then why don't you do it?"

"Regina," Father said, his tone sharp, "there's no need for that.

Philip investigated Sergio's death at my request. He's here at my invitation."

Though Regina didn't respond, her look adequately conveyed the position she'd taken during our conversation in the billiard room. Father was a fool to trust me.

Audrey and Aunt Charlotte arrived together. Aunt Charlotte wore a satin robe over a long nightgown. Audrey was in jeans and a sweatshirt. She looked more like Charlotte's maid than her daughter.

When Audrey asked what the gathering was all about, I let Regina explain, ignoring her nasty tone while I concentrated on Maggie. Her eyes were moving from Beckett to Beckett, while her hand rested on my knee.

Frieda came in a moment later, pushing a cart loaded with carafes of coffee and hot water, cups, saucers, dessert plates, and a stack of Danish pastries. The room went instantly silent, the shift so dramatic that it broke the tension.

"We're assembled," Father said once Frieda was gone. "As you asked." His voice was grave, his face ashen. It was going to be very bad and he knew it. He turned his palm up, sighed. Now it was my turn.

"I'm going to begin with a question." I kept my tone deliberately sharp. I wasn't asking anybody's permission. "Regina, do you know when the Beckett family sold its majority interest in Beckett Industries?"

"In September of 1985." Regina's unhesitating reply made two things clear. First, the decision was made so long ago that Regina could legitimately avoid all responsibility. Second, the issue had come under discussion in the recent past.

"So let's start in 1985. In September. Prior to then, the Beckett family's position was unassailable, its control of Beckett Industries subject only to the laws of the land. Any threat, no matter how well organized, was doomed to failure as long as the family owned more than fifty percent of the stock."

I glanced from face to face, finding my listeners (with the exception of Regina, who was feigning boredom) attentive. "More than likely," I continued, "it seemed perfectly safe, this move to . . . to what, Regina? To forty-seven percent? Forty-seven?"

"Philip, please," Father intervened. "The point is conceded. In hindsight, things might have been done differently."

"There must have been an awful lot of hindsights since 1985," I insisted, "as more and more of the stock was sold off to maintain the Beckett lifestyle. It might have stopped at any of those hindsights, but it didn't, and the unthinkable may now happen. The Beckett family, after nearly two hundred years, may lose control of Beckett Industries. As Sergio D'Alesse, Graham Winokur, and Vivian Walpole have lost their lives."

This time, as I looked from one member of my family to another, I was forced to admit that I'd gone too far. They had no interest in the dead, not with so much still on the line for the living.

"What's sad," I began over, "is that even the sale of the Beckett stock wasn't enough to cover personal expenses, that the need to create additional income became as all-consuming for the Beckett family as for senior citizens living from one Social Security check to another. That was when individual Becketts became 'consultants' to Beckett Industries' subsidiaries. It was also when the family began to explore the market for initial public offerings. Risky business, IPOs, but so rewarding when they pay off. Like Halstead Financial Services is about to pay off. The *Wall Street Journal*, for example, estimated that the initial offering of Halstead common shares will pump more than a hundred million dollars into the company. That will make the value of the retained shares worth approximately nine hundred million."

I stopped long enough to drink from a cup of coffee that Maggie had thoughtfully poured. Regina was making tea, no doubt annoyed at having to use a tea bag. "Tell me, Philip," she said, "exactly when did you become a financial genius? I thought you'd walked away from all that."

"Put it out of your mind, Regina," I replied. "I won't be deflected and I won't be made the issue. Remember, it was you who contacted me. What you're getting is what you paid for."

"Philip." Aunt Charlotte waited until I turned to look into her eyes. Though I knew her lids had been tucked, and her cheeks rounded with collagen, I found myself drawn into her rather imploring gaze. Charlotte's large eyes were a very dark blue that bordered on indigo. In her youth, ever so poor, yet ever so impeccably bred, she'd been quite the beauty. "Couldn't you simply tell us whom you suspect?"

"I think the answer to that question is pretty obvious," Regina said.

It wasn't, of course. Regina hadn't hired John Caroll, and I shouldn't have been riding her. I just couldn't resist.

"Enter Sergio D'Alesse," I said, changing the topic without answering Aunt Charlotte's question. "Charming Sergio. Hapless Sergio. Sponging Sergio. How much, over the years, Audrey? How many times were you forced to come to the family? How did it feel to go down on bended knee? To beg for a check to cover Sergio's excesses? How did it feel when you were finally refused? Lord knows, it's hard enough to play the supplicant, even when you're successful."

"You tell us," Audrey replied. "You're the detective."

Never ask a question unless you know the answer—sage advice that I have somehow never been able to follow. I turned to Father. "That last straw, the forty-thousand-dollar gambling debt, who decided that enough was enough?"

"It was a family decision, Philip. As I told you."

Perhaps bolstered by the bottom line on Sergio's insurance policy, Audrey turned her anger on her uncle. "It was you," she declared. "You made the decision."

Father sighed, then gently said, "There was no end to it, Audrey. No matter how much he was given, Sergio always needed more. It had to stop."

Audrey's eyes, two small circles within the larger circle of her round face, widened in outrage. "What right did you have to tell my parents what to do with their money? What right? Wasn't snatching Beckett Industries for yourself enough? Isn't it enough that you've bullied my father for all these years?"

"Please, Audrey."

Audrey shrugged off both her mother's hand, and her attempt to intervene. "Answer the question, Uncle Philip. What right?"

"My family came to me," Father said. "All I did was advise."

The claim was so without foundation that it brought a moment of silence into which I injected myself. "Uncle Alfred," I said, "if your brother had *advised* you to pay Sergio's gambling debt, would you have done it?"

Uncle Alfred shook his head. "My brother was right. Enough was enough."

"That's not what you said at the time, Alfred," Aunt Charlotte reminded.

"No," he admitted, "it's not."

"Good," I said. "Then it's settled. Father refused Sergio, leaving the count to accept responsibility for his actions—an object lesson that was long overdue, as I'm sure even Audrey will admit."

I paused to give Audrey a chance to respond, but she refused to look at me. "So we have three seemingly unrelated lines converging. The proxy fight for control of Beckett Industries, the profit to be turned by the initial public offering of Halstead Financial Services, and the increasingly violent threats being issued by John Caroll."

"We know all this, Philip." Father, for the first time, betrayed a hint of impatience.

"True enough," I said. "With the exception of Maggie and myself, everyone seated at this table was aware of all three developments. But not everybody was aware of a fourth development, which would meet the others head on." I turned to Audrey. "Why did you tell your husband that you were HIV-positive? Why did you advise him to be tested? You're in the earliest stages of the disease. Even if you'd already infected Sergio, it would be years before he developed symptoms, years before he knew."

Audrey stared at me, so angry she couldn't speak at all. The question hadn't been asked for her benefit, or even intended to draw a response. I was primarily interested in Father's and Regina's reactions.

Neither disappointed. Father's shoulders slumped, and his blue eyes rose to the chandelier suspended above the table. The breath he released through his patrician nose was close to a moan. Regina, on the other hand, drummed her fingers on the table, then yawned. My revelation was yesterday's news. If I was the last to know, it was my own fault.

I winked at Regina, then said, "In a sick way, Audrey, you have to admire Sergio. If I tested HIV-positive, I'd more than likely retire to bed and cry for a week. But ever the intrepid opportunist, Sergio had a more positive reaction. And why not? What with protease inhibitors and new drugs coming on the market every year, and Sergio being in his fifties, he knew he'd most likely die of something else before developing full-blown AIDS. And guess what? He was right."

"You're a bastard," Audrey said. "You're enjoying this."

I acknowledged her comments with a smile. Audrey had confirmed one of those items for which I had no direct proof. "I don't know how much Sergio demanded, though I suspect it was a lifetime settlement. What I do know is that Sergio's blackmail—what with Beckett Industries and the Halstead offering on the line—created a major problem. One can only imagine the scandal unleashed by a public divorce charging that Audrey infected her husband with HIV, which she'd gotten from her black lover." I was skipping ahead now, deleting any mention of who or how. That would come later.

"In retrospect, I think even John Caroll would admit that he was a bad choice for an assassin. He was a tough guy, sure, but murder wasn't his game. And he would, of course, be the prime suspect." I shook my head. "No, it wouldn't surprise me to learn that Caroll initially turned the job down and that his co-conspirator increased the payoff until it became an offer that could not be refused. But whatever the sordid details, Caroll eventually agreed, and a plan was developed to divert suspicion, if not to someone else, at least away from Caroll. Enter Philip Corvascio Beckett, gumshoe to the ruling class.

"If Caroll was a bad choice for the job of assassin, I was a far worse choice for the job of patsy. I was supposed to approach Caroll, as one

gentleman might approach another, and politely request that he forgive Sergio's debt. Instead, I showed up at the club with an agenda
of my own. While there, I met a sweaty little man named Graham
Winokur who bragged about his connection to the Beckett family. 'I
have a piece,' he told me, 'of one of their IPOs.' "

Regina straightened in her chair. I had her attention now, and I
directed my remarks directly to her. "Now, why would the Beckett
family allow a small-time fool like Graham Winokur to handle any
aspect of their affairs? Halstead was not only being underwritten by
Salomon Brothers, it also was being touted by the most powerful
houses on the Street. What could the Beckett family want with
Graham Winokur?"

After a moment, Father responded. "Shares in Halstead were
used to pay for Sergio's . . . for his murder. They were funneled
through Winokur as a matter of convenience."

"Creating, in the process," I added, "a paper trail that leads from
the Beckett family, to the firm of Winokur, Champion, Berwick, to
a woman named Angelina Carollo." Another fiction. The paper trail
was pure surmise. "As I said, Caroll was unskilled in the art of assassination. When things began to go wrong, as they did from the very
beginning when I arrived at Caroll's home with Graham Winokur in
tow, Caroll began to panic. I waited in the car while Graham went
up to Caroll's apartment. There was still time for Caroll to back
away, or at least postpone. Instead, he let me sit in Regina's Rolls for
almost forty minutes while he arranged to have a kid named Tony
Farelli visit Sergio.

"Tony, he was a goofy-looking kid, very small and very thin, but
with an appetite for violence. I don't know how he convinced Sergio
to allow him into the apartment. Maybe he pretended to be
returning Sergio's markers, or maybe he was so unthreatening that
Sergio never considered refusing. What matters is Audrey found me
at Sergio's door and told the police that the door was unlocked. That
made me a suspect. It forced me to get involved.

"Graham Winokur, at that point, had to go, and before I got to
him. Caroll still had enough self-control to make his death resemble

a robbery, but the connection was obvious. Vivian Walpole—Sergio's long-time lover, for those of you who don't know—also had to be eliminated once she'd been seen with me. Caroll got lucky here because I was already a suspect in another murder. Thus no care was taken to make the hit appear other than a pure assassination.

"Marcus Packard, who'd given HIV to Audrey, was next on the list, and that's where the police caught up to John Caroll. But it's not the end of the story. Caroll, you see, tried to kill me at least twice and missed both times. The only reason Marcus Packard is alive is because Caroll was using him in an attempt to get to me. But Packard *is* alive, and John Caroll is going to be charged with kidnapping and attempted murder, and sooner or later he *is* going to crack. Something to think about."

Regina was staring at me, her gaze frankly evaluating. I don't know what she was thinking, but her voice, when she interrupted me, betrayed curiosity and not contempt. "How," she asked, "did you find Marcus Packard? How did you know where to look?"

I glanced at short, thick, homely Audrey D'Alesse. Audrey D'Alesse the ugly duckling, the debutante who stood against the wall sipping punch, the daughter cast off. Abused by friends and family until she married. Abused by her husband from that moment forward. "I met with Sergio immediately after you hired me, Regina," I explained, "and he told me that he expected his fortunes to improve. Naturally, in light of Caroll's threats, I found the statement provocative. So I went to his friends, hoping he'd bragged to them, as he generally bragged to everyone. Sure enough, he'd also told his buddies that things were looking up. What he hadn't told them, however, was the means by which this rise in fortune was to be brought about. That, in itself, was suspicious.

"Nevertheless, I was close to a dead end until I reached a player named John Simone. Simone was Sergio's buddy. He told me that Sergio, going back six weeks or so, had appeared to be quite depressed. This caught Jones's attention because Sergio was ordinarily quite cheerful, no matter how difficult his circumstances. Then Sergio asked Jones for the name of a doctor, which again surprised Jones because Sergio had a doctor of his own. Finally, a week or so after making this odd request, and presumably after visiting this doctor, Sergio's spirits improved. He began telling Jones, and the rest of his friends, that good times were just around the corner."

Regina was smiling now, that familiar smile so close to a sneer. "And you went from there to Audrey having given Sergio AIDS? A plausible jump, but it doesn't explain Marcus Packard."

"By that time," I told her, "I knew that Audrey spent a good deal of time at Project Rehab, a drug treatment center. Marcus Packard is a social worker at Project Rehab."

"But that still doesn't explain Audrey's choice," Regina insisted. "Audrey was socially active. Why not one of her friends?"

Regina's gaze was focused directly on me, as if we were discussing a business matter in her Sixth Avenue office. Nothing I'd said thus far had come as any surprise.

"First," I said, "Marcus Packard was Audrey's friend. Her friend and her lover. As to why I focused on Project Rehab, the answer is quite simple. I didn't believe that Audrey, given her general appearance and her personal psychology, could find a lover among her peers."

Maggie's grip tightened on my knee. I'd been deliberately cruel and she didn't like it. Audrey jumped to her feet, her fists clenched. "How could you?" she demanded.

"That question is better put to you," I replied. "How could you not tell the police why Sergio was killed? If Mulligan had known the motive for Sergio's murder on that first day, Vivian Walpole, and perhaps Graham Winokur, would still be alive. Now they're dead, and the sad truth, as I read it in your eyes, is that you don't give a shit."

Father took that moment to speak up. He'd recovered from his earlier shock and his mouth was set in a thin, determined line. He would protect the family. It was all he knew how to do. "I commend you, Philip," he said. "You found Sergio's killer in three days. Quite an accomplishment, as I'm sure all present will concede. But more importantly, you came to the family, as I asked you to do." He cleared his throat. "What I'm trying to say is that I want to know who hired John Caroll."

"Well, it wasn't you, Father. You were the fly in the ointment, the man who turned down Sergio's original request for a loan to pay off his gambling debts. If you'd been told about Sergio's illness, and the payoff he was demanding, there was every reason to believe you'd turn that down as well."

"And that's the only reason?" Father's voice was gentle.

"No, Father. Hiring me to aid Sergio wasn't your decision, but hiring me to find his killer was. If you'd been conspiring with John Caroll, the juxtaposition would necessarily have been reversed."

"Neat," Regina said. "And now for me. I can't wait."

"You didn't know," I said, "but—"

"I already know that *I* didn't know," Regina interrupted. "Tell me how *you* know that I didn't know."

The answer was simple enough and I ticked the reasons off on my fingers. "In the course of a phone call that took place on the morning after you hired me, you made it very clear that you'd opposed my involvement from the beginning. If you'd been working with Caroll, hiring me would have been an absolute necessity. When I asked you exactly what it was you wanted me to do, your response was along the lines of, 'You'll think of something appropriate.' If you were conspiring to kill Sergio, you would have tried to arrange the gentlemanly meeting Caroll was expecting." I was attempting to ignore Regina's admiring grin. I couldn't possibly, or so I told myself, have any need for my sister's approval. Could I?

"Finally," I continued, "you compensated me with a check drawn on Halstead Financial Services. If you'd just paid off John Caroll with Halstead shares, you'd certainly have been more careful. After all, on the forty-seventh floor of Beckett Industries, you're fondly known as the Queen of Details."

"That's only," Regina said, "when they don't refer to me as 'that Beckett Bitch.' "

I nodded. "The check, by the way, played a large part in my investigation. Somehow I associated it with Winokur's IPO comment, then made Halstead the object of a media search. Once I knew that Halstead was the only Beckett IPO that Winokur could have been involved with, it was an easy jump to how Caroll was paid off. I was already certain that the figure was too large to be withdrawn from a bank account without attracting attention. But a block of shares in a closely held corporation funneled through an obscure brokerage into the hands of Angelina Carollo? The cops might never have found the trail."

"You already said that," Audrey noted. "You're repeating yourself."

"My apologies, but I think it was a good stroke. I don't believe the police would have gotten it on their own."

"They still won't," Regina interrupted, "if you don't tell them."

I ignored Regina's poor timing. "You seem very amused," I told her, "but you're not off the hook. You also knew why Sergio was killed. You made that clear when you said that Father was a fool to trust me. You knew and you could have prevented Vivian Walpole's death. But you didn't. You let her go to her death."

"In that case, perhaps I should summon an attorney before I say anything else." Regina was still smiling, but her smirk was now a good deal more contemptuous. She could admire me and she could dislike me, but she could not fear me. I was too far beneath her.

"Audrey," I began, again anxious to be finished, "you—"

"How did I know," Audrey interrupted, "that it was going to come down to me? Tell me how I knew?"

"But it doesn't," I explained. "It goes through you, and the police will probably suspect you, no matter what's said here, but I know you aren't guilty of anything more than an indiscretion. You really should have kept that list of Sergio's friends to yourself."

"I would have," Audrey admitted, "but I was sure that you'd killed Sergio and I thought it didn't matter." After a moment, she added, her tone softer, "Plus I needed someone to talk to."

"Yes, I guess you did." I straightened in my chair, then directed my comments, not to Audrey, but to her mother. "I became confused, Aunt Charlotte, by your daughter's claim that the door was unlocked and my hand was on the knob."

"It's the truth," Audrey insisted.

I waved her off. "I went over those moments in the hallway a thousand times. Where was my hand when the elevator opened? Did I hear the dead bolt retract when the key was turned? Or did I hear only what I expected to hear? Was your daughter trying to set me up? Or did she really believe that I'd killed her husband?

"My obsession with these questions was a big mistake, which I now freely admit. What did or didn't happen in that hall isn't really important. No, what matters now is Audrey's shock and grief when she found Sergio's body. I can believe Audrey capable of feigning grief, but her look and her actions that afternoon were those of a child who's lost her way. She wasn't surprised, so much as befuddled. She didn't know whether to strike out or break down.

"The bottom line, Aunt Charlotte, is that your daughter loved her husband despite all the ugliness. That's why she told him to get tested for HIV, and that's why, despite the pressure, she refused to file for divorce." I paused long enough to glance at Maggie. She'd taken her hand from my knee and was now re-filling my cup with tepid coffee. If she disagreed with anything I'd said, she didn't show it.

"If I hadn't been so preoccupied," I continued, "with the business of the unlocked door, I would have put things together a lot sooner than I did. I would, for instance, have realized that Audrey's pointing the finger in my direction was not part and parcel of some evil plot to have me take the fall. My job was to blow a little covering smoke in John Caroll's direction, then vanish. Regina virtually admitted as much when she told me that I'd never be convicted of any crime. It simply could not be allowed to happen. Audrey's accusation was exactly what the conspirators didn't want."

Charlotte tightened the belt on her robe, then crossed her legs. The robe, of royal blue satin, nicely complemented her eyes as she raised them to meet mine. She was wearing a pale blue nightgown beneath the robe, and pale blue slippers on her feet. "I knew you'd eventually get to the bottom of things," she said. "I told you that. Do you remember?"

"I do, Aunt Charlotte, but I'm not quite finished." I paused long enough to allow her to respond, but her eyes dropped to her lap, and she became still. "As Audrey just told us, she needed someone to talk to, a confidant to whom she could vent both her grief at her husband's death, and her anger at the pressure I was putting on her. It was in the course of those conversations that Audrey gave me a list of Sergio's friends, a list that went from Audrey's confidant to John Caroll. So, to whom did Audrey confide? To whom did she turn for solace? To my father? To Regina? To her own father? Or to her mother? The answer, Aunt Charlotte, is obvious."

"My wife did nothing." Uncle Alfred spoke for the first time since entering the room. "I contacted John Caroll. The Halstead shares I sold to Winokur were in my name. I was the one who updated Caroll after Philip began investigating."

Uncle Alfred spoke as if in great pain, but his apparent suffering was lost on his daughter. As she tossed her coffee in his face, then cursed him through a rising storm of tears, I settled back to enjoy the show. I was done at last.

Aunt Charlotte came to her feet and tried to restrain her daughter. Father also rose. His face was tomato-red and his fists were clenched. Only Regina—calm, cool Regina—kept her place. At one point, if I remember correctly, she yawned.

I shifted my chair closer to Maggie's and put my arm around her waist. "We did good," I told her.

"We did," she returned, her eyes sparkling, "but somehow I don't think your client's going to be in any hurry to pay your bill."

Audrey's tantrum gradually subsided, and a few minutes later the family was again seated around the table. I expected the conversation to turn to the obvious question of what came next, but Father surprised me.

"What a fool you are," he told his brother. "Beckett Industries isn't going anywhere."

Uncle Alfred, thoroughly cowed, kept his eyes on the floor. Regina, on the other hand, rose to the bait. "That remains to be seen," she declared.

"I'm talking to my brother," Father said. His tone was very

controlled, and I was reminded of the chairman who'd dispatched Mercer Fredricks, CEO of Giant Paper, with a flick of a finger. "Are you listening, Alfred?"

"I heard you," Uncle Alfred muttered.

"On Tuesday morning," Father continued, "before the opening of business in New York, I will purchase a large block of Beckett shares from a European institutional investor. At that point, the proxy fight will end. As for your precious Halstead Financial Services, with Beckett Industries finally stable, there's no reason to believe that a messy divorce between two individuals uninvolved in the firm's affairs would affect the offering. So what you did, Alfred, you did for nothing."

Father let the ensuing quiet build for a moment before turning his attention to Regina. "I've known for some time," he told her, "that you planted the rumors that have you assuming the chair of Beckett Industries, and that you contacted Mercer Fredricks just after Sergio was killed. Do you deny it?"

"Mercer is a pissant," Regina replied. Though her face had drained of blood, her voice was strong, her tone almost casual. "As for your stepping down, it's past time. You were late getting off-shore, and you were late getting into the IPO market. As I've told you on many occasions." No longer willing to look over her shoulder, Regina finally shifted her chair to face her father. "Your strategies were formed in a world of high inflation, oil embargoes, and persistent recession. They don't apply to the first decade of the third millennium. Do you deny it?"

"Don't return to your office," Father snapped.

"I've had everything I need out of there for weeks." Regina's gaze was as cold as I'd ever seen it. "But while we're at it, you can say good-bye to your grandson."

"You're holding your breath."

It took me a moment to realize that it was Maggie, and not one of the combatants who'd spoken. She was right. I wouldn't be able to relax until I was away from my family. "The more things change," I told her, "the more they stay the same."

"We're almost finished here," Maggie replied. "Just as well, because I need a hot shower. Do we have any of that soap left?"

"A sliver."

"Bath oil works just as well."

"And it bubbles, too."

"Philip?"

I looked away to find myself transfixed, not only by the expectant eyes of the living Becketts, but also by the eyes of our male fore-bears. Fortunately, Mother's eyes were behind me. I was afraid that if I turned, I'd find that her small ironic smile had vanished at last.

"Father?"

"I want to thank you again for bringing this to the family."

"Yes, well, I thought you'd want to know."

My father acknowledged my evasive response with a narrow smile, but his glance was razor sharp. Somehow I would have to be brought into line. "There's no legal reason," he told me, "why you can't refer the police to your attorney. I—"

"That not quite true," my attorney interrupted. It was time for a reality check. "Philip can be subpoenaed to appear before a grand jury. He could then attempt to assert his Fifth Amendment rights, but if he's no longer a suspect, the prosecution will grant him immunity. At that point he will either testify or go to jail."

Far from angry at being interrupted, Father's smile warmed as he turned to Maggie. "And how long will that take?"

"As little as a week."

"And as much as . . . ?"

"A month, six weeks. It depends on how fast the district attorney wants to move."

"And you think the decision will be made by the district attorney? And not one of his assistants?"

"The case is too big for assistants."

Father turned his gaze to me, though his smile remained in place. "The district attorney is a personal friend," he declared, "and I know him to be a reasonable man. I'm sure he'll concede us the benefit of any doubt."

"It's not," Regina added, "as if anybody's asking you to lie, Philip. You've got your attorney with you. Let her speak to the police. I don't think even the cops will expect you to voluntarily give evidence against your family."

"And what about Audrey?" I asked. "Can we count on her to forget about her husband's death?"

The question was rhetorical. The last thing Audrey needed was to have her lover and her illness proclaimed by every media outlet in the nation. Beyond that, she was still a Beckett, and while she would dash a cup of tepid coffee in her father's face, she would never be so unforgivably crude as to deliver him into the hands of the police.

"All we're asking for," Father cajoled, "is time. If you're forced to give testimony . . . well, no one is suggesting that you go to prison."

Maybe not, but if I was forced to testify, someone, probably Father, would most certainly suggest that I perjure myself. I looked at Uncle Alfred. His gaze had moved from the floor in front of his feet to the ceiling overhead. Still, I could read him well enough to be sure the dominant emotion flooding his consciousness was fear, not remorse.

The door opened at that moment, and Calder Hallmark's head appeared. He coughed, then announced, "Detectives Mulligan and Aganda are outside."

"Did they say what they wanted?" Regina asked.

"They wish to speak to Master Philip."

Maggie and I rose together. She took my arm but asked no questions. I let my eyes run around the table for the last time. Aunt Charlotte's gaze was beseeching, Audrey's fearful, Father's firm and reassuring, Regina's again contemptuous.

"Tell Detective Mulligan," I told Calder, "that I'll be right down."

I picked up my briefcase and slung it over my shoulder. It felt a good deal lighter without the Browning. "Which do you prefer?" I asked Maggie. "The mountains or the sea?"

"The sea," Maggie declared. "Definitely."

As we passed through the doorway and into the Beckett ballroom with its twenty-foot-high walls and frescoed ceiling, the last thing I heard was Regina's voice. "Father," she called, "was such a fool to trust you."

THIRTY-FIVE

WE MADE IT TO THE sea just in time for the summer's first extended heat wave, specifically to a small house in the community of Saltaire on Fire Island, a barrier island some thirty miles east of New York City. It was still early in the season and the beach was nearly deserted.

Maggie took to the sand and the Atlantic Ocean surf without hesitation, browning beneath a hazy sun while I protected my Waspy white skin with thick layers of greasy sunblock. Though I feared for her long-term health (in which I was now certain I had a stake), I must admit that I found the contrast between the tanned and protected areas of her body profoundly erotic. Maggie, I think, was aware of my interest, because as time went on and her bathing suits became more and more skimpy, her tan line consistently retreated.

We were staying with Benny Abraham and his wife, Shelley, in a house lent to Benny as partial payment for a gambling debt run up by its owner. Built at the apex of a rolling sand dune, the white clapboard house had a broad porch that faced the ocean. On that porch, in the late afternoon, with Maggie at my side, I felt completely at peace, every hard edge softened by the summer haze. There was no horizon, and no horizons that I wanted to think about.

Maggie stirred alongside me. "I'd better go in and help with dinner," she said.

For reasons known only to herself, Shelley, an old-school Jewish housewife, had taken sole responsibility for cooking dinner. The meals she prepared were invariably heavy, and the air in the kitchen, which might have been filled with the odor of grilling salmon, reeked of pot roast and cabbage.

"Why don't we take a walk along the beach instead," I suggested.

"I can't," Maggie replied. "As you know."

I did know. I knew that Maggie felt compelled to offer her help, and that Shelley would allow her to prepare the same tossed salad we'd been eating all week. I knew, also, that Shelley would regale Maggie with tales of the Abraham and Moscowitz families, members of which had been involved in various criminal activities for the past hundred years. A thoroughly intrigued Maggie would repeat these tales later in the evening, then demand to know if they could possibly be true.

Benny Abraham emerged from the house a moment after Maggie went inside. He was carrying bottles of Bass Ale on a small tray. There were no glasses.

"What's the story with the trust fund?" he asked as he squeezed himself into a wicker rocking chair. Benny had spent the past several days in Manhattan, and it was the first chance we'd had to talk.

"I'll get it restored," I told him. "Eventually."

"And how long is 'eventually'?"

"Six months, a year, maybe longer. It depends on how hard they want to fight."

I should note that the firm of Turcotte, Pendleton, Brown, at Father's behest, had declared me unfit to receive the benefits of my inheritance, then cut off my quarterly dividend. The charge was completely without merit, as I'd been cleared of any involvement with the killings, but even with Maggie aggressively pursuing the matter on my behalf, I'd thus far gotten nowhere.

Still, not all the news was bad. Father had promptly paid the bill I submitted two days after I confronted the family. I suppose it was his way of salving his conscience. He was a good man, a *just* man who was pulling my trust fund because I'd truly proven myself unworthy. Whatever his reason, it enabled me to pay off Arthur Howell, then attend the auction at Christie's, where I lost my dragon-fish vase to a high roller who ran the bid to double the estimated selling price of twelve thousand dollars. Already, I had my eye on another piece, a rabbit carved from pink and white jade currently in the hands of a private collector.

I sipped at my beer, then took a longer swallow. It was wonderfully bitter. "We'll move to have the judge appoint a neutral executor if we ever get into a courtroom."

Benny grunted in commiseration. In fact, he'd recently cut a deal with his nephew Paulie, and would shortly be out of the bookmaking business. "What's happening with the uncle? He been arrested yet?"

"Not yet."

"What's the problem?"

The problem was that John Caroll was lying in a neurological ward. The problem was that when his eyes finally opened a week after his battering at the hands of Marcus Packard, they were without sentience. "If Caroll wasn't part of an ongoing investigation," Kirk Mulligan had told me one day, "the docs would pull the plug."

At the time of that conversation, Zoe had already turned on Tony Farelli, whereupon Farelli had been marched from an open ward at Bellevue Hospital to the facility's prison unit, then charged with three counts of murder. But Zoe claimed to know nothing of Caroll's relationship with any member of the Beckett family, and Tony wasn't talking.

The only evidence against Alfred Beckett, aside from his spontaneous confession, was the transfer of forty thousand shares of Halstead Financial Services from Alfred's account at Salomon Brothers to the account of Angelina Carollo at Winokur, Champion, Berwick. Alfred's attorneys were now claiming that the shares had been offered to Caroll in payment for Sergio's gambling debt, while his confession had been rendered in a moment of powerful emotion to protect his wife, whom I appeared to be accusing.

"Alfred Beckett's a big fish," I told Benny, "and the district attorney is a friend of the family. Alfred won't be arrested until—and unless—he's formally indicted by a grand jury. That's according to Kirk."

Benny Abraham bristled at my use of Detective Mulligan's first name. Having little trust in cops, he wouldn't have liked the idea that we'd become friends, even if he wasn't jealous.

We sat in silence until we finished our beers, watching a young woman in an orange bathing suit play with a diaper-clad toddler at the edge of the water. The scene was very peaceful, the girl's laughter as she was swung out over the waves as remote as the piercing cries of the banded gulls soaring overhead. Nevertheless, I found myself drifting back to John Caroll in that alleyway, to the flash and reek of gunfire in a confined space. For all my talk of a cold, hidden place at the bottom of my psyche, I'd been unable to kill, or even to attempt to kill. I could not readily take human life. That was why (or so I'd been telling myself) I hadn't withheld a single detail from Detective Kirk Mulligan. That was why Father was punishing me.

"Regina called me today," I finally said. "Early this afternoon."

"What'd she want?"

"She wanted to tell me that I'm not invited to the Becketts' annual Fourth of July party in Vail, a disappointment to which I'd already resigned myself."

"But she's going?"

"She and Father have reconciled," I explained.

"Yeah, it figures they would."

"It figures?"

"Hey, Phil, wake up. She's carryin' the ultimate insurance policy in her womb."

It was nearly sundown when Maggie and I finally took our walk on the beach. The breeze off the water had picked up, but it was still warm enough for shorts. In the failing light, Maggie's chocolate-brown T-shirt was only a shade darker than her skin. Her teeth, when she smiled, were sparkling white. We shared a mutual need to touch, walking shoulder to shoulder, arms about each other's waists. Maggie was finished with Exxon, and had been for nearly a month. Like me, she was living on her savings while she figured out what to do next.

"I've decided not to go public," I told her. We'd touched on this question in the past, with Maggie insisting that my trust fund would be instantly restored if I merely threatened to expose the facts to the media. Somehow I couldn't imagine myself on the front page of a supermarket tabloid, or on the talk show circuit discussing my tell-all book, even if a threat of that kind didn't amount to blackmail. I'd had enough of blackmail for the time being.

"I'll never be free of them," I continued, "as long as I jump whenever they tighten the ties that bind. I have to stop reacting."

"You're suing them," Maggie pointed out. "That's about as reactive as human behavior gets."

We walked in silence until it was fully dark. The rolling mist, which would soon be fog, smelled of salt, and of an eternal (and inspiring) fertility. I walked Maggie away from the water, to a hollow in the warm sand where I spread a blanket. Benny's house was very nice, but it was small, and our shared bed protested even the slightest movement with a series of creaks and groans audible throughout the upper floor. In desperation, we'd taken to the beach.

I stretched out on the blanket and felt the warm sand beneath it mold to my body. Maggie knelt beside me, then flicked off her T-shirt. She wore no bra, and the breeze drew her nipples instantly erect. I reached out to cup her breasts, thinking that despite the pressing need for cash, I hadn't done too badly. I'd had a great adventure and come through with my honor and with Maggie. I could live with that.